P9-ELF-821

A HEALTHY GLOW

Something made a noise outside. He crept toward the window. The moon was half full. It painted the rocks a weak silver.

The sound was repeated, mixed with laughter.

Something caught his eye. He got very cold. A girl was running along the dry, opposite bank of the creek bed. Occasionally she would glance back over her shoulder and try to stifle a giggle. She was wearing a simple white dress and sandals. Her blonde curls fluttered with each little jump she took. Her complexion was pale as incoming fog. She was truly beautiful, not *Vogue* fake or *Cosmo* creepy, but as beautiful and pale as the white gypsum sands of the national monument to the south.

And she glowed like a torch.

By Alan Dean Foster
Published by Ballantine Books

THE ADVENTURES OF FLINX OF THE
COMMONWEALTH
    For Love of Mother-Not
    The Tar-Aiym Krang
    Orphan Star
    The End of the Matter
    Bloodhype

NOR CRYSTAL TEARS

CACHALOT

ICERIGGER

MISSION TO MOULOKIN

SPLINTER OF THE MIND'S EYE

WITH FRIENDS LIKE THESE...

...Who Needs Enemies?

Alan Dean Foster

A Del Rey Book

BALLANTINE BOOKS • NEW YORK

A Del Rey Book
Published by Ballantine Books

Copyright © 1984 by Thranx, Inc.

All rights reserved under International and Pan-American Copyright Conventions. Published in the United States by Ballantine Books, a division of Random House, Inc., New York, and simultaneously in Canada by Random House of Canada Limited, Toronto.

Library of Congress Catalog Card Number: 84-90858

ISBN 0-345-31657-6

Manufactured in the United States of America

First Edition: June 1984

Cover art by Barclay Shaw

ACKNOWLEDGMENTS

"Swamp Planet Christmas" copyright © 1976 by James D. Denney; first appeared in *Art & Story*.

"Snake Eyes," copyright © 1978 by Random House; first appeared in *Stellar 4*.

"Bystander," copyright © 1978 by Davis Publications, Inc.

"What Do the Simple Folk Do? . . . " copyright © 1979 by Alan Dean Foster.

"Gift of a Useless Man," copyright © 1979 by Davis Publications, Inc.; first appeared in *Isaac Asimov's Science Fiction Magazine*.

"Surfeit," copyright © 1982 by Thranx, Inc.; first appeared in *Speculations*.

"The Dark Light Girl," copyright © 1981 by Davis Publications, Inc.; first appeared in *Isaac Asimov's Science Fiction Magazine*.

"Instant With Loud Voices," copyright © 1982 by Thranx, Inc.; first appeared in *Perpetual Light*.

"Communication," copyright © 1981 by Alan Dean Foster; first appeared in *Rigel*.

"The Last Run," copyright © 1982 by Mercury Press, Inc.; first appeared in *Fantasy & Science Fiction*.

"Wu-Ling's Folly," copyright © 1982 by Fantasy Book Enterprises; first appeared in *Fantasy Book*.

"Village of the Chosen," copyright © 1983 by Omni Publications International Ltd.; first appeared in *The Best of Omni*.

Contents

Introduction   ix

Swamp Planet Christmas   1
Snake Eyes   18
Bystander   63
What Do the Simple Folk Do?...   77
Gift of a Useless Man   106
Surfeit   124
The Dark Light Girl   151
Instant with Loud Voices   173
Communication   188
The Last Run   195
Wu-Ling's Folly   210
Village of the Chosen   239

Introduction

Why write short stories?

I mean, why should a working writer bother? Unless your last name happens to be Bradbury or Ellison, there's no way you can make half a living writing short science fiction. Even if one were to persist and be successful, it still takes years to build up enough of a backlog of stories to keep more than a couple of collections in print. Furthermore, most publishers are convinced that single-author collections don't sell—a truism you are proving wrong by buying this book. Anyone writing science fiction today knows that in order to make any real money, you have to write novels.

That was not always true. In the golden age of the science fiction pulps and digests it was possible to do reasonably well if you could sell a sufficient number of shorts. Sadly, that time is history, with most of the magazines that publish sf today paying rates not much in advance of what they paid thirty and forty years ago.

There are three exceptions to this rule of poverty: *Omni, Playboy*, and *Penthouse* magazines. In the first example short science fiction is included as a diversion from the real core of the magazine, which is devoted to highly visual explorations of current scientific events.

The other two magazines are devoted to highly visual explorations of a different nature entirely, and short science fiction, along with other short fiction, is provided to give the reader an excuse for picking up the magazine in question where said reader would never think of buying a copy of *Hustler* or *Latent Image* ("No, dear, I'm not looking at these nudes, I only bought this issue because there's a new Arthur C. Clarke short story in it.").

Uh-huh.

This leaves us with the question of why so many established

writers of science fiction continue to pour so much energy into a literary form that provides so little financial return.

For an answer you have to seek returns that can't be read in dollars and cents. Because what the writer gets out of executing a good short story can't be cashed at the bank. It's a little item called Satisfaction.

See, there's something so *clean* about a good sf short, so spare and unencumbered by wordy baggage, so personally gratifying to a writer that the form would exist even if there were *no* market for it. It's the same kind of delight a contractor who builds shopping malls might derive from constructing an ornate dollhouse, or a fine jeweler would get from making a pair of tiny earrings instead of a massive necklace. There is a joy in the pure form an idea must take to be expressed in the brief format of a short story. Those of us who operate within the peculiar closed universe of science fiction—a literature of ideas—are addicted to that kind of satisfaction. Novels can't always give it to us. Short stories can, no matter what the Rolling Stones say to the contrary.

There's no room for laziness, no margin for error, in a short story. An author can't make the reader forget a bad bit of exposition by burying him or her under a twenty-page space battle in the next chapter. There's no next chapter, no tomorrow, in the short story. It's live television versus taped, with the same attractions. An author has to do things right the first time, because he can't fix any problems on a nonexistent page hundred and fifty.

When the author has done his job right, there's nothing to compare with a good science fiction short. Long-time readers often remember shorts after hundred-thousand-word novels have long been forgotten. Storms last longer, are more varied and impressive, but what onlookers often remember most are the rainbows. Brief, affecting, bright.

That's what a good sf short story should be. If any of the tales told herein meet those criteria, then I've done my job.

Alan Dean Foster
Prescott, AZ '83

Swamp Planet Christmas

One of the more popular formats for short sf in the heyday of the digest-size magazines of the 1950s was the open "letter" story. Letters were exchanged by an astonishing assortment of humans and aliens in the pages of everything from *Astounding* to *Startling Stories*.

Eric Frank Russel was the master of this kind of interstellar communication, just as he was the master of the bureaucratic foul-up tale, the most notable example of which is his Hugo-winning story "Allamagoosa."

We've progressed beyond the days when that type of misunderstood long-range communication could affect not only individual lives but the histories of whole worlds. Because now we have computers to straighten out any little semantic difficulties we sloppy humans are heir to.

Or was that "air" to? . . .

FROM: HQ, Colonial Office
     Myraville, Myra II
     Michael Sjonstrom
     Acting Advisor

TO: MASTUREXX CENTRAL
     Sangeles, Terra
     Annex 119-ab

SUBJECT: Aboriginal Conflict

Dear sirs:

I'd like to remind you again (officially this time, as my unofficial inquiries seem to have met with oblivion) of our situation here.

Myra II is, as you have been notified, a tropical planet. Several rare foods and drugs are found in plenty in its swamps and rainforests. Unfortunately most of the ground, if such it can be called, lies under an average of five to fifteen feet of water. The mud at the bottom is not much thicker. Through considerable skill on the part of our engineers we have managed to construct a fairly stable series of stilt towns. A similar style was once utilized in the tropical areas of Terra. Our transportation is by boat and swamp-skimmer.

However, Myra II is also the home of a rather mean-tempered race of amphibians whose natural abode is the swamp and shallow lake. They have been rated at least Grade III intelligence. They possess a language, tools, and uncomfortably effective weapons. Singly they are no problem and in fact they seem to prefer moving in solitary couples, coming together in large groupings only for religious festivals and defense. Collectively they display somewhat greater intelligence.

Which brings us to the problem.

In our harvesting the wild flora they have somehow gotten it into their soggy skulls that we've violated their swamp-gods, or whatever. Anyhow, that's what the anthropologists feed me. Especially in our depredations (their word) of the wild *pingrov* tree. The *pingrov* just happens to be the source of Tyone. Tyone is not duplicable under laboratory conditions. When used in small quantities it has the property of strengthening worn or damaged heart muscle. Over 85% of our export revenue is derived from the harvesting and initial processing of raw Tyone from *pingrov* sap.

Or was. Since attacking our harvesting boats they've refused conciliation attempts. Under the prodding of their herb-doctors they have made it their aim to drive us off the planet.

Your suggestions and assistance are therefore urgently solicited.

SIGNED: Michael Sjonstrom
    Capt., Colonial Service

FROM: HQ, Colonial Office
    Myraville, Myra II
    Michael Sjonstrom
    Acting Advisor

TO: MASTUREXX CENTRAL
    Sangeles, Terra
    Annex 119-ab

SUBJECT: Aboriginal Conflict

Sirs:

Once again I call your attention to our problem here. Under a great herb-doctor named Umoo, several neighboring tribes have banded together with the locals in their efforts to wipe us out. Harvesting of raw Tyone and other products has nearly ceased. All attempts to negotiate the situation have been repulsed.

The natives are difficult to spot in the murky waters and the innumerable submerged logs, rocks and other objects render tracking by sonar almost impossible. The Grimps are extremely quick in the water and their darts, fired from long tubes by powerful wooden springs, can penetrate nylon armor at an impressive distance. Due to its clumsiness, hunting in spacearmor is impractical.

I implore you once again to send us your suggestions and any material aid the department can spare. We are being driven back to Myraville, our original base. If help is not forthcoming I fear I shall be forced to recommend abandonment of the colony.

SIGNED: Michael Sjonstrom
    Capt., Colonial Service

FROM: HQ, Colonial Office
    Myraville, Myra II
    Debbie Sjonstrom, age 8½

TO: MASTUREXX CENTRAL
    Sangeles, Terra
    Annex 119-ab

SUBJECT: Christmas

Dear MASTUREXX:

Hi! My name is Debbie Sjonstrom and I will be nine in three months. My daddy is in charge of our colony here. Do you know my daddy? Maybe not, even tho he says you know just about everything and everybody.

I am not supposed to be talking to you but I thot it

would be fun to talk to Earth again. Daddy thinks I don't know how to use the comspactyper but I've watched him lots of times and it looks pretty easy. And it *is*! Everyone says I'm awful smart for my age and I guess they're probably right.

Anyhow, daddy says you sometimes help people out in the colonies get what they need really bad. Well, it's almost Christmas time and I need some things *real bad*! Not lots, just a few. Daddy is so busy that I thot maybe you could get them for me. Or write to Santa Claus about them. He could help. He can get *anything*.

I need a Dolly and a swamp-bike and a real Mark XX laser rifle so I can help daddy shoot the bad Grimps and that nasty mister Umoo.

THANK YOU: Debbie Sjonstrom

FROM: MASTUREXX Annex 119-ab
　　　Colonial Control

TO: MASTUREXX CENTRAL

SUBJECT: Request from Myra II colony

An inquiry has been received reporting apparent native hostilities on the planet.

Request for one (1) Mark XX laser rifle forwarded to Shipping, Colonial Armaments section 26 (medium single-person armor). Coded cr#14925-A

Request for one (1) swamp-bike forwarded to Shipping, Colonial Luxury Items. Coded cr#14925-B

Request for one (1) Dolly, type unspecified, forwarded to Shipping, Colonial Luxury Items. Coded cr#14925-C

Noted by Terminal 44, Annex 119-ab

P. S.: Inquiry is directed concerning individual identified only as Claus, Santa. Suggest follow-up.

No reference exists in Annex files.
END NOTICE—cr#14925-ABC

FROM: MASTUREXX CENTRAL
TO: Shipping, Colonial Armaments (section 26)
SUBJECT: Order

Request for one (1) Mark XX laser rifle received cr#14925-A. Action directed: Approved. Forward.

FROM: MASTUREXX CENTRAL
TO: Shipping, Colonial Luxury Items
SUBJECT: Order

Request for one (1) swamp-bike received cr#14925-B. Action directed: Approved. Forward.

FROM: MASTUREXX CENTRAL
TO: Personnel, Colonial Service
TO: Personnel, Civil Service
SUBJECT: Personnel Inquiry

Inquiry received from Annex 119-ab per cr#14925-ABC concerning one Claus, Santa. Annex recommends follow-up.

Action directed: Approved. Complete dossier to be forwarded to MASTUREXX CENTRAL for evaluation. File Code SCX.

FROM: MASTUREXX CENTRAL
       Sangeles, Terra
       Annex 119-ab
TO: Receiving, Colonial Office

Myraville, Myra II

SUBJECT: Requests

Dear sirs:

Encl. find one (1) Mark XX laser rifle, one (1) gross Mark XX-i energy packs, one (1) Mark XX-ii cleaning kit.

Encl. find one (1) swamp-bike, energized, 2095 model supreme, suitable for pre-adolescent bipeds ages 4 to 12.

END NOTICE

FROM: MASTUREXX CENTRAL
    Sangeles, Terra

TO: HQ, Colonial Office
    Myraville, Myra II
    Debbie Sjonstrom, age 8½

SUBJECT: Requests

Dear Miss/Mrs.:

Shipped: One (1) Mark XX laser rifle with energy packs and cleaning equipment, plus one (1) model 2095 supreme swamp-bike, as per request cr#14925, coded A and B, respectively.

Action request: Specifications in detail required for processing of cr#14925-C, otherwise identified as 'Dolly.'

Action in process: Request any further information available on person identified as Claus, Santa, in previous notice, in compliance with Combat Areas Act, section IV.

END NOTICE

FROM: HQ, Colonial Office
    Myraville, Myra II
    Michael Sjonstrom

Acting Advisor

TO: MASTUREXX CENTRAL
Sangeles, Terra
Annex 119-ab

SUBJECT: Aboriginal Conflict

Sirs:

The laser rifle is of course welcome and ought to bolster our defense somewhat as well as our morale. I don't mean to sound ungrateful, gentlemen/machine, but we've tried lasers and they're just not good enough. We've got a unique situation here. Uniquely dangerous. And we need a new-type response. We've tried small subs. Too easily trapped. We've tried aquatic jury-rigged armor. Insufficiently maneuverable.

Understand, we need a new approach here. Yesterday I lost two more men. Natives surprised them by attacking from the trees while others apparently used diversionary tactics in the water. *These are not animals we're fighting!* Their adoption of new and sophisticated tactics like that is making for a critical situation here.

Send us something *new*, damn it! And it better be soon!

SIGNED: Michael Sjonstrom
Capt., Colonial Service

P.S. Thank whoever sent the swamp-bike to my daughter. Maybe someday she'll be able to use it safely.

FROM: HQ, Colonial Office
Myraville, Myra II
Debbie Sjonstrom

TO: MASTUREXX CENTRAL
Sangeles, Terra

Annex 119-ab

SUBJECT: Christmas

Dear MASTUREXX:

Thank you for the swamp-bike, even if I can't ride it yet. Ema and Davy are all over it already. Little brothers and sisters can be a pain!

Daddy kept the laser but he must need it real bad so I didn't say anything. I got your letter when I was watching the compspactyper for the operating man. We don't get much communication that way so he lets me watch it for him when he goes out for lunch and other things. I told him I'd always call him when something came in but this was my own letter so I didn't.

Don't you know who Santa Claus is? Boy, and I thot you were so smart! Santa stays up at the North Pole (the one on Terra, I guess) and every Christmas he flies down and gives toys and things to all the good little boys and girls, even big ones, like me. He flies in a big red sleigh which is pulled by reindeer. Reindeer are 'arctic terran ungulates,' which is what my cyclopedia says.

I want a Little Miss Nucleon Dolly, one that walks and talks and has her own remote-controlled sky-scoot! THANK YOU: Debbie Sjonstrom

FROM: MASTUREXX Annex 119-ab
    Colonial Control

TO: MASTUREXX CENTRAL

SUBJECT: Request from Myra II colony

Reply received to action request per cr#14925-C.

Request for Dolly, Little Miss Nucleon, with auxiliary sky-scoot, remote-controlled, forwarded to Shipping, Colonial Luxury Items, child, minor.

Reply received to Action-in-Process per File Coded SCX per cr#14925-ABC. Data forwarded to Masturexx Central.

Noted by Terminal 73, Annex 119-ab.
END NOTICE

FROM: Masturexx Central

TO: Shipping, Colonial Luxury Items, Child, Minor

SUBJECT: Order

Tangent to request cr#14925-C (unfilled):
Request is for one Dolly, Little Miss Nucleon.
Action directed: Approved. Forward.
Addenda: Included with order formal apology for failure to comprehend initial request.

P. S. Be certain to include one (1) sky-scoot, remote control, for same.
END NOTICE CR#14925-CS

FROM: Masturexx Central
    Sangeles, Terra
    Annex 119-ab

TO: Receiving, Colonial Office
    Myraville, Myra II

SUBJECT: Request

Dear sirs:
Encl. find one (1) Dolly, Little Miss Nucleon, with remote-controlled sky-scoot for same, as per cr#14925-CS.

Encl. find one (1) standard ICC Data apology #14.
END NOTICE

FROM: Masturexx Central

TO: Personnel, Colonial Service

TO: Personnel, Civil Service

TO: War Department

TO: Civil Defense Department

SUBJECT: File Coded SCX

Encl. find additional data on individual known as Claus, Santa.

Report follows:

To date no department has been able to locate any significant information on subject. Data newly received from colony on Myra II during hostilities suggests person may be involved in attempt to indoctrinate Terran youth (probably pre-teen). Said individual is reported to be operating in an area on Terra itself suitable to such operations.

Suggest subject be treated with utmost secrecy to avoid unnecessary panic among populace, until this unusual situation has been clarified.

Action directed: Continue investigation.

Action directed: Research into levitational capabilities of Terran herbivore known as REINDEER. See reference files LAPLAND, SIBERIA, CANADA/ALASKA.

END NOTICE

FROM: War Department
    Central Computer

TO: MASTUREXX CENTRAL

SUBJECT: File Coded SCX

Information received and appropriate action initiated.

Evaluation: Concur.

END NOTICE

FROM: Muknuk-on-Baffin
    NA Territory
    Servan ThreeRivers
    Chief of Police

TO: Central Police Terminal
    Information
    Bermuda

SUBJECT: Robot Insanity

Dear sirs:

    What in the seven great flaming hells is going on? Look, I operate a nice, peaceful little village, guys. No muss, no fuss, no trouble. Too cold to fight, even. Not like Bosyork or Crasaw. We like it. *I* like it.

    So why are we suddenly deluged one morning with enough machine armor to blow up half the continent? Kindly remove your [CENSORED] robots from my village or my neighbors will [CENSORED] your [CENSORED CENSORED].

SIGNED: Servan ThreeRivers
    Lt., Police

FROM: HQ, Colonial Office
    Myraville, Myra II
    Debbie Sjonstrom, age 8½

TO: MASTUREXX CENTRAL
    Sangeles, Terra
    Annex, 119-ab

SUBJECT: Christmas

Dear MASTUREXX:

    Golly, I almost forgot! While you're finding my Dolly, maybe you could help us get rid of these nasty Grimps. Daddy is having all *kinds* of trouble with them! I'm sending you the official town printout on them because it uses a lot of big words that I don't know (yet).

Please help my daddy for his Christmas present!

Also, big sisters should be nice to their little brothers and sisters (even if they are a pain), so I want to tell you that Ema wants some guppies for her aquarium and Davy wants a Pallurium transceiver set, a real one. SIGNED: Debbie Sjonstrom.

P. S. Merry Christmas!

FROM: MASTUREXX Annex 119-ab
TO: MASTUREXX CENTRAL
SUBJECT: cp#2335 Myra II

Encl. find fax of transbeam comuspac report on outbreak of hostilities on Myra II colony. Emotional analysis of content suggests speed essential. Implementation AAA priority.
END NOTICE

FROM: MASTUREXX CENTRAL
TO: War Department, Research
SUBJECT: cp#2335 per Annex 119-ab-12AAA

Action directed: AAA implementation on enclosed request for solution to problem of native amphibian uprising.

ENCL.: 1 local report/request.

1 Breakdown/analysis of suggestions embodied in local report/request (110 copies).
END NOTICE

FROM: War Department, Research
TO: MASTUREXX CENTRAL
SUBJECT: cp#2335 per Annex 119-ab-12AAA

Action directed: Solution to problem contained in analysis of suggestions from local report/request breakdown/analysis. Devices prepared. Special handling requirements will delay shipping slightly. Degree of effectiveness of solution est. 96.354% probable. Rating: superior.
END NOTICE

FROM: Central Police Terminal
    Strategy and Dispersement
    Albert Tuambo
    Asst. Commdnt.

TO: Muknuk-on-Baffin
    NA Territory
    Servan ThreeRivers
    Chief of Police

SUBJECT: Overreaction

Dear Lt. ThreeRivers:

Sorry for the inconvenience. Apparently a computer nexus blew a fuse unit somewhere and became convinced the bogeymen were descending in your area. All robot peace enforcers should by now have withdrawn.

I still don't know what the heck happened myself. Driving my best techs up the wall.
SIGNED: Albert Tuambo
    Col., C. P.
ENCL.: 1 check, payment for damages by local peace-enforcers.

1 bill, enumerated, for damage by inhabitants of Muknuk-on-Baffin, NA Territory, to Tank, Medium, serial #175AWE.

1 civil suit, registered, for unprovoked attack on person of official investigator.

1 bill, cleaning, for removal of foreign substances (tar and goose feathers) from uniform of same.

FROM: Personnel, Colonial Service
TO: MASTUREXX CENTRAL
SUBJECT: File Coded SCX

Reply: Santa Claus?
Comment: Suggest re-examination of your logic circuits and complete overhaul of central rationality paneling.
END NOTICE

FROM: MASTUREXX CENTRAL
TO: War Department
TO: Civil Defense Department
SUBJECT: File Coded SCX

Reply received from Personnel, Colonial Service.
Action directed: In view of nature of data received, file coded SCX is hereby closed and sealed.
Response: Certificate of censure is hereby entered into official records of Annex 119-ab against future computer promotions.
Addenda: Subordinate computers are reminded that levity directed towards MASTUREXX CENTRAL and/or MASTUREXX CENTRAL directives is in violation of Computer Code Basic of 2046, para 83, sub-sections 4-8.
END NOTICE

FROM: HQ, Colonial Office
    Myraville, Myra II
    Michael Sjonstrom

Acting Advisor

TO: MASTUREXX CENTRAL
Sangeles, Terra
Annex 119-ab

SUBJECT: Congratulations

Dear sirs:

Well, for a while there I must admit you had me worried. Confess I'd almost given up hope of being noticed. When your new weapons system arrived, the Grimps were in the process of undermining our central support shafts. Never would have found out until too late if your stuff hadn't shown up when it did. My apologies, but sometimes you people cut it too damn close!

Never would have thought of it here. Kudos to the man/machine that thought it up. Eeesh! Didn't believe it myself until I'd finished the instruction booklets. Radio-controlled mutated piranhas indeed! Stroke of genius there, somewhere. We completely neglected the angle of bio-weaponry. But it was almost worth all the trouble just to see old Umoo fly up a *Pikma* tree, picking up thorns at every step!

Our Bio-boys didn't think Grimps could swim that fast.

It didn't take much to get them to sign a treaty. Next shipment of Tyone is due out on the 5th, local. We've turned off the piranhas, and with the treaty the kids can go swimming and swamp-bike riding now. But we'll keep them in case they're needed again—though I doubt it, judging from the way those frogs *moved*.

SIGNED WITH THANKS: Michael Sjonstrom

Capt., Colonial Service

ENCL.: One (1) scroll, commemorative, signed by populace of colony Myra II.

P. S. Off the record, any idea who's been sending my eldest expensive gifts?

FROM: MASTUREXX CENTRAL
    Sangeles
    Control
TO: MASTUREXX Research and Development
    Roma
    EU Territory
    Edwin Aliyah
    Programmer-in-Charge
SUBJECT: MASTUREXX

Dear Ed:

I think you ought to fly up. Something fishy going on here.
SIGNED: Bob Golles
    Master Technician

FROM: Interspace T&T
    Billing Department
    Ebostone City
    Tau Ceti IV
TO: HQ, Acctg., Colonial Office
    Myraville, Myra II
    Acting Advisor
SUBJECT: Cash

Dear sir:

Been busy, you folks, haven't you?
SIGNED: Simwa Agryopopulous
    Director, Accounts
ENCL.: One (1) bill, interspace beam commu., for period fiscal 1 December through 30 Lastmonth T-standard 2094: 12,342.77 credits.

Noel.

17

Snake Eyes

The mysterious young man Philip Lynx, better known to his readers as Flinx, and his empathic flying snake Pip have gallivanted through five novels written over a span of twelve years. They've become good friends of mine. I feel I know Pip, for instance, as well as I know my own six-foot-long Colombian boa constrictor, Samuel.

I wish I knew whether Samuel was a he or a she, though. It's tough to tell with a snake, and after they get to be Sam's size it's tricky to press the point. Not that it really matters. Sam feels like a he to me, and so far he hasn't bothered to argue about it. It's just a feeling I have, of course. I'm often chided for believing that anything as lowly as a snake can project any kind of feeling.

But it's sure fun to imagine one could, and

many's the time in those tales that Flinx has been glad Pip could sense what he was feeling. Never more so than in the story that follows...

Her name was Pip. She was a minidrag, or flying snake. She was barely two-thirds of a meter long, and no bigger around than the wrist of a sensitive woman. Her venom could kill a man in sixty seconds. In a hundred if she missed the eyes when she spat.

Until a few seconds ago it had been an unremarkable day. Then unexpected and overwhelming emotion-thoughts had struck her like a wave bowling over an unprepared crustacean. Her own feelings tumbled up and over, spun and submerged and overpowered by other thoughts. Pip was a sensitive empathic telepath, and the emotional outburst she'd just received was not to be denied.

Through slitted pupils she could see the slim form of her young master, an adolescent named Flinx, asleep on the park bench below her perch. He dreamed pleasant mind-mirages devoid of fear or worry while fuguelbell leaves tinkled overhead, crisp as the damp morning air. Pip shivered slightly. Moth, Flinx's home world, was always cooler than the comfortable jungle and veldt of her own Alaspin.

Their surroundings, a park in Drallar, Moth's capital city, were familiar and empty of menace. Nor did her roving senses detect anything like a threat in the immediate mental vicinity. Pip decided she could safely leave Flinx for a while.

The other objects of her concern, the offspring of her recent union on Alaspin with a solidly muscled minidrag named Balthazaar, were presently elsewhere, busily engaged in the hunts that were part of a minidrag's early education. She would have felt better about leaving Flinx had her progeny been around to watch over him in her absence, but the call swept over her again, insistent, mournful.

Slowly she slid free of her branch. Below, Flinx snuffled in his sleep, dreaming of matters as incomprehensible to her as they were important to him. Flinx's own mental abilities often weighed heavily on him.

Children playing nearby saw the brilliant pleated wings of pink and blue unfurl. They stared openmouthed at the leathery, supple beauty of the flying snake, ignorant of the lethal danger those wings represented. They watched with guileless fascination as the exquisitely jeweled creature climbed into the cloying dampness of Moth's air, spiraled above the chiming treetops, and soared southward out of the city.

Knigta Yakus would have traded a twenty-carat hallowseye for a glass of water. As events had developed, the sunken-chested old graybeard was one of the few men in the Commonwealth who could readily have made such an offer.

After eight despairing months in the High Desert of Moth's Dead-Place-on-Map he'd discovered a pocket of the rare orange gems extensive enough to support a dozen people in baroque splendor for the rest of their lives. Now he survived partly on the thought of the expressions his discovery would produce on the faces of the boasting rheumy wrecks who inhabited the sandy dives of Edgedune Town.

They had assured him he'd find nothing but sand and a dessicated death in the vast wastelands of Dead-Place-on-Map. And they'd laughed at him.

One hand reached into the left pocket of his torn overalls and fondled what would be an eloquent rebuttal to every taunt and cheap joke. It was the single crystal he was bringing out with him: an electric-orange translucent lump of basic alumina-silicate weighing some two hundred and twelve carats. Properly cut, it would display a remarkable simulacrum of a human eye in its center, an eye that would stare back at whoever looked at it. A well-cut hallowseye also produced an emotional response in whoever saw it, a response generated not by beauty but by peculiar piezoelectric fields within the stone itself.

This particular gem would finance his return to the High Desert, a decently equipped return with proper equipment. After that, he'd mine-out the lode and then he would never have to work another day of his life. But if he didn't find water very soon, he might not have another day of his life left not to work in.

For the hundredth time he reminded himself that this desperate situation was his own damned fault. With ten months' supplies he'd confidently marched into Dead-Place-on-Map, knowing full well that in the desolate reaches of the High Desert he could anticipate finding no water and precious little game.

Five days before, he'd shot a skipgravel. Only hunger had enabled him to eat all of the tiny quasi-rodent, down to the last bean-size organ. That had been his last solid food. His water...when had his water run out? His brain said yesterday. His tongue and throat argued for a week.

Leaning back, he glared at the cloud-mottled sky that had become an unfriendly, unavoidable companion. It was overcast, as always. Few regions on the winged world of Moth saw the sun more than a couple of days a year. But the homogenized clouds overhead

21

held on to their slight moisture content with the tenacity of a bereaved mistress guarding her benefactor's will.

Towering on the western horizon, broken-toothed mountains prevented any substantial moisture from reaching the High Desert. It all fell heavily on their eastern slopes. None fell where it could revive Knigta Yakus.

Painfully he squinted at the distant snow-capped spires of five-thousand-meter-high Mount Footasleep. Beneath it and several kilometers to the north lay Coccyxcrack Pass and the town of Edgedune. Both were unbearably far away, impossibly out of his reach.

In his youth, when his body was made of braided duralloy cable insulated in hard flesh, he might have made it. Bitterly he cursed his eighty-two-year-old frame. The insulation was battered, the cables of his muscles corroded away. Dehydration gave his naturally thin form the look of a dead twig. Once-powerful muscles hung slackly from old bones like slabs of exfoliating shale.

A sad snort caused him to look backward. Even though he had already abandoned all his equipment, the dryzam was beginning to fail. The ten-meter-long scaly quadruped stumbled along faithfully in his wake. Its long anteaterlike snout swung slowly from side to side over the rocky ground. Absurdly tiny eyes glowed behind the snout. There were five of them, set in a curve across the top of the skull. Like the sails of an ancient ship, twin dorsal fins moved on the back. They helped to cool the tired creature, but that was no substitute for a long drink.

Oddly, the starving dryzam no longer made Yakus nervous, though his desiccated human carcass would make a welcome snack for the omnivorous beast of burden. A more faithful creature Yakus could not imagine. It had never complained about its load, or about the always slim rations Yakus had allowed it. Despite its evident thirst, the prospector was convinced it would die before it turned on him. The animal was the best purchase he'd made on Moth.

Yakus had a great deal of respect for such loyalty. He eyed the slightly swollen belly of the green-and-yellow beast sadly. Its meat and blood could keep him alive for some time, maybe even long enough to reach Edgedune. Idly he fingered the needler slung at his hip. Could he kill it?

"I'm sorry, Dryzam." He'd never bothered to name it.

The creature halted when Yakus did. It wheezed painfully, sounding like a badly tuned oboe. Already it had gone weeks without water. Its supremely efficient, streamlined body had extended itself as far as could be expected.

Five tiny eyes blinked expectantly, patiently back at him, ready to try to respond to his requests. "Tooop?" it inquired hopefully. "Too-whoop?"

"Stop that. Quit lookin' at me like that, you dumb dinosaur." Come on now, Yakus. No place to get sentimental. That's all it is, a damn dumb animal that's goin' to die soon anyhow.

Just like himself.

Yakus had spent most of his eighty-two years struggling to exist in a universe which made it much simpler to be dead. The crystals offered him a chance to spend his few remaining days in comfort. That is, they did if he could only bring himself to slaughter this ugly, staring, urine-colored heap of—

Something which was not a piece of cloud moved in the sky above him.

"Concentration's goin'," he muttered to himself as he fought to identify the object. Lately he'd been muttering to himself a lot.

The shape dipped lower, cruised near on convenient thermals. Yakus was a much-traveled, observant man. He recognized the intruder. He didn't believe his eyes, but he recognized it. It didn't belong in this desolate place, that tiny half-legendary dispenser of instant death. But there was no mistaking that shape and size and coloring.

Yakus was too debilitated, too worn out and despondent, to wonder what an Alaspinian minidrag was doing in Dead-Place-on-Map in the High Desert of Moth. All he could consider now was its reputation. No known antidote, natural or cultured, existed to counter the flying snake's venom.

He had to kill it first.

Riding air currents, the creature swooped lower. Yakus raised the needler. Reflexively his gaze went to the weapon's handle, automatically took in the reading on the built-in gauge.

Empty.

Despair.

He'd used his last charge in the weapon to kill the skipgravel.

Too frustrated to scream and too dehydrated to cry, he reversed the weapon. Hefting it by its narrow barrel, he wielded it like a club. It was an impractical gesture, but it made him feel a little less helpless.

"By God, it figures," he murmured exhaustedly. "Kill me then, apparition," he instructed the approaching winged form. "You'll be quicker, at least."

Despite his seeming resignation, Yakus didn't want to die. He wanted very much to live.

Rowing air, the minidrag stalled and regarded both

man and dryzam with unwinking eyes. Fluttering exquisite wings, it came closer, paused, darted away.

"Playin' with me." Somewhere Yakus found the strength to be disgusted. "Snake-an'-mouse, is it, you scaly little bastard? Disappear, vanish, you don't belong here."

Minutes went by. The minidrag did not disappear. Instead, it moved neither at him or away, but continued to hover. This wasn't right. If the creature was taunting him it was going about it in a most peculiar fashion. Likely it had wandered here from some inhabited region. It had to be lost. Didn't it want to drink Yakus's blood?

The minidrag moved much nearer, and Yakus saw something falling from wings and body, saw it glistening beneath wing pleats. He gagged a little.

The minidrag was dripping wet.

Thoughtlessly Yakus threw himself at the poisonous flier. It slipped easily back out of his reach, continuing to stare at him. Yakus fell to the ground, scrabbling at the sandy soil and gravel where droplets had struck. One pebble he touched was still noticeably damp. So—he was no madder than usual.

For a terrifying moment his legs refused to obey and he feared he wouldn't be able to get up. Hope made a powerful crutch, however, and he fought to rise to his feet.

"Where?" he pleaded dumbly, staring at the snake. It stared back at him. "Still wet." He was mumbling again, a little wildly now, as he threw undisciplined glances in every direction. "In this heat, that means that water has to be close by. But which way...oh God, which way?" His attention focused again on the hovering snake.

"You're not lost. You're with someone, aren't you?"

He glared dreamily at the minidrag. "That's it, there's an encampment nearby. Where? *Where!*"

As mute as its less-sensitive ancestors, the flying snake continued to regard him silently.

Yakus started to laugh. Here he stood, in a region no sane being would venture into on foot, conversing with a snake. Why stop with asking for water? He giggled. Why not request linzer-torte and lemonade while he was asking?

Unexpectedly the minidrag made a sudden turn, flew ten meters westward, and turned to regard Yakus expectantly. A little frightened, the old prospector ceased giggling. The minidrag flew back at him, hissed, then whirled and flew to hover once again ten meters off.

The situation was crazy, of course, Yakus assured himself. But then, so was the very presence of the minidrag. If the snake was a mirage, it was acting as sensibly as he'd been. Perhaps he ought to try following the mirage for a while.

"Hup!" His call produced a wheeze like a leaky balloon as the dryzam swung to follow the man following the snake.

Fly ten meters and wait for man and beast to catch up. Fly and wait, fly and wait.

Near the end of his endurance, Yakus had no idea how long he'd been following the insistent minidrag. But he soon knew he could go no farther. If the minidrag's water was real, it was too far off for him. No one knew he was about to become the wealthiest corpse on Moth. Desperately, his weakened mind sent walk messages to his legs. Water-starved cells rejected the request. Old knees struck unyielding gravel and sand as Yakus's torso toppled forward and splashed into the surface.

Splashed?

26

He opened his eyes and discovered he couldn't see. The water was too murky. As he raised his head he heard a deep gurgling sound nearby. The dryzam was sucking up water like a skimmer taking on fuel.

Murky water... Yakus would gratefully have accepted a feast made of mud. Anything possessing moisture.

The pool rested in a low hollow beneath a shading, upthrust blade of gray-white phyllite. The pool was barely two meters wide. An ocean.

Crawling in, he lay on his back against the sandy bottom. His throat hurt from the unaccustomed act of swallowing. He felt ten years old.

After half an hour of luxuriating in the life-giving liquid, he thought to thank his benefactor. "Hey, snake, Knigta Yakus gives life to you! Snake?"

Sitting up in the shallow water, he glanced around curiously. The minidrag was nowhere to be seen.

"Oh, well, the motives of a little snake-thing..."

Something nearby coughed unpleasantly. Yakus tensed, the hidden sun drawing water off him. The cough was repeated. Getting to his knees, Yakus looked around warily.

A head peeked out from behind the far side of the overhanging rock. It was a big head, square and nasty. Mostly black, it was spotted with patches of gray and yellow that enabled it to blend in well with the predominant colors of the High Desert.

Yakus had wondered during his long dry march about the possible presence of scavengers. Now he didn't have to wonder anymore. Coming around the stone, the head was followed by a thick, powerful turtlelike body moving on six lean legs. The predator was half the mass of his dryzam.

Ordinarily the big dorsal-finned beast of burden

27

would have pounded this menace into the sand. But the dryzam was so weak from hunger that it could barely stand, and this dark gleaner of the dry sands instinctively sensed the larger creature's helplessness. Once it was finished with the dryzam, the spotted killer would undoubtedly have Yakus for dessert. As rare as substantial prey probably was hereabouts, the prospector was convinced the dryzam would not be enough to satisfy this monster.

Turning to confront the smaller beast now stalking it, the dryzam lowered its head and tooted a feeble warning. Yakus was sure the temporary revitalizing effect of the water would dissipate quickly under the demands of combat.

While the carnivore's attention was focused on the dryzam, Yakus backed deeper into the pond and hunted for the largest rock he could lift. Maybe while the hunter was occupied with his beast, Yakus could sneak up behind and crush the thick black skull. It seemed to be his only chance.

He located a good-size boulder. The dark predator continued to circle the dryzam, tiring it, worrying it. Sheer exhaustion would finish the dryzam's chances before a single blow could be exchanged.

Struggling with the large stone, Yakus discovered that his own reserves of energy were unequal to the task. He might lift it, but he could never carry it and strike with it. The predator yawned, displaying double rows of pointed, curved-back teeth. Yakus groaned at his own stupidity. A water hole! Where better for a lone hunter to make its den? He should have anticipated such a possibility and prepared for it.

Then suddenly something thin and winged darted between the dryzam and the hexapod closing in. It spat, a thin sound in the dry desert air. The hexapod halted, blinked—then screamed.

Yakus half swam, half ran in his attempts to stay out of the predator's path as it tumbled over and over, clawing at its eyes where the corrosive venom had struck. In doing so, the creature sped the poison into its own bloodstream.

Kicking convulsively, the beast sprawled into the pool. One clawed hind leg barely missed the retreating prospector. Then it scrabbled clear of the water, crawled a few meters, and lay twitching on its belly. The twitches grew fewer and fainter, but several minutes passed before they ceased altogether.

As Yakus watched, the minidrag settled itself on a nearby wind-scoured boulder and started to preen. His gaze then traveled to the substantial corpse lying on the sand. Slowly the dryzam wandered over to it. Several long sniffs apparently satisfied the patient creature. The first bite of tough dark flesh was difficult. After that the dryzam ate with increasing ease and gusto.

When a quarter of the predator had vanished down the dryzam's gullet and it still showed no ill effects, a salivating Yakus drew his knife and moved to join in the feast.

After the clouds had turned black and the screened sun had set, Yakus found himself sitting contentedly against a dry rock next to the pool. He'd felt this good exactly three times previously in his life: when he'd defeated Jorge Malpaso, the famous null-ball player, at arm wrestling; when he'd escaped from jail on Almaggee; and four years ago, when on a dare and a bet he'd shown a certain saucy barmaid on Kansastan that aging can improve other things besides wine.

For three days the pool was home, during which

time he rested and recovered his strength. Despite his inevitable worries, no other carnivore showed up to claim the oasis. Yakus watched the harmless ones who came to drink and let them leave in peace. He already had as much meat as he and his dryzam could handle.

On the fourth day he rose, secured the rest of the meat as best he could between the dorsal fins on the dryzam's back, and started off confidently in the direction of Edgedune. When the minidrag settled onto his shoulder he wasn't too surprised. Still, he was only partly successful at hiding his fear at the proximity of so deadly a creature, however friendly it had proven itself to be.

The minidrag seemed content to ride there. On the sixth day Yakus tentatively reached out to touch it. It did not threaten him. The prospector smiled. It was several days later that he first noticed the tiny tag clipped beneath the rear of one wing.

IF FOUND ALIVE OR DEAD, the tag read, PLEASE RETURN TO . . . It gave a name and several addresses. The first lay reasonably close to Edgedune.

Yakus might die soon anyway, but not before he had returned his leathery savior to its proper owner.

Flinx was drinking at an outdoor stall. A slim youth, red-haired and dark-skinned, he concealed many secrets and unusual abilities beneath an unremarkable exterior.

Only a loud commotion among the stalls lining the upper street roused him from his thoughts, which had been soured with concern these past days. Curious, he turned along with the vendors and other shoppers in the marketplace to see what the cause was. As he did so, something landed with familiar pressure on his right shoulder.

"Pip!" He stroked the minidrag's neck as it curled close to him. "Where have you been? You worried me crazy. I thought—"

"Don't be harsh on your pet!" Flinx looked toward the source of the imploring voice, saw a straight if aged form crowned with curly black-and-white hair striding toward him. The principal source of the commotion which had first attracted him trailed behind the old man. It was a peculiar, high-finned creature that barely managed to squeeze itself between the closely packed street stalls. Children ran alongside, gesturing and poking at the unfamiliar monster.

The oldster regarded Flinx speculatively. "I am Knigta Yakus. I owe your pet my life." A hand like a gnarled piece of firewood indicated the relaxing minidrag. "Later I will make you rich. But I must know—if this place is your home, and you this minidrag's master, why did it seek me out in Dead-Place-on-Map to save me?"

Flinx murmured reprovingly at his pet, "So that's where you disappeared to." He peered past the gray-beard to inspect the oldster's beast of burden. "A dryzam."

Yakus had thought he was beyond surprise. He discovered otherwise. "You know this creature? I purchased it here, but it is not of this world, and few recognize it. You do."

"Yes. Oddly enough, this creature comes from the same world as my minidrag—Alaspin." He patted the creature's flank, and it tootled in pleasure. "But that doesn't explain why Pip went to you. Minidrags are empathic telepaths, sensitive to powerful emotions. Ordinarily Pip responds only to mine. This seems to be an exception. I wonder why."

"I think I can explain." Yakus sounded satisfied. "I

was dying, you see. Your snake sensed that, over all this distance, and came to rescue me." He expanded his chest proudly. "I didn't know old Yakus could feel anything that strongly."

Flinx shook his head in confusion. "No. People have died all the time around me." The way he said that made the perceptive prospector eye him narrowly. Perhaps this boy was not the innocent he looked. "Pip never left me to save any of them. And she has reasons for staying especially close to me now. I don't understand." Turning, he eyed Yakus. "I'd like to know why she did leave me to save you."

Yakus decided it no longer mattered. "She saved me. That is what is important. She saved me to make you rich. Come with me, help me do a little hard work, and you will have more credit than you can imagine."

The reaction was not quite what Yakus expected from a simply dressed lad only a few years removed from urchinhood. "Thanks, but I already have enough credit for my needs." He seemed embarrassed by the admission.

"However," he continued, before a stunned, disbelieving Yakus could respond, "I'll come with you anyway. You see, it's important for me to know why Pip—my pet—left me. No offense, but I just can't believe it was to save you. Whenever Pip leaves me it becomes a matter of intense interest. There've been too many times when I had to have her around. So . . . I'll go with you." Flinx grinned. "Anyhow, I've never seen the High Desert, much less Dead-Place-on-Map, though I've heard a lot about it. It's not a very appealing place, I understand."

When Yakus was through laughing, he showed Flinx the crystal. Surely he had nothing to fear from this boy, who seemed honest and deserved well, if only because he was not quite right in the head. "A hallows-eye!" Flinx was properly impressed. "I've never seen one that big."

Yakus winked conspiratorially. "There are many more this size and larger. The emotions from the deposit are so strong I could hardly bear to work the lode. This"—he tapped the magnificent orange gem—"will outfit us for the work and the journey. We will bring back crystals enough to bow the back of my dryzam. When can you come with me?"

Flinx shrugged, gestured. "When my curiosity's at stake, my impatience matches it. Come on, I'll introduce you to a reasonably honest outfitter."

They walked off down the street, conversing amiably, the dryzam trailing behind. The woman buying jewelry from the stall next to the foodshop edged aside as the bulky beast of burden slid multiple hips down the narrow avenue. She had the slim, lithe figure of an adolescent, but was a good deal older. Flowing clothes obscured all skin save face and hands, which were the color of milk-rich fudge.

A diamond ornamented one pierced nostril. She turned to regard the receding procession with much interest, robes of water-repellent silk shuffling like frozen wind about her. So intent was she on the two retreating male figures that the jeweler was prompted to ask if anything was wrong.

"Wrong? No, no." She smiled at the man, teeth flashing whitely, bright enough to form two small crescent moons in her face. She pointed absently at a pair of wormwood-and-onyx earrings. "I'll take those. Deliver them to this address." She handed the jeweler a card on which was impressed her name, a personal identification number, and the address in question.

While the jeweler hastened to process the transaction through his cardmeter she turned to the man standing patiently nearby. He was short, no taller than she, but perhaps ten years older. Face and body showed globules and bulges of fat. Their surfaces were taut, however, without age wrinkles or the true signature of the hopelessly obese. The man simply had the physique of a baby never grown up.

"You heard everything, Wuwit?" inquired the woman Savaya.

He nodded once. "I did. I'll go get Michelos."

"No." She put out a hand to restrain him, then gestured down the street at the disappearing convoy. "Follow that carnival. See where they go, learn who they talk to, stay with them. I'll find Michelos myself." They parted.

Wuwit watched her progress for a moment, then turned and ambled off after the two men with a speed startling to those not familiar with his abilities. One of the men, he'd noted, was old, the other much younger.

They were an easy pair to trail inconspicuously, since the docile dragon's rump rose and swayed above the ground. So intent was Wuwit on his assignment, however, that he failed to notice the tall, gangly ornithorpe pacing parallel to him on the other side of the street. Nor did the feathered alien notice Wuwit.

A rounded, swaybacked body was mounted on two long, feathered legs. These fitted into boots which reached to the knobby knees. Those knees reached to a normal man's waist. A long thin neck ended in the elongated skull, from which protruded a short, curved beak in front, ruffled plumage behind.

In addition to the boots, the creature wore a slickertic cape designed for his shape. A lightweight garment that kept off the perpetual moisture of Moth's atmosphere, the slickertic did not cover the headdress, a construction of blue-green-yellow foil which complemented the alien's natural gray-and-brown plumage.

Various gems, some real, some imitation, dotted the long weaving neck, the chest, and the long thin arms which had evolved from ancient wings.

The ornithorpe's name was Pimbab. He'd been taking his ease in the same drinking establishment as Flinx. Despite the absence of external ears, the alien's hearing was acute—which was why he was presently shadowing the two humans and their lumbering beast, his mind filled with visions of ornithoid larceny.

Roly-poly human and attenuated bird-thing ignored each other with a single-mindedness of purpose matched only by a similarity of intention.

Flinx wiped the back of his left hand across his brow. Moisture-wrung clouds obscured the sun, but he could feel its veiled heat. Yakus was beginning to draw slightly ahead of him, and Flinx touched his spurs lightly to the flank of his muccax. The squat two-legged toad-creature gave a grunt and hopped to close the distance.

"You walked this?" Flinx asked in admiration.

Yakus nodded, his expression colored with pride as he turned to glance back at the supply-laden dryzam. "I did that. Walked in and walked out, though I couldn't have done the last without the help of your pet." He gestured at the curled, sleeping snake-shape on Flinx's right shoulder.

Flinx glanced backward, past the plodding dryzam, to the distant ridge of the Snaggles, over which lorded Mount Footasleep. They'd come a long way since leaving somnolent Edgedune, and according to Yakus still had a good distance to go. Heat made the terrain and horizon ahead soften and run like multicolored butter.

"I still don't quite understand why you insisted on these muccax"—Flinx rapped the broad, bony skull of his own mount affectionately—"instead of having us hire a good skimmer."

"Too much dust and gravel in the air here. Skimmer's a mistake too many first-timers make," Yakus explained. "Usually they're last-timers as a result." He tapped his visor. "Grit in the air is full of all kinds of abrasive dissolved metals. Chews the hell out of any skimmer's air intakes. No thanks, I'll take my chances with live transport. I like the flexibility a muccax gives me. You get to be my age, boy, and you learn to appreciate flexibility. Besides, in an emergency, you can't eat a skimmer..."

Well behind the lecturing Yakus three other humans rode. "How far?" asked Michelos. He was a big man with a deep voice to match, athlete-tall and muscular. His legs nearly touched the ground on either side of his muccax.

Savaya had shed her traditional silks in favor of a more practical desert jumpsuit. She frowned at the sweating figure riding alongside her. "I haven't any idea. All the time they were talking, he never mentioned distances or location. Only that the mine's out here some place."

"'Out here some place.'" Michelos waved a thick, fuzz-covered arm at the vaporous horizon ahead. "That's more hundreds of square kilometers than I like to think about, Savaya." He squinted at her. "I'm not sure how I let you talk me into this in the first place."

"Yes, you are." She allowed herself a thin grin. "You joined up because you're just as greedy and selfish as Wuwit and me." She indicated the pudgy little figure partly behind them, who was suffering more from the heat than his two thinner companions. "You joined because I told you I saw a rough hallowseye of good quality that must have weighed two hundred carats."

Michelos started to reply, was interrupted. "It's all right, Mick," Wuwit insisted in his slightly squeaky voice. He was perspiring profusely. "This is easier than knocking vendors over the head and then trying to run from the gendarmes and the crowd. It can't be a total loss even if there is no mine. If we don't find any gems we sneak up behind them"—he nodded forward in the direction of the unseen trailbreakers—"kill 'em both, take the animals and the supplies. They bought plenty of supplies—I know, I saw them doing the ordering. Enough to more than pay for this trip."

"That makes sense, Wuwit." Michelos calmed down and turned his attention back to the dull seared plain undulating before them. Wuwit always managed to cheer him up when he was feeling bad, which was frequently. Michelos was not a man given much to happy thoughts, unless they involved the distress of others.

Savaya nudged her muccax with spurs. "Come on, we don't want to fall too far behind. Hallowseyes aren't found on the surface. Any mine would provide good cover, and in this flat country that could make a big difference if it comes to a fight. We want to get to them before they can get into it."

Michelos spurred his own mount viciously. It bleated and jumped forward. "Don't quote strategy to me, Savaya," he growled. "I'm no pimple-faced novice at this..."

Knigta Yakus halted his muccax on a slight rise of sand that was too high to be part of the plain, too tired to be called a hill. He pointed. "There it is, lad. Bet you'd thought we'd never reach it. Bet you was wondering if old Knigta was a liar."

"Oh, I believed you all the time, Yakus," Flinx told him. "I was just beginning to worry how much meat I'd have left on me by the time we arrived."

The hillock gave way before them to a gentle downslope. This abruptly turned into a sharp but not high drop, falling for a couple of meters to a flat, wide surface that might have been a sunken road. It was not, though it was gravel-paved across much of its surface, with streaks of darker ground forming ridges here and there.

The dry riverbed they were approaching was impressively broad. At one time a considerable amount of water must have flowed through this part of the High Desert, and recently, judging from the still-uneroded banks.

On the far bank lay a darker spot, which Yakus was gesturing at excitedly. It stood out clearly against the lighter material of the banks: unmistakably a gap in the rocky soil.

"And there's the pocket!" Yakus's excitement was evident in his voice. His hand moved to the south, tracing an invisible path along the extinct river. "Downstream the river floor divides. I found the first piece of crystal a dozen kilometers down there. Had to dig my way upstream. There are twenty other caves, not as big as that one, lining the stream bed in that direction." He nodded at the excavation across the riverbed.

"That hole's the twenty-first. I didn't think it would be the last, but it was. Let's go."

They started toward the river. Flinx regarded the

nearing bank warily. "I've never ridden muccax before. You sure they can handle this drop?"

"They're not fast and long-legged, but they're durable." Yakus looked behind them. "They'll handle the bank all right, but I'm a little worried about the dryzam. Seems kind of tired."

"That doesn't surprise me," Flinx replied, "considering the weight of those supplies it's carrying." He looked over a shoulder, saw the placid five-eyed creature trailing dutifully behind them, packages piled high between the stiff dorsal fins. "It's big enough. It should be able to put its front legs all the way down to the bed while its back legs rest on the bank top. As long as it doesn't break in the middle, I think it can make it."

"Hope you're right, boy. We'll have to try it. I don't feel like packing and unpacking half that stuff out in the midday sun..."

Savaya peered over the crest of the sandy ridge. Next to her, Michelos was raising the muzzle of his rifle. She motioned cautioningly to him. "Not yet. Wait till they start crossing the riverbed. Out there they'll have no cover at all and no place to retreat. I don't think a muccax can hop *up* that bank with a man on its back."

Michelos grumbled but held his fire.

The little party of two started down a slight break in the dry river wall where the parched earth had crumbled. As Yakus had predicted, the muccax made the bone-jarring jump down without difficulty. The dryzam made their worries seem absurd by floundering elegantly after them, taking part of the bank with it.

When they were a fifth of the way across the wide dry river, Savaya raised her needler. Michelos had

39

risen to his feet and was aiming his own weapon carefully when something shattered rock before him, sending emerald sparks flying at his boots.

He dropped, and scrambled on his belly back behind the protective rise. "What happened? What the hell happened?" He was looking around wildly.

"Over there." Wuwit fired his own needler in the direction of a pile of boulders looming in the distance. Michelos glanced down at Savaya angrily.

"I thought there were only supposed to be two of them!"

"Did you see more than that?" She too was furious at the unexpected opposition. She raised her head slightly for a look, ducked back fast as another green energy bolt sizzled over their heads to impact on the ground behind them.

"Neither the old man nor the boy said anything about having a separate escort, I suppose?" Michelos's tone was accusing. "If they suspected they might be followed they wouldn't want to advertise their protection, would they?" Then he frowned, thoughtful. "But in that case, why mention the mine so boldly at all?"

"It doesn't make sense, I'm telling you!" Savaya glared at him as she hugged sand.

"Someone's trying to kill us and you two lie there arguing." Wuwit sounded disgusted. Rising, he snapped off a shot from his weapon. More green bolts answered. Soon the three of them were exchanging steady fire with whoever lay sequestered in the tall pile of rocks.

When the first energy bolt had exploded behind them, Flinx and Yakus had reined in their mounts and turned sharply to look behind them.

"We've been followed!" Yakus was more upset than panicked. "We're under attack and—"

40

Flinx shook his head crisply. "Followed, most likely." He sounded puzzled. "But they're shooting at each other, not at us."

Yakus had learned long ago not to question providence. "Come on, boy!" He spurred his muccax and called a loud "*hup*!" back to the dryzam. Then they were racing full speed for the still-distant mine...

Once, a green fragment of lightning skimmed close enough to singe Michelos's shoulder and send him spinning in pain. His anger overrode the sting, however, and he resumed his position quickly.

A shot of Savaya's was rewarded with a scream from the high boulders. A very peculiar scream.

"That wasn't a man or thranx," she said confusedly. "Something else. This is crazy."

Michelos got off another angry burst from his rifle. When he looked at Savaya again he saw she was tying a piece of white cloth to the muzzle of her needler.

"What do you think you're doing?"

"Isn't it obvious?" She started to wave the cloth-clad muzzle over her head.

This display produced a couple of querulous bursts. Then the firing ceased. Taking a chance that the quiet was intentional, she rose and called out, "Hey... who are you?"

"Who are you, chrrrk?" came a reply from the distant rocks. The voice was high, thin, and grating on the ear. "As you are with the miners, whill you wantt to kkill us so badly?"

"Wait a minute." Wuwit threw Savaya a confused stare. "They think that *we're* working with the boy and the old man."

"We're not with the miners!" Savaya yelled. "We're..." She hesitated a moment. "We're hunting!"

41

A high tippling laugh sounded from the tiny natural fortress of their antagonists. "Huntting, are you? Whell, lady woman, we're 'huntting' ttoo. Tthinkk I we're huntting the same ggame." A pause, then, "You're ttruthful sayingg you're nott whith man and boy human?"

"On the contrary, as you've guessed," Savaya admitted, her extemporaneous ruse having failed. "Let's both of us call a truce, at least long enough to talk this out!"

"Very whell," the voice finally agreed. "Whee whill advance ttogetther and meett unmountted att tthe center place bettwheen our respeccttive positttions."

"We agree!"

"Just a minute," rumbled Michelos softly. "If this is a trick, then we—"

Wuwit put out a plump hand and gripped his friend with surprising strength. "Listen, Mick, if you were in their position"—he gestured toward the river bank and the retreating Flinx and Yakus—"and you knew we were following and trying to kill you, would you suggest truce with us?"

"No." Michelos conceded the point grudgingly. "You're right." He looked up at Savaya and nodded as he started to rise. "Okay, let's risk it."

Together the three of them walked over the ridge and started down the opposite side. As soon as they did so, a pair of tall thin shapes started climbing down the rock ramparts.

"Not human. You were right, Savaya." Wuwit thoughtfully regarded the two figures, noticed a third join them in descending. "Chikasacasoo ornithorpes, I think."

Michelos looked at his friend in disbelief, then back across the plain. "What are those birds doing out *here*?"

"The same thing we are, idiot," Savaya told him.

When the two groups were roughly five meters apart, the aliens halted. "Is cclose enough for preempttory disccussion, I thinkk," said the lead creature. He held his beamer loosely cradled under one delicate arm. "I singg tthe name of Pimbab. Tthese are my remainingg companions, Kisovp and Ttor. Boonoom and Lessuwhim were botth reccckless and paniccckky durring tthe fightting. Bad ccombinattion when facing ones of your markksmanship." The inflexible beak could not form anything so facile as a smile, but Savaya had the impression of one. "I feel tthatt should increase odds of nexxtt kkill in our favor."

"Forget this business of killing each other. That won't profit anybody. What are you doing out here in Dead-Place-on-Map?" Wuwit wondered.

"Same as you, if I singg tthis sittuattion rightt." Pimbab's head bobbed gracefully on the long stem of a neck. "I was drinkking att a sttall in Drallar when tthere was menttion nearby me of hallowseyes. Being something of a gem fancier—"

"Yeah, we're real big gem fanciers ourselves," Michelos broke in.

"There's nothing to be gained by killing one another," said Wuwit forcefully, despite his high voice. "I think a temporary alliance would be a good idea."

"Just a second," said Savaya, "who's in charge of this—"

Pimbab did not let her finish. "I singg likkewise, man." He gestured with a willowy limb across the dry riverbed. "They have reached ccover now and whill be much hardder tto dislodge. Ttwo or tthree of us would have a difficcultt ttime doing so. Five should do much bettter. If cconversattion I overheard was half ttrue, tthere should be much plentty wealtth for all of us."

"Yeah, suits me." Michelos nodded. "Makes sense. Money's no good to a dead man . . . or bird."

"Well, I don't agree." Savaya looked furious. "I still think we're better off operating separately."

Wuwit eyed her strangely. "Maybe you're right, Savaya."

"And you," she snapped, "just remember who started this when—"

"Starting's finished," the unjolly little man reminded her. "But I'll go along partly, with what you say about proceeding separately." His needler came up. The ornithorpes twitched, but the muzzle wasn't pointing in their direction. "So why don't you go start your own group, Savaya?"

"Look, you fat little—" She took a step toward Wuwit, froze when one finger tightened slightly on the trigger. She looked around in outraged disbelief. "What is this?"

"You're so smart." Michelos was grinning as he stepped over to stand next to his short companion. "You figure it out."

"All right. All right." She was backing away slowly and cautiously. "Have it this way then. Between you you haven't got the brains to last two days against them." She jerked a thumb in the direction of the mine.

"I know my limitations." Wuwit nodded toward the watching ornithorpes. "The bird folks' penchant for games and strategies is well known. I happen to think we'll do better with them than with you. Besides, I'm sick of taking orders from you, Savaya. You've flaunted your smarts a little too often over me. See how much good they do you without anyone muscling for you."

"Ttruly the female seems exxccitted," observed Pimbab.

"You can take your muccax and head back to Edgedune," Wuwit continued magnanimously, "or you can form your own separate party, as you want." For the first time since they'd started the trip, he smiled.

Flinx and Yakus lay down in the cool shade of the excavation. Both rifles rested in front of them, on top of the mine edge. Behind them, down and dug deep into the earth, was an open circular area large enough to conceal both muccax and the dryzam. The dorsal-finned beast of burden was exhausted from the short sprint across the riverbed. Flinx worried that they might have overloaded it with supplies.

Once when the sun pierced the cloud cover, there was a suggestion of orange fire near the back wall of the excavation.

"Sounds like they made peace among themselves," observed Yakus, peering over the rim. "I'll bet both groups were plenty surprised, all nice and set up to ambush us only to find out somebody else had the same ideas." Flinx was staring at him reprovingly.

Yakus looked away, embarrassed. "I know, I know... I talk too much. Someone must have overheard me some place. Well"—he fingered the trigger of his rifle—"they'll have an AAnn of a time trying to winkle us out of here."

"Do they have to try?" Flinx scanned the relatively flat horizon outside the mine. As usual, when his mental talents were most needed they chose not to function. He couldn't sense a thing. "They've got us trapped in here."

"That's a matter of argument, boy. To you, we're trapped. To me, we're comfortably protected." He gestured at the dry river. "If they've got any sense among them they'll come at us tonight." He paused, and frowned as he eyed Flinx. "Say, boy, where's your pet?"

Flinx continued to watch the stream bed. "She flew off when we started our sprint for here. Once it would have bothered me, not anymore. She's left me a couple of times previously—once to come after you, remember? She always comes back."

"I'm glad you're not worried, but I've seen what your little fly-devil can do. I'd feel better if she were here."

Flinx smiled gently. "So would I, but Pip goes and comes as she pleases. Still..." He looked puzzled. "It's not like her to take off when I'm threatened like this. I expect she'll show up fast when they do attack."

"She'd better," said Yakus feelingly. "No telling how many there are out there..."

Night amplified the stillness of the High Desert. Even the insects were silent here, baked into insensibility, Flinx thought.

Careful not to keep his head exposed for long, he periodically surveyed the riverbed. There was little to see in the near-blackness. The perpetual cloud cover shut out the starlight and the faint glow of Moth's single tiny moon, Flame. Even if their attackers possessed light-concentrating gunsights, they'd have to be extraordinarily powerful to pick up enough illumination from the dark desert sky to see by.

"Think they'll wait until just before morning, when they'll have a little light?" Flinx asked.

"Can't tell." Yakus too was gazing out across the dry wash. "Depends on how impatient they get."

There was a tiny click of stone on pebble. Yakus whirled, bringing his rifle around to cover the left side of the talus hill. Behind them the two muccax slept soundlessly, balanced on the tripod of feet and tail, their heads bent over onto their chests. The dryzam lay motionless on its side, curled against the back of the mine and several million credits of fiery orange crystal.

Flinx also jerked around, an instant ahead of Yakus. Sensitive as he was, the emotional feedback effects of the raw hallowseye behind him was making him more nervous than normal. The proximity of so many emotion-amplifying gems was having a dangerous un-steadying effect on his mind.

"You can hold it right there," the prospector ordered.

"Look, I'm throwing my gun in." The voice was unmistakably, and unexpectedly, feminine.

A long needler landed on the rocks in front of them, clattered to a halt near Flinx's feet.

"I'm coming in unarmed. They threw me out. If I try to go back to Edgedune they'll kill me." A pause, then a hopeful "Can I come closer?"

"Into the light?" asked Yakus testingly.

"No, no lights! They'd use them to shoot by. There's enough for you to see me."

And that was enough to satisfy Yakus. "Okay, come on in . . . but keep your hands over your head and your fingers spread."

A slim outline materialized from the darkness. "My name's Savaya," the figure told them. "I was out there, in this with *them*." This last uttered with contempt. "I don't want your gems anymore." She sighed. "I just want a chance to live and get back home . . . and back at them."

"Neither of those is a good enough reason for me

not to play it safe and shoot you where you stand," said Yakus evenly, raising his needler.

The voice spoke again, hurriedly, desperately. "I told you, I'm unarmed. That's my only weapon, there in front of you."

Flinx kneeled and picked up the needler. "That's what you say."

A touch of amused indifference colored the woman's next words. "Go ahead and search me, if you don't trust me."

"Watch her close, boy." Yakus put his own rifle down next to Flinx and walked over to the shadowy form. Several long minutes passed. There were indecipherable murmurings and one muffled noise that might have been a giggle. Flinx finally tired of it.

"I can't watch the both of you and the riverbed too, Yakus."

"All right, all right," came the impatient reply. The old prospector returned and hefted his weapon.

"Thank you," the woman said simply. "Will you let me help you kill them?" She motioned for her needler. Flinx gave Yakus a questioning glance. The prospector shook his head, watching the woman.

"You can stay. If we live, you live. But no gun."

"I'm a good shot," she argued, coming closer. "There are five of them out there: three ornithorpes and two men-things. If they decide to all rush you at once, another gun could make the difference."

"Especially if it was directed at us, from behind," said Yakus pleasantly. "No thanks, Savaya. We'll take our chances."

Flinx slid down and rested his back against the talus slide. "I don't think they'll rush us tonight."

Black eyes studied him curiously in the darkness. "I can't see you too well, whatever your name is."

48

"Call me Flinx."

"You seem a little young to be making those kinds of pronouncements with such surety."

"I do all right." Flinx took no offense. If the woman *was* planning some treachery, it would be best if she thought of him as an overconfident child.

Something with the intensity of a green star erupted against the roof of the mine. Both muccax came awake, bleating throaty objections. The dryzam barely stirred, however, as a shower of gravel fell from the scorched pit in the stone ceiling.

Another energy bolt shot by well overhead, while a third exploded against the pile of talus shielding them. Flinx fired in response. Unlike what happened with the energy beamers, it was impossible to tell where his needler was striking. He could only fire in the direction the energy bursts had come from.

By the same token, however, the needler didn't reveal its user's presence. The manipulators of those beamers had better keep moving from place to place as they fired, or Flinx would use their discharges to pinpoint them.

"See anything?" he asked tightly.

"Not a thing, boy," Yakus replied. Flinx noticed that Savaya was curled close to the old man and he didn't appear to be in a hurry to push her away. Well, Flinx had her needler, and he didn't think she could wrestle Knigta's weapon away from him before Flinx could bring his own gun to bear. Nor was the old man a fool . . . he hoped.

"There, to your right!" she suddenly shouted. Flinx spun to face that direction, saw a shadowy form partly outlined against the rocks. He fired, and was rewarded with a cry of pain. The shape retreated into the darkness. Flinx fired again, but the sound wasn't repeated, and he wasn't anxious to leave the safety of the mine to pursue the wounded figure.

He remembered the source of the warning. "Thanks," he told the woman.

"I told you," she said, a touch impatiently, "I'm on your side now. Can I have my gun back?"

"No. That could have been a trick designed to let you gain our confidence."

She responded sarcastically. "Do you think one of them would risk his life for that? How could they know your shot would only wound and not kill?"

Flinx had to admit she had a point. But he was too concerned about moving shapes in the near-blackness to consider her request. Better to keep the weapon a little while longer, until they could be absolutely sure the woman wasn't faking.

As expected, the energy bolts soon ceased their futile, distracting assault. Yakus looked satisfied. "Tried to draw our fire and attention while one of 'em flanked us," he observed. "If that's the best they can do, we'll have no trouble holding them off indefinitely."

"That's just it," Flinx pointed out. "We can't hold them off indefinitely. With five of them out there, they can send a couple back to Edgedune for supplies and leave three here to keep us pinned down. Sure we've got a stock of food and water, but indefinite it's not. They can afford to wait us out."

"That's so," admitted Yakus solemnly.

"I'm impressed," confessed Savaya, sliding close to the old prospector in the darkness.

"Really? Where would you like to be impressed?"

"Come on now," she chided him gently. "I had a different kind of alliance in mind when I came here."

"I'd say what you need, then, is a good dose of moral support." Yakus moved toward her.

Flinx turned away. Someone had to keep an eye on the dry riverbed. To his horror, he realized that the men he'd thought were asleep had been fully awake and readying for an attack—so much for his intuition. He glanced back into the depths of the mine. A powerful surge of feeling resided back there, a reflection of his own emotions magnified by the hallowseyes. If they were cut, he knew, he'd be a nervous wreck by now. Fortunately they were still in their raw state.

For the first time in years, he felt he couldn't trust his talents. Was that why Pip had flown away?

Worried, he strained to stay awake...

A loud, sharp sound woke him from his half-sleep the following morning. It did not come from outside the mine. Both Savaya and Yakus also woke at the noise, hastily disengaged, and looked down into the excavation.

Both muccax had backed up against the far wall as much as their tethers would permit. They were staring blankly at the dryzam. It was making long hooting noises, and they could hear high-pitched screams seeming to come from all around it.

"What's wrong with the beast?" Yakus wondered. "I've been through a lot with it. I'd hate to see it—" but Flinx was already scrambling down the talus slope. Then he was walking cautiously across the floor of the mine. The dryzam didn't *look* violent, but that screaming and hooting...

All was quiet save for that intense howling.

"Flinx, lad?" Yakus called in the early-morning air. The back of the mine was still clothed in blackness.

"Leave him be," suggested Savaya. "If he gets hurt it's his own fault."

Yakus glanced at her sharply. "This little alliance

51

of ours can be dissolved as fast as it was made, you know."

"Sorry." She was quickly apologetic. "I didn't know you and the boy were so close."

"As close as partners can be."

"It's okay. I'm all right," Flinx's voice floated up to them. A moment later he was alongside.

"Did you find out why it's screaming like that?" Yakus asked.

"Not it—them," Flinx explained with a grin. "Your dryzam was pregnant, Knigta. As near as I can tell in the dark, there are eight offspring."

"Pregnant! I thought she'd been acting sluggish, but nothing to indicate—"

"Knigta, not all animals show pregnancy as blatantly as humans do. It explains a lot." He stared out across the lightening desert. "It explains, for example, why Pip came to rescue you in the first place, which was what I couldn't figure out."

"I don't follow you, boy."

"What's he talking about?" Savaya inquired. The prospector motioned her to silence.

"On Alaspin the minidrag and the dryzam are associative creatures. I told you that, back in Drallar. Pip *was* drawn to the High Desert by an overpowering emotion all right, but it wasn't yours, Knigta. It was the dryzam's. A pregnant associative animal was in danger. I wouldn't be at all surprised to learn that on Alaspin dryzams have been known to save or protect young minidrags."

Yakus looked crushed. "So it wasn't me at all that your pet considered worth saving, just that animal." He gestured with his rifle back into the mine, still resounding with unnurserylike howling and screeching.

"No need to feel slighted," said Flinx consolingly.

52

"You were saved, after all." He turned to regard the desert. "I also think this explains why Pip left and where she's gone off to, and why she's been gone so long."

Yakus shook his head. "You're making less and less sense, boy."

"I know what to do now," Flinx murmured, not hearing him. He stood up, cupped his hands to his lips, and yelled, "Hey, can you hear me out there?"

"Get down, boy, are you gone crazy?" Yakus was crawling over, tugging at Flinx's boot.

Flinx looked down at him. "Trust me, Knigta Yakus." He turned and shouted once more. "Can you hear me?"

A voice drifted back to them, faint but distinct. And nonhuman. "We ccan hear you quitte whell. Which of you is itt tthatt speakks?"

"I'm called Flinx. I'm the younger man."

The voice sounded elegantly in the clear morning air. "Whee have notthingg tto ttalkk aboutt, man."

"Listen, I'm not ready to die for a little money."

"Speak for yourself," grumbled Yakus, but he let Flinx talk.

"How do you propose tto avoid itt?" the voice called back to him with a touch of amusement.

"By trading this place for our lives," Flinx responded. "On your word," and he added something in birdtalk, so bright and sharp that Yakus jumped in surprise.

"You singg of *tthatt* oatth!" the ornithorpe shouted admiringly. "You are whell ttraveled, fledglingg!"

"Your word on that oath then," insisted Flinx once more, "that we and our captive—"

"What captive?" demanded a deeper, human voice.

"That's Michelos," whispered Savaya. "He thinks

53

he's . . ." She stopped, looked sharply at Flinx. "What 'captive'?"

"Just play along, will you?" said Flinx irritably. "Better to let them think we're getting something out of this . . . namely you. It'll make our offer to trade sound more logical if they think we have something to gain besides our freedom." He turned his voice back to the desert.

"Let us leave with her, the woman who came with you. She'll be our . . . compensation for our trouble here. You can have the mine if you let us go safely back toward Edgedune. I'm not ready to fight for it!"

"We'll consider your offer," came the inhuman voice.

"They'll accept," said Flinx confidently, sliding back down behind the protecting wall. "It's a good deal for them."

"I'm not sure I accept, boy," said a frowning Yakus. "What's possessed you?"

Flinx eyed him firmly. "It's important that we get out of here before they do rush us. We can't handle a rush, I don't think. And if we get out, we can afford to wait."

"Wait for what?" Savaya wanted to know.

Flinx didn't smile. "You'll see. Trust me, Knigta."

Yakus grumbled, and finally peered hard at Flinx. "I don't know what you're up to, boy, but you'd better know what you're doing."

"We acceptt tthe offer, if tthe oldd man whill singg tthatt he does also," came a call.

Flinx rose to reply, but Yakus beat him to it. "Yeah, I do, you wormeaters!" and he added another, more pungent comment.

"Give us a couple of minutes to load our supplies,"

Flinx responded after Yakus had finished, "and then we'll leave. We'll be heading south toward Edgedune!"

"Itt shall be so," the bird-creature answered.

"What about dryzam?" asked Yakus as the two muccax were packed for departure.

"She has to remain," Flinx said. "I wouldn't think she could travel immediately after giving birth."

Yakus looked at him shrewdly. "You've got another reason, haven't you, though I can't figure it."

"They won't kill it," Flinx insisted. "The dryzam and her young represent a source of meat; besides, the dryzam's a valuable beast of burden. They'll want her to carry out the hallowseyes they mine. Speaking of which, I'm betting they'll be too involved with the gems to worry about much else."

"This'd better work, boy."

Savaya's gaze traveled from man to boy. "You're both mad, but I haven't any choice now. I have to go with you."

From a hidden place off to the south, the five anxious attackers waited as a pair of muccax shapes moved toward them.

"Here they come."

"Yeah," said Michelos with relish. As the footsteps came closer he and his companion readied themselves.

When it sounded as if the two muccax were directly abreast of them, the five jumped from their various places of concealment. Pimbab and his friends watched as the two humans fired.

Two muccax died, beamed instantly. That was all.

"They're not here." Frantically Michelos searched around the two corpses. "They're not *here!*"

Flinx, Yakus, and Savaya, their backs heavy with food and water, were running across the dry riverbed.

They'd waited until the five figures had crossed to the south of the mine before starting their sprint in the opposite direction.

"Lousy bastards," rumbled Yakus, panting under his load.

"I told you they wouldn't risk letting you get away. Much easier to kill you." She threw Flinx a venomous glance. "What about that wonderful oath you had that lead bird swear to?"

"I'm sure," Flinx replied, "he took no part in the shooting. His oath bound only him and his companions." He looked sad. "I hated to sacrifice the muccax, but it was the only way I could be sure we'd get out safely. First I had to convince them that we were convinced they would let us go. That was the purpose of the oath."

"I wish I knew what you had in mind, Flinx." Yakus was starting to scramble up the bank, at the place where the dryzam had partly crumbled it. "We're not going far on foot. And they've got the mine. They can hold it and send others after us."

"Why should they, Knigta? Like you said, we're not going far on foot. They know that. They'll trust the desert to kill us, and reasonably so. Besides, I don't think any of them trust the others enough to split up to chase us. No, they'll leave us alone now, and we can wait in safety."

"Wait for *what*?" Savaya demanded to know. But Flinx ignored her as he started up the bank.

Michelos continued to rage until Wuwit said with calm authority. "Shut up, Mick." He turned to the watching Pimbab. "Tricked us."

"Itt does nott matter," insisted the tall, imperturbable ornithorpe. "Whee have gained possession of the mine, and their animals are dead. Tthey cannott walkk

56

outt of tthe desertt, nor can tthey attackk us, as whee outtnumber tthem. Tthe sand whill beccome partt of tteir bodies. Whee need only kkeep alertt while whee mine tthe ccrysttals."

"The crystals," Michelos said, his attention shifting abruptly.

"Yes." Pimbab also turned to look back in the direction of the mine. "I tthinkk itt is ttime whee ttookk a lookk att tthem."

Flinx squinted across the riverbed from his position atop the pile of columnar boulders once held by Pimbab and his companions. "There they are . . . two of them, anyway." He could see one ornithorpe and a human resting on the parapet of talus fronting the mine. "Keeping watch."

"They know we're liable to hang around," muttered Yakus. "I'm sure the rest of them are in back, chipping away at my crystals."

"Our crystals," Flinx corrected quietly.

"We can't wait here forever," Yakus pointed out.

"Give me a couple of days." Flinx had raised his gaze. "If what I'm expecting doesn't happen, we'll think of something else."

They waited, conserving water, all that searing day and night, and through the next day. Flinx remained expressionless, didn't comment on the blatant way Savaya coddled Yakus. The prospector was obviously pleased by the woman's attention and made no attempt to ward her off. On the contrary, he welcomed her advances.

Flinx was very good at minding his own business. If the old man hadn't learned enough by now to know when . . . He shrugged silently. He had more important things to worry about. He was beginning to be concerned by the absence of the activity he'd anticipated. Suppose he was wrong in his feelings? In that case he'd placed them in a tough position.

He wouldn't blame Yakus for never forgiving him.

Flinx was a light sleeper. So was Yakus. They woke simultaneously that night.

"Did you hear it?" Flinx strained at the darkness.

Yakus was looking around curiously. He confessed, "I thought I heard *something*, boy."

"What was it like? A sort of buzzing or whirring sound?"

Yakus nodded slowly. "Maybe."

"What's going on?" a sleepy voice inquired.

A terrifying shriek sent the groggy Savaya exploding from her resting place. The shriek was followed by the crackle of an energy beam discharging, then more screams. Some of them were not human. All came from the direction of the mine.

Flinx and Yakus scrambled for a better view of the distant excavation. A woman who'd always thought of herself as cold and strong put both hands over her ears and broke out in a cold sweat.

"Would've been kinder if we'd done the killing, boy." Yakus's voice was almost accusing.

"I know. But it would probably have been us who'd have died."

Green energy bolts flared in all directions from the depths of the mine. They struck walls and roof, speared the desert sky futilely. None stabbed in the direction of the concealed onlookers. They ceased quickly.

"They're dead," Flinx announced calmly when all had been silent for several moments. "We can go back now."

Yakus eyed him oddly. "How can you be so sure?"

"Those yells." Savaya shivered despite the warmth of the night. "What happened?"

"You'll find out in a minute." Flinx glanced at the sky, where clouds were beginning to brighten. "It's almost morning." He started down the rock tower.

Halfway across the dry wash a small winged shape that shone pink and blue in the dawning light swooped to meet them. Savaya started, was reassured by Yakus.

Pleated wings collapsing, the minidrag came in for a landing on Flinx's shoulder. Her coils whipped around under his arm, tightened to a firm perch. The triangular head nuzzled Flinx's jaw as the trio continued their march across the riverbed.

Yakus pointed downstream. Several muccax were standing blankly in the middle of the riverbed, panting with fright.

Savaya fell behind, shortening her pace, and Yakus dropped back to comfort her. His hand tensed on his weapon as they followed the youth up the talus slope leading into the excavation.

Five bodies lay scattered about the floor of the mine. Two were human, three nonhuman; several sprawled in positions easily achieved only in death. Yakus turned one of the human corpses over as they started down the inner slope.

"That was Wuwit," Savaya whispered. Part of the pudgy schemer's left cheek was gone, eaten away as if by acid. "What did this thing?"

"This," Flinx called up to her from the floor of the excavation, indicating the coiled reptilian shape on his shoulder.

"But if she could do this," a puzzled Yakus asked as they moved toward the boy, "why did she leave? Why didn't she stay to help in the first place instead of flying off?"

"Pip's not stupid," Flinx explained. "She probably could have defended me, but only me, against five attackers. She couldn't have saved you and, more importantly, the dryzam—and her offspring."

Yakus grunted. "That animal again."

"So she responded," Flinx continued, "as she would have on Alaspin. Look for yourself."

Moving hesitantly, the old prospector and Savaya walked toward the back wall of the mine. Orange fire was growing there, kindled by the rising sun. Against that fiery wall lay the dryzam and eight miniature replicas of herself, reproductions as precise as those that might have come from a machine.

Circling above those eight shaky young dryzam were six tiny, darting winged forms.

Flinx stood nearby, stroking the back of Pip's head. "Pip knows what it is to be a mother, Knigta. She could have protected me, but what about these newborns? It was important to her to save them, too. But sometimes it takes a family to save a family..."

It was a most peculiar procession which ambled into Edgedune several weeks later. Startled out of their perpetual lethargy, heat-soaked residents came running to gape at the parade.

Leading it were an exquisitely beautiful young woman and a grizzled old man riding a pair of muccax. Accumulated filth and dust couldn't hide the woman's perfect features or the old man's high-powered grin.

Behind them lumbered a strange dual-dorsal-finned apparition, a young man seated on the thick neck behind five staring eyes. A poisonous flying creature circled watchfully above the youngster's tousled hair. In their wake trooped eight duplicates in miniature of the dorsal-finned creature, flanked by six darting, twisting shapes that looked like leathery wasps.

The old man saw some aged figures he recognized. Without dismounting, he took a small sack from the saddleband of his muccax. Reaching in, he brought out a stone the size of his fist that gleamed in the sunlight.

For the first time, a sigh rose from the crowd...

A night of revelry was followed by dawning disaster. Flinx discovered the missing muccax first, the absent Savaya second, and the loss of a very valuable sack last of all. He rushed to wake Yakus.

"I thought you knew better, Knigta," Flinx said accusingly. "Did you really think she meant everything she told you, that she was after anything but the gems? She took the sack you put the pick of the diggings in, the stones you told me were the purest and finest." He shook his head sadly. "I didn't have the heart to tell you what she was doing. I couldn't believe you didn't see through her."

"Now, boy, take it easy." Yakus sat up in the bed and ran his hands through hair the consistency of baling wire. "She only took the one sack, eh?"

Flinx calmed Pip, who'd grown nervous at the surging emotion in her master. "You don't look very upset."

"Oh, boy, you're pretty smart-savvy for your age, but you don't know it all, not yet you don't." He yawned and smacked his lips. "She was prettier than most, and a bit smarter than most... but not that pretty, and not fifty years smarter."

"But the jewels!" Flinx pleaded.

"What jewels?" Yakus was smiling. "I knew from the start what the tart was after, boy. So I dug out a nice batch of linedie along with the real hallowseyes. Linedie's a different type of silicate, though it looks just like the real thing. Usually found together. Takes an expert to tell the raw stones apart. Linedie's also called false hallowseye, also idiot's delight.

"It was a bit of a risk, but I really hoped she'd turn out to be honest." He shook his head disgustedly. "We don't have to go after her, boy. If you want to look Savaya up, you'll probably find her in jail back in Drallar, for trying to market linedie as hallowseye."

"Why, you treacherous old scabby dirtgrubber!" Flinx eyed the miner closely. "You were using her all the time, weren't you. You knew just what she was doing and so you used her."

"Fair's fair, boy. I haven't turned a lady's eye in some years." He turned over and lay down again. "Now leave me alone."

Flinx hesitated. There was something...oh, yes. "But this linedie, if it's different in composition it can't have the emotion-feedback qualities of real hallowseye. Why didn't Savaya sense that?"

"She provided her own emotional feedback, boy," Yakus growled from somewhere beneath the sheets. "She was so swamped with greed she couldn't have sensed anything else."

Flinx turned to leave, hesitated. A scaly head nudged him impatiently, and so he forgot his remaining questions.

Pip was right. They had a big nursery to check on.

Bystander

At the World Science Fiction Convention in Washington, D.C., in 1974, the finely textured airbrush paintings of an aspiring young illustrator named Rick Sternbach captivated everyone who saw them in the art show. Rick has subsequently moved on to do work not only for all the major science fiction magazines but for the straight science publications as well. Not to mention his standout work for PBS's show "Cosmos."

Rick was kind enough to give a struggling young science fiction writer a ride from Washington into New York. Along the way the writer tried to construct a scene suited to Rick's way with astronomicals. It took most of Maryland and New Jersey for the both of them to work out an image, but by the time they arrived in Manhattan in the middle of the night,

a prospective picture had begun to take form.
I wish I could show you the painting Rick did for the story that follows...

Sleepy...he was so sleepy....

Existence was proven by the depth of his dreaming, dreams of endless green plains across which he ran in slow motion. The dream faded. He clutched at it as it faded. Then it was gone.

He awoke.

Chapman sighed, waited motionless and logy until his vision had cleared. Revitalizing liquids stirred in his veins. There was the expected swabby-cotton taste in his mouth, as if he hadn't swallowed in a thousand years.

The clear domed lid of his suspension lounge slid back smoothly. He unlatched one side. Moving deliberately, with muscles groggy from several years' suspension, he eased himself into a sitting position on the lounge edge and stared around the empty pilot's pocket.

All the other seats were empty. He was the sole occupant of the gigantic bulb ship. Must be in orbit around Abraxis now, he mused. In an hour or so the endangered colony there could begin shuttling its members aboard. Then he could turn over responsibility to the colony leaders.

That was the second dream to be shattered.

"Position?"

"We are slightly more than five standard days out from Abraxis," replied the even voice of the ship's computer as though it had last spoken to him only yesterday and not three years ago. Chapman considered this unexpected news, forced his long unused tongue and palate to work.

"Then why have I been awakened now?" Not that a few days' wakefulness would hurt him, but there was no reason for early revivification. No programmed reason, he reminded himself.

"We are presently being paralleled by a Dhabian," the ship explained, "and there—"

"Scope first." Chapman curtly interrupted the computer. He drew a globe of energized water from the lounge dispenser, squeezed it down his throat.

Obediently, the ship complied with the order. A small viewscreen set into the emergency pilot's console flickered alight. Displayed on the screen was a massive cluster of red-orange blocks. The blocks were connected according to some elegantly inhuman design to form a ship. A Dhabian ship.

Earthmen had encountered the Dhabians over two decades ago. Since that time the relationship between the two races had been an uncertain one. Mankind's curiosity about the Dhabians was met with what was best described as cordial indifference on the aliens' part. Since the Dhabian vessels, for all their ungainly appearance, were faster than those of men, the aliens' privacy had thus far remained inviolate.

Whenever one of the infrequent encounters between human and Dhabian ships did occur, the Dhabians would sometimes communicate and sometimes not. They were never hostile, only uninterested. It was hinted that they had much of value to offer mankind. But neither pleading, threatening, nor a matching indifference had managed to inspire them to talk.

No one had ever seen an individual Dhabian. Chapman couldn't repress a slight thrill of excitement. Maybe he would be the first.

Yet the silent Dhabian was a known factor. The presence of one did not constitute a sufficient reason for revivification. He told his ship as much.

The ship proceeded to tell him about the new flare.

Flares were the reason for his hastily programmed mission. Astronomers had predicted several years ago that the Abraxis colony would have to be evacuated from its world at least temporarily because its sun was about to go through a period of brief but intense activity. That activity would produce enough high-energy radiation to kill any human on Abraxis's surface or even slightly beneath it.

For the four to six months of dangerous stellar activity, the population would have to live aboard a rescue ship. This information being communicated to the proper authorities, a properly prepared and provisioned vessel was dispatched with barely enough time to arrive and take on the population before the onset of threatening activity.

What was the problem, then? Were the astronomers wrong? No, the ship informed him, the figures given were correct. The cycle of stellar outbursts was not beginning dangerously early. This new flare was an anomaly, a freak not accounted for in the earlier predictions. It would not endanger the colony, safe beneath its amorphous atmospheric shielding.

However, it would be severe enough to critically damage certain vital components and instruments. The bulb ship would be crippled beyond hope of performing its mission. And, incidentally, Chapman would die.

"When?" the dazed pilot muttered.

"Twenty-four to forty-eight hours from now." The reply was quiet. The ship was sophisticated enough to take its pilot's emotional state into consideration and generate appropriate vocoder impulses in response.

Chapman requested more information. In the time remaining to him, the bulb ship could not flee far enough to escape the crippling burst of energy from the star. Nor could he reach the sheltering darkside of the colony world.

"Check computations." The ship did so, repeated what was already known to be inevitable. "Check again."

It was no good. Wishing had no effect on the realities of physics. Hoping failed to reduce either the critical distance to Abraxis or the number of energetic particles the star would generate. Chapman considered thoughtfully, analytically. The mission, then, would fail. The two thousand settlers, scientists, and technicians on the colony world would not be rescued in time. They would die. He would die a little sooner. And he was at once frightened and ashamed, because the last item of the two was the more important to him.

A light winked on, on his console: an incoming call for position from the still-distant world. An automatic relay would reply to it, since he wasn't expected to be awake yet. However, the computer inquired, since he *was* awake, did he perhaps wish to...?

No, he shouted emphatically, he did not. He did not. There was nothing he could tell them, nothing he could tell anyone. Let them enjoy a last couple of days of peace and confidence. There would be ample time for their shuttle pilots to board the orbiting bulb ship when it arrived on automatics. Time enough for them to find a dead man in the pilot's pocket, the vital instrumentation around him ruined beyond repair.

There was a backup for the main computer, and a backup for the backup. Last of all the backups was a man, an emergency pilot, a Timothy Chapman. One man, kept in suspension for the entire journey, hopefully to be awakened only at journey's end to turn over his self-piloting temporary coffin to its real passengers.

It was a good job, he told himself. Safe, peaceful, rewarding. You lost little real time in suspension, traveling comatose across the cosmos in an empty cavern of a ship. There were no bosses to yell at you, no daily schedules to keep.

Now, though, he'd been resurrected. For the first time in his placid career he was called upon to do what he'd been trained for, and it was beyond his ability to cope with. It was maddening, depressing. He wanted to cry.

The light on the console continued to blink. Possibly the astronomical laboratory down on Abraxis had also sensed the incipient flare and they were trying to warn him.

Reviewing what might be done, he decided he could do nothing. He could not outrun the flare. He could not hide from it. There was nothing for him to do now but accept...and maybe satisfy some personal curiosity.

"The Dhabian ship," he inquired. "Will it be able to escape the effects of the flare, based on what we know of their abilities?"

A pause, then, "Barring as yet undemonstrated speed, predictions are that it cannot."

He might have company, then. "Offer them the

standard 'exchange of information request,' ship." It would be interesting to learn if they were doomed, too. They seemed to be if his ship was right and they didn't possess some extraordinary particle shielding. Maybe they'd come to the Abraxis system to study the activity of its star prior to eruption and had been shocked and trapped by the same coming, unexpected burst of radiation that would finish him.

Anyway, it was something to do. The idea of returning to suspension, to await the end in ignorance, appalled him.

He did not really expect the alien to reply. He was surprised when a voice of oddly modulated tone whispered at him from the speaker. *"We will exchange with you, man."*

"This star will soon generate a burst of highly charged plasma which will be fatal to me." After a moment's thought, he added, "My ship will also be severely damaged."

"Information." The response was Dhabian-brief. *"No query?"*

"What will happen to you?"

"Will with us be the same as with you, man."

The first intimation of Dhabian mortality, Chapman mused. He felt no elation at the discovery. No one else would learn what he might discover here.

"There's no way you can survive? I thought your ships were fast."

"Not enough. But there may be a way." What seemed an uncertain pause before the Dhabian spoke again. *"You have not detected it?"*

"Detected what?" Chapman was more confused than excited.

"The onu."

69

"What the hell's an . . . !" Chapman calmed himself. "Can you give me position?"

"Your figurings correspond not well, but from what we have learned," and the Dhabian shot some figures at him.

"Ship? What do they mean?"

"A moment, Chapman." He thought he could hear the machine thinking . . . too long in suspension, he thought. "Using maximum amplification focused on region given by alien vessel, it is determined that a large though faint object is indeed located in the position suggested. Alien mass sensors must be more efficient-powerful than our own. Present position precludes visual identification of comet from this angle of observation."

"Comet? Question, ship. *Is it big enough* to provide adequate protection from the anticipated flare?"

"Yes, Chapman."

"Second question: is it big enough to provide shielding for *both* vessels?"

"Some delicate close-range maneuvering by each ship to prevent damage from the other's exhaust particles will be required. It can be done. But there is a difficulty."

Chapman's hopes scattered like children at playtime. "What difficulty?"

"Drive time to cometary umbra estimated at thirty-nine hours."

"We are going, man," the Dhabian informed him. *"Shall we prepare to adjust position to accommodate your own ship?"*

Chapman considered very quickly. Thirty-nine hours was stretching the upper limits of the time alloted before the expected stellar flare. In thirty-nine hours he could be a good deal farther out than the comet's position. Yet his computer informed him he would still be well inside the fatal radius of the flare radiation.

It was an easy gamble to take.

"Yes, I'm trying for it too." The Dhabian apparently accepted this without replying.

"Ship, adjust position to place us behind the cometary nucleus. Keep heading of the Dhabian in mind."

"I will be careful, Chapman," the ship replied confidently.

The ensuing hours passed busily. Studying and recording the Dhabian vessel as it moved past and ahead of him at close range would provide much that xenologists would find of value. It also kept his mind pretty much off his slim chances. After the twenty-four-hour limit passed and he knew the flare could occur at any time, he found himself working steadily more intensely.

It was a large comet, all right. At least fifteen kilometers across the head. At thirty-two hours he had his closest glimpse of the Dhabian ship. It was eight hundred meters long, a hundred less than his own craft, but far more massive. It passed ahead of him, racing at its greater speed for the sheltering safety of the cometary bulk.

At thirty-five hours he permitted himself to hope a little. At thirty-six he was planning a full report to the Commission on his narrow escape.

At thirty-seven hours the ship told him he would be too late.

"Surface stellar activity is already showing signs of impending eruption, Chapman. If local conditions do not change, we will arrive behind the cometary nucleus one hour twenty-two minutes ten seconds too late."

"What's the maximum we can take flare radiation for without sustaining irreparable damage to the ship?" Somewhat to his surprise he did not ask about himself.

"Ten and a half minutes."

That was it, then. Drowning, he'd been tossed a rope, and it had fallen short. He turned, let himself collapse in the chair opposite the main viewscreen. His head slumped forward, cradled in the crook of his right arm, to rest close by the cool metal.

He knew the fire would singe his wings, but it was so beautiful, so clean. Just a little closer, that was all, just a little closer. Through the quiet roar of the flames he thought he could hear the computer babbling precisely at him. Which was absurd. Computers did not talk to moths. Computers did not babble. He ignored the meaningless noises, dipped closer to the beckoning succubus. Fiery fingers touched his wings.

He woke up sweating.

And that was wrong. Very wrong. He couldn't have fallen asleep for more than a few hours, he felt. Even so, he had no business being awake and alive. He ought to be dead, snuffed out in a single incendiary *poof*, like a moth in a furnace. He blinked, looked around wildly.

"Ship! The flare, what...?"

"Commencing countdown to arrival of first energetic particles," the computer said calmly. "Twenty, nineteen, eighteen...."

Chapman stared dully at the viewscreen, tried to comprehend what he saw. To one side drifted an object that seemed assembled from the remnants of some ancient construct: the Dhabian ship, its quiescent drive glowing blue-white. Ahead was a dim green mass that, as he watched, concluded eclipsing the sun of Abraxis: the backside of the comet. In the

reflected light from his own bulb ship it shone icy
green and sharp. One moment it appeared solid, the
next shifting and unstable.

"Four, three, two, one...." The computer concluded. Chapman sucked in a startled breath.

The coma, the thick gaseous envelope which surrounded the cometary head, was shining so brilliantly
it almost hurt him to look at it. The tenuous ribbons
of gases and particles streaming back all around both
ships took on a vibrant, purplish-red hue. In the storm
raging off the surface of the star ahead, the streamers
assumed a near-solid look, like the silken veil of a
Spanish dancer.

While the view from several million miles away
would have been even more impressive, there was
something in the knowledge that he was *inside* the
comet's tail which made him feel very small.

For five and a half hours the two ships rode the lee
of the comet. Fiery colors danced around them. Dev-
astating energy sheeted against the head of the comet,
producing beauty instead of death.

Then the computer announced that the level of
stellar radiation was dropping rapidly. Soon it fell to
an acceptable level. At the same time the Dhabian
ship began to move. It passed beyond and through
the subdued but still dramatic cometary flow before
Chapman thought to consider what had happened to
him.

His ship could not have reached the safe position
behind the comet by itself. Therefore the Dhabians had
somehow helped him. Why?

"Initiate request for information, ship!"

After a moment, "They do not respond, Chapman."
The alien vessel continued to move away.

"Try again!"

73

The computer did so, several times more before Chapman spoke directly into the pocket's pickup. "Dhabians! Why? Why save me? I owe you. Two thousand and one owe you." Silence, as the great blocky ship continued to recede from him on the screen. "Why don't you respond? Answer!"

A lilting, stilted voice. *"Multiple query inappropriate. Query elsewhere. Nothing here, man."*

Try as he would, Chapman was unable to elicit further communication from the alien.

Several weeks later, when the colony had been transferred easily and safely on board the ship and they were well out of the Abraxis system, it occurred to Chapman to ask hesitantly of his computer, "Ship, the Dhabians saved us and I don't know why. Do *you* know *how* they accelerated us in time to get us safely behind the comet?"

"Question inappropriate, Chapman."

He frowned. "Why?"

"No evidence to show Dhabian vessel affected our motion in any way."

He felt a little dizzy. Relief, he decided, and too many days on stimulants to stay awake. "What do you mean? If the Dhabians didn't adjust our velocity, then how did we get behind the nucleus?"

"Dhabians occupied fully with own maneuvers," came the reply. "Evidence indicates that comet shifted position to place us within its umbra. Dhabians had to slow, not accelerate, to match altered cometary position."

"You mean the Dhabians moved the *comet*?"

"Negative, Chapman. No evidence to support such hypothesis."

"But the comet changed position."

"Correct."

"That's impossible," he said with finality.

"Event occurred." The computer sounded slightly miffed.

Chapman considered. His eyes grew very wide. Then he raced through the ship until he located its present commander, colony-leader Otasu. The colony-leader was chatting with several other colony officials in the cramped confines of the pilot's pocket. He looked up uncertainly at Chapman's anxious entrance.

Chapman went immediately to the viewscreen. It showed only a view of star-speckled space and the slightly brighter distant spot of Abraxis's sun.

"We've got to go back, sir."

"Go back? We can't go back, Chapman, you know that." Poor fellow, he thought. Suspension does funny things to men. "Our sun's entered its eruption cycle. We'd all be fried."

Query elsewhere, the Dhabian had said before going finally silent. *Elsewhere, elsewhere* . . . where else had there been to query? The comet had changed position. . . .

"Fifteen hours," he mumbled, staring at the screen. "Fifteen hours."

"Fifteen hours for what?" prompted the colony-leader kindly, humoring the hyper emergency pilot. Chapman's face did not look up from the screen.

"I had fifteen hours during flare-time and I used it to make observations and notes about the Dhabian." He sounded numb.

"And very valuable observations, I'm told," acknowledged Otasu, trying his best to be reassuring and approving.

"But you don't understand!" Chapman stared harder at the screen. The comet was back there, somewhere, moving about in the way of comets; and what did they know about comets, after all? Very little, very little.

"I spent fifteen hours studying the wrong alien. . . ."

What Do The Simple Folk Do?...

This story grew over the years out of a teleplay I did while I was a senior at UCLA. Pure science fiction. The idea of interactive television, of an audience able to make its opinions known instantly to the producers of a certain program, was nothing more than a flight of fantasy.

A number of years ago, Warner Amex Cable established its QUBE channel in Columbus, Ohio. QUBE permits viewers to vote on issues while they're being discussed on the air—thus making their opinions known to a central site via special cable hookups to their home TVs.

Harmless enough technological advance, isn't it? Of course, the less-than-harmless extrapolation that logically follows could never happen. It's pure science fiction. A flight of fantasy.

Besides which, this is *America*...

Once there was a box that held a thousand worlds. It reproduced like nobody's business.

The particular world on display in a particular box just now was one familiar through long use. A number of men dressed in blue uniforms are engaged in the defense of a pile of hewn logs known universally as a "fort." They contest with respectable ferocity a large group of wailing aborigines.

What occurs next, however, is the result of the box-world's maturation. Aborigines and soldiers alike are replaced by a pert young blond female whose obviously mammalian development is perhaps her most prominent feature. A number of colorful charts and photos appear on the wall behind her. She refers to them as she speaks.

"Good evening, tri-vee viewers! It's that time again. The time when you, our faithful audience, must determine how tonight's episode of 'The Commanche' is to conclude.

"As you have seen, the Commanches, led by their valiant and enormously virile chief, Red Hawk, have been provoked into attacking Fort Resolution by numerous treaty violations and land incursions of gold-hungry miners. Alternately, Red Hawk and his vicious savages are staging an unwarranted sneak attack on the Fort and its innocent, stalwart occupants.

"It is up to you to decide the outcome! Will the chief and his braves overcome the bluecoats? Or will Colonel Jepson and his beleaguered defenders succeed in staving off their barbaric assault! Who shall prevail?"

Although repeated in similar form hundreds of times during the Season, this deposition nonetheless holds leechlike the attention of a number of well-dressed businessmen seated at a long table. The table is inlaid, hand-carved mahogany and was fashioned by an unknown artisan in sixteenth-century France.

Seated near the far end of the table is a young man who seems rather out of place. Not only is he set apart by his comparative youthfulness, it seems the drama of the box-world holds little delight for him. In fact, he appears quite absorbed in detailed inspection of his own hands.

Somewhere in the box-world a bell has chimed. The prominent young lady has been studying a notebook in front of her but now looks up.

"I'm afraid our time is up. Have you all made your decisions? Good! Those of you favoring Red Hawk should have pressed the red button on your kinovoter; that's button number one. Those of you favoring Colonel Jepson should have depressed button two, the green button. If you have not done this, please do it now."

The noble face of the Commanche chief appears on the screen, followed by a picture of the girl's hand reaching down to the arm of a chair and pressing a red button. This is followed by a picture of the noble Colonel Jepson, and the striking of the unlucky green button. Each button flashes slightly when depressed.

"Remember, that's button one for Red Hawk and his braves, button two for the colonel and the cavalry."

The young man looks up briefly at the screen of the tri-vee. His name is David Texas. The large bald man seated to his immediate right, the one with the fat cigar billowing narcotic haze, is named Don Texas. He is David's uncle. David might possibly have changed this if he could, but he had no say in the matter.

Don leaned over and whispered sardonically to his nephew.

"The Indians'll win. Normally it'd be a toss-up, but there are women and children inside the fort this time. No contest."

A map of the North American Union has appeared in the tri-vee. Glowing figures in red and green begin to appear within each province and state.

"And here they come, ladies and gentlemen!" reports the blonde breathlessly (no mean feat). "Your votes, *your* decisions, tabulated with lightninglike speed by the latest generation of CBC computers! The final results should appear any minute . . . now . . . !"

Two numbers glow on screen. The first, in red, reads: INDIANS: 32,657,894. The second, in green: CAVALRY: 19,543,255.

"There are the results, beloved viewers, as brought to you instantly by CBC and Frosty-O's, the breakfast cereal that provides all the vitamins, minerals, and tranquilizers prescribed for a normal, healthy adult. Now, the exciting conclusion of tonight's episode as determined by you, the audience."

As though nothing had happened, the box-world returns to its stasis-frozen conflict. But something has indeed happened, for the savages have suddenly been reinforced by another tribe under the leadership of Red Hawk's cousin, Little Sparrow. The cavalry is unable to cope with this second onslaught. They weaken, the gate is breached, and the battle becomes a most realistic massacre of the Fort's inhabitants. Over which the camera lingers lovingly. It continues for quite some time. Instant replay is utilized extensively, as are close-up and slow-mo. Eventually and inevitably, the credits flash on, backed by the series' stirring theme of the Old West.

Gradually the atmosphere around the rich-grained table relaxes. The box-world is commencing to detail the adventures of Rock Steele, intersteller scout, but he hurriedly vanishes from the confines of the brightly lit office. Rock Steele is a pariah, one of the unwashed. His series is not of the CBC and none present shall watch.

A slim, elderly gentleman rises at the head of the long table. His kindly blue eyes sweep its length, commanding the attention of allies and secret enemies alike. He has a few wrinkles and a full head of white hair like serrated cream. He has the appearance of a saint and the mind of a puff adder.

"Gentlemen, I think we have a hit on our hands."

The assembly murmurs approval.

"That was the tape of last week's episode of 'True Tales of the Old West.' For the third consecutive week our voting audience has exceeded fifty million. What do you think?"

"Not much doubt about it, R.L.!" blurts the comptroller. "The public is eating it up. As word gets around, our ratings can only skyrocket."

"I agree, Sam. Frosty-O's thinks so also, and they're willing to renegotiate for a three-year contract. What do you think, Will?"

"Despite the expense, R.L., it seems to be holding at slightly over the projected budget."

"Excellent, Will. Marple?"

"Outstanding production, R.L.! Modesty aside, I think everyone connected with the show deserves our unrestrained commendation for an idea well executed."

"Quaint choice of words, Marple," said David. "In fact, if memory serves, aren't you the man directly responsible for having 'True Tales of the Old West' put on our production schedule?"

"Well, I have that honor, yes," Marple replied modestly.

"And it doesn't bother you that dozens of actors and actresses are maimed and horribly killed to satisfy your sense of artistic endeavor and some bloated cereal manufacturer's advertising department?"

Marple had never encountered this argument before and was so put off by its uniqueness all he could say was, "Wha-a-t?"

David stood abruptly and stared down the table at the startled creative programmer. "I asked you whether or not you feel any remorse over having hundreds of performers a year murdered in cold blood!"

"*Really*, R.L.," said Marple, "I must protest, I...I..." With great dignity he turned to face David. "I'll have you know, Mr. Texas, that I personally interview every performer who appears on 'True Tales of the Old West.' They all know what to expect. Union rules are scrupulously adhered to. CBC has, I might add, the finest autotechs and restorers in the business. Once in a great while someone will come out of a show with a small scar or nick, but that's the risk of the trade."

"What about psychic scars, Marple? Sure, no one is permanently injured. But they *feel* those bullets and arrows penetrating their flesh, they feel the hurt and the pain, the—"

"That will be quite enough, Mr. Texas," pontificated R. L. "This isn't the twentieth century, you know. So a little pain is involved. No one is forced to become an, actor. For what they're paid, they can tolerate a little mutilation here and there. Have you ever watched 'Claudius of Rome'? Now *there's* a show takes a strong stomach to sit through! I think you owe Marple, here, an apology."

That worthy sits with the air of the first martyr.

"I'm terribly sorry, gentlemen," says David, pushing his chair aside, "but I'm feeling a bit ill." He gives the table a ghastly grimace. "If you'll excuse me?"

He turns and heads for the exit, ignoring the forty pupils focused on the back of his head.

Don Texas is on his feet. "Please excuse my nephew's little outburst, gentlemen, R.L. He hasn't been having an easy time of it lately. Production problems and all that, you know." He grins knowingly. "Ah, the problems of youth!"

The executives seem to relax a little, even R.L.

"All right, Don. But have a talk with the boy, hmmm?"

"Sure thing, R.L. Right away."

The hallway is broad and well lit by flourescent paneling. Busy people are pacing off dollars and cents. David enters one of ten elevators and addresses the air.

"Ninety-five, please."

"Ninety-five, sir," says the elevator grid eventually.

He exits the lift and turns down a series of corridors, nodding absently to acquaintances and a rare friend.

David's office is all stainless steel and plastic. Real vines and creepers cling hopefully to transparent sculpture. Impossibly, the office has a faintly homey look. Completing the tin jungle are a few cabinets, a low desk, a couch that is much more, and the inevitable computer annex.

He slouches disconsolately behind the barren desk, devoid of the usual multitude of personal bric-a-brac. After several soft moments he sighs and punches a button. It offers up a sheaf of paper, which he begins reading.

Another button produces a small grid.

"Miss Lee, may I see you a minute, please."

The grid disappears into the desk as the secretary enters.

"Sir?"

"Please cancel any appointments I have scheduled for today, will you?"

"Very well, sir."

She turns to leave, hesitates.

"Uh, Mr. Texas . . ."

David does not look up. "Ummm?"

"That same gentleman, Mr. . . . .uh, Mr. Slappy Williams, has been around several times again today."

"Him again? No, no visitors whatsoever, Miss Lee."

She seems about to say something else, but David is already back to his notes. The pneumatic door closes silently behind her.

He reaches out and hits another of the omnipresent buttons. A small microphone pops out of the desk, swivels, and focuses on him. The words come off the paper.

"Pursuant to the development of the new series 'The Making of the Presidents,' let me first say that Congressional actions extant last June the fourth make it unadvisable at this time for us to proceed with exploitation as per articles seven through nine of—"

The door slides back and a rotund, bedraggled figure bursts into the room. Panting heavily, the man's attitude is one of determination and desperation, a direct counterpart to the roly-poly, unshaven face.

David puts down the papers and turns to face the intruder.

"Don't feed me your clever lines, David. I've been trying to see you for weeks!"

A harried, distraught Miss Lee stops in the doorway. "I'm so sorry, Mr. Texas! He wouldn't listen to me and he forcibly opened the door!"

"Don't worry about it, Miss Lee. Would you please call Security and have them send a couple of men up?"

She nods at him and gives Williams a quick, unapproving glance before ducking back into the outer office.

"Well, Slappy. You seem to have gained a few minutes."

The comedian walks over and puts both hands on the gleaming desk.

"Dave, I want you to void my contract!"

"That's all?" He leans back into the lounge, which shifts to adjust to his new configuration. "You know I haven't got the power to do that, Slappy. It takes a majority vote of the board. The next contract session is three weeks off, yet."

"Look at me, Dave. Take a good look."

He backs off, swings into a comical clown-dance.

"Happy flappy Slappy Williams! Notice anything amiss with the image, Dave? If the odor of scotch carried over the tri-vee I'd have been cancelled months ago. Want to know why I look like this? A touch different from the promising young comedian you signed eight months ago? God, only eight months!"

David watches him steadily.

"You know what the ratings on my show have been?" he mutters nervously. "You follow the Nationals? They're low, Dave, low. They're so low you'd need carbon-arc lamps to find 'em! But that's not the prize, oh no. The show's been *renewed*."

He stops and leans over the desk again. The sweat from his hands stains the polish.

"Renewed, low ratings. Any idea what that stems from?"

He mimics a well-known director.

"'We find that this show has great *potential*; however, there does seem to be one teensy flaw...which is...'" He breaks down into sniffles. "I tell you I can't take that, Dave! It's bad enough, the firecrackers, the crappy practical jokes! Some guys can take that sort of thing, regrowing an arm or leg after each show. I can't handle that kind of pain anymore, Dave. For God's sake, when they write me out of the series, they'll get rid of me with every trick in the book! There'll be no limits, since I won't have to show up for next week's work. I can't take that, don't let—"

"I know what it means, goddamn it!" explodes David. "You think I like it? But you knew what it meant when you signed that contract, too! What the holy hell do you expect me to *do*, man? If I could do anything, don't you think I'd have done it weeks ago when you started to sink? Don't you think I *tried*?"

He stops, out of breath. Williams's lip begins to tremble and he steps back.

Two husky young men enter and immediately split, one to each side of Williams. Each one gently grasps an arm.

"Hello, Mr. Williams. Won't you come with us? We won't hurt you."

"You've got to do something, Dave!" he screams painfully. "I won't live through it, I know I won't! I can't take that kind of pain! For God's sake, Dave!"

It's only an illusion—the office is perfectly sound-proofed—but David imagines he can still hear the comedian's moans long after the cushioned doorway has shut tight. He sighs deeply and begins replacing papers, mike, and lounge in their former locales before leaving the office.

Miss Lee looks up as he passes.

"Where are you going, sir?"

He pauses. "I am going, Miss Lee, to reflect on the meaning of life, on the futility of existence, on the relationship of my pitiful self to that large, vast cosmos which I have the misfortune to be a part of. In brief, I am going to get drunk as a skunk. Please note and file."

Alas, she does not understand.

SKIT-SKAT CLUB.

The consonants exert a strange pull. He enters.

Clouds of perfumed and narcotic smoke have driven out much of the breathable, but he finds his way to the bar by instinct. Imperiously, he beckons to the bartender.

That worthy appears as magically as any djinn, wearing an expression that has not changed in six thousand years.

"Scotch and soda, my good Brutus. And hold the soda."

The lamp has been rubbed. Djinn disappears, reappears instantly, the glass in front of him full of molten mica. David samples it and turns like an old windlass to survey the crowd.

The majority are gathered around a large tri-vee cube suspended from the ceiling. Just now a four-hour history-film of the second great war is coming to a close. The camera dwells lingeringly on death, just like real war.

David, who has been floating rather lightly of late,

turns sullen again. The bartender turns money into booze, voilà. David sips moodily.

There is a moan from somewhere in the audience at a particularly crimson explosion on screen. Dulled cheers rise from the crowd.

Disgusted beyond measure, David turns to the mass of fellow sots.

"Souuu-eeee! Hey, animals!"

Somehow shocked, perhaps by the uniqueness of this outburst in their midst, their attention is diverted.

"An inspiring spectacle, my fellow grunts, is it not?" he babbles. "Here's to human blood, may it always be red, and there be plenty of it!" He drinks.

"Death has always been an amusement, we've but commercialized it, eh? A few violent moments to spice your otherwise mundane existences. Mutilation massages the cortex!" He turns away suddenly.

One chap, of considerable size and scant intelligence, is not to be so put off. He confronts David.

"Who are you calling an animal, squirt?"

David responds. He giggles.

"Selective hearing! And I thought alcohol an inhibitor."

"All men are animals today, my obese obtuse compadre. We all dance to the same rhythm of destruction."

The man tosses a loosely controlled thumb in the direction of the tri-vee.

"That's my favorite show you're insulting, buddy."

David reacts with an outpouring of utter astonishment.

"Your favorite show! My heavens, how ignorant of me. And I lacking in proper response. *Attiens*! I shall improvise."

He whirls and heaves his shotglass at the cube. For

an aspiring executive his aim is remarkable. The screen is shattered.

The man takes a step closer to David, raising his fists.

"That wasn't nice."

"What ho? A challenge to combat? One ape against the other in a battle for survival. From management to the limelight in five easy bottles! Up technology! For Frosty-O's!"

He turns slightly and salutes the shattered tri-vee cube.

"We who are about to die salute you!"

A sudden twist and he belts the startled belligerent square in the chops. That worthy, objecting, recovers and throws himself at David. Shortly they are as one.

The other patrons of the watering hole crowd around at the prospect of real live entertainment.

The bartender is not appeased. He signals to two large gentlemen at the back of the room. With practiced care they peel the two combatants apart, hold them harmless.

"Throw the skinny one out the front and the big one out the back."

David is given a protein-assisted exit but somehow manages to keep his feet. Turning, he hurls a few choice invectives at the bouncer. The man's skull is impervious to such weapons. They bounce off like raindrops.

At this, more liquid enters David's mouth than leaves it. Examination reveals that he is bleeding from a fair gash on the forehead. He takes out a handkerchief and begins mopping at himself, glancing around.

With the aid of the rapidly working sober-up pill he manages to locate a telebooth. It is painful just to remove his credcard and slip it into the telebooth slot.

The receiver pressures his shoulder as he waits for the machine to respond.

"Private number code four-six-two. Number now, please."

"767-44533." He grabs his head with the other hand and winces. The video screen in front of him clears.

Static vanishes, to reveal Uncle Don Texas seated on a wide couch in silk lounging pajamas, martini in hand. Music filters over the audio pickup, along with the sounds of feminine giggling. The picture abruptly zooms in to a closeup.

"Bad video at this end. Is that you, David?"

"Yeah. Listen, Uncle Don, I've got to come up and have a talk with you."

A pair of long-nailed hands enter the picture. Don slaps them away amidst more giggling.

"Now? Are you crazy?" says his uncle.

"It's important, Uncle Don. I...I'm thinking of quitting."

"What! You *are* crazy!" He stares hard into the pickup. "Say, what happened to your face?"

David touches the coagulated blood on his cheek.

"It's nothing. Damages incurred while discussing the merits of current programming. Happens to critics all the time."

Uncle Don grunts disapprovingly. "Looks like you were part of the show yourself. All right, come on up. But if this is part of some gag, Sarnoff help you!"

There is no click as his uncle hangs up, breaking the connection. David stares at the now blank video screen for a while before exiting the booth.

It's two A.M. and a mild cold front is passing over the Eastern seaboard. David gets wet.

* * *

The hallway of his uncle's maximum security building is done in pseudo-fur and knotty pine.

David approaches his uncle, grimacing.

"Hi, Uncle."

Don gives his nephew the once-over and around.

"Tch! Are you sure they returned all your parts when you were reassembled? Well, come on in."

Don's apartment is sumptuous and extensive. He sits David down in front of a low table with three free-form steel decanters on it.

"You sit there and work at breathing while I try and forage something to cement your skull with." He leaves the room, pauses at a crescent doorway.

David stares after him. After a moment, he pours a tiny bit of brandy, sips it. He glances around the apartment.

Nothing is changed. The heavily erotic red and purple furnishings still contrast strikingly with the early American desk in the far corner. Paperwork is piled deep on its shoulders and to one side a microtape player drools thin plastic impregnated with minor thoughts.

Don returns. "Success." He holds up mediseals and a spray can.

While David winces and twists, Don cleans the wound and sprays assorted bruises.

"Before you die, I'd appreciate it if you'd tell me what was so urgent as to require interrupting a conference session for."

"Some 'conference session'!" He grinned. Then, seriously. "Don, since my parents died, you've been half like a father to me and—"

Don stands in disgust. "Oh, for Nielsen's sake!" He goes falsetto. "'Since mumsy and dada went bye-bye, you've been *just* like...'" He stares down at David.

"If you came up here to slobber off your drunk, just pick yourself up and haul out, nephew!"

David smiles. "All right, Don, all right. Easy down." He stares at his drink.

"Like I said, I'm considering leaving the business."

Don stares intently at him. "Say, you *are* serious, aren't you? I thought that was just part of your binge."

He pours himself a drink and sits down.

"Now then. *Why* are you thinking of quitting the industry? I suppose your ridiculous outburst at the board meeting this morning had something to do with it, umm? Gave me a hell of a time placating old Mousseface and the others."

"Don, hasn't it ever occurred to you that there might be a, well, an excess of violence on the tri-vee today?"

"Oh, so *that's* what's been bothering you! Listen, David. All we do is supply the people something they want. Their home kinovoters indicate their desires, and we do our level best to provide the kind of shows they say they want. Do you want us to end up with tiny, ultra-conservative audiences like the movies have? Nobody goes to the movies anymore. Not only aren't they live; nothing ever *happens*!

"Another thing. Why do you think modern tri-vee is so successful? You know, there was once a time when everything on the air was *taped*. Can you imagine?"

"But why is it so necessary, Uncle Don, to use live actors and live ammunition?"

"First off," Don began seriously, "people are sophisticated enough to tell the difference between robots and real actors, David. No robot can writhe like a man in pain, or bleed as realistically, or cry as convincingly, no matter how well he's programmed. And when the audience votes for a man to die, well, he has to die, doesn't he? We get them to the resurrection chambers on time. The fatality rate is very low, lower than for construction workers. It's in every contract. You wouldn't want the FCC down on us for offering an inferior product, would you?"

David is confused, as always, by his uncle's evaluation of things.

"No...no."

"Of course not!" Don leaves his chair and begins pacing. "The people get what they want. What they need, in fact. Do you know that since the advent of world-wide tri-vee there hasn't been even a minor war? Because everyone can now safely sublimate his normal, healthy desire for homicide via his own tri-vee, in the comfort and privacy of his own living room. Would you trade tri-vee for war? Cameras for cannons?"

"No," sighed David, downing the rest of the brandy. "Of course not."

"Well then." He gives David a hand up, walks him toward the door.

"Now, you go back to your place and take a Quik-Nap and another good dram of something warmish and tomorrow you can get right in on those two new series we've been discussing. Right?"

"Yeah, sure."

They are standing in the doorway when Don remembers something.

"By the way, did you happen to catch the 'Slappy Williams Hour' this evening?"

"No. Why? I was soused from late afternoon on."

"Great show, great! Real trouper, that guy. They bowed him out according to voter demand. Finished by choking a full-grown lion to death with his own body. Hysterical! Laugh index was over eighty-five.

Unfortunately there wasn't enough left for the resurrectors to work on. His own fault. Didn't handle it well. They think he might have been drugged at the time. Too bad."

"Oh."

Don is shaking his head in admiration.

"Yeah, well, that's show biz. See you tomorrow, kid."

The door closes, but David doesn't leave for several minutes yet.

David's desk has acquired a thin film of papers. He looks up from a bundle in hand as a chime sounds, followed by the appearance of the miniature speaker.

"What is it, Miss Lee?"

"Your uncle is here to see you, Mr. Texas. And a young lady."

"Send them in."

The grid is retracted and he returns to his papers.

"Yo, David."

"What's simmering this morning, Uncle Don?" He does not look up from his work.

"I think, lad, that we've found the girl for that new spy series. Say hello to Oriel Vanity." David looks up.

The girl has the face of a madonna and the body of a succubus. Red hair flows into a curved frame around an innocent face that hides little of it. He stares for a long time before rising embarrassedly to his feet.

"I know how you feel, my boy. Our little girl has that effect on people."

"How do you do, Mr. Texas," she said, extending a hand. He took it and eventually remembered to shake it. Her touch was enough to wake him completely.

"Just fine, thank you."

Don has been surveying the scene with undisguised

pleasure. "Well, I'll leave the two of you to get acquainted. Don't hold her too long, David. She has a screen test in thirty minutes."

David waves vaguely in the direction of his departing uncle.

"Won't you please sit down?"

"Thank you."

"Uh, what did my uncle send you to me for, specifically?"

She lights a pastel narco-stik. "He said that you were handling the contracts for the cast of the series ... Dave."

"Quite so, I am. Indeed. As a matter of fact ..." He begins rummaging through an open drawer. His efforts slacken and he looks across at her.

"Well?" she offers.

"Listen, are you tied up this evening." She shakes a negative. "No? Good. I'd like to take my time discussing this with you. How about dinner?"

She leans forward, smiling coquettishly.

"I'd like that very much, I think."

"Seven-thirty?"

"Just fine. In fact, I'm sure everything will work out just fine."

There is just enough light for David's reclining form to show, had anyone cared to look. He is lying on his back on the cream-filled water bed, quite naked.

"What time is it?"

There is motion to his left, and the flame-haired Aphrodite rolls onto his side. She is half awake.

"Ummm. Who cares."

"This is important."

She groans in mock indignation. "Well, thanks!"

"No, really. If your contract isn't ratified and approved by twelve noon today, the Guild can demand that another actress be given a try at the part."

He smiles then and turns to her. He rumples her hair, but he is staring over her head.

"A series contract is an unimaginably vital document these days, you know. Like the contracts for indentured servants hundreds of years ago."

"Never mind contract. How about a little contact?"

She silences him with a twisting kiss and he returns it enthusiastically. But it is he who breaks the clinch and again finds fascination in the dark ceiling.

"Oriel, I can't let you sign that contract."

"Well now," she murmurs interestedly, "and why not? You can't stop me anyway, you know."

He turns to face her.

"Dammit, Oriel," he began angrily, "you've no idea what they can put you through, once you've signed that contract! You'd do better to sell yourself to the devil."

"Now listen," she said firmly. "I'm fully aware of what I'll be asked to do. I'm also aware that it's only a three-year contract. I can quit at the end of that period, with more money than I'll be able to spend the rest of my life. I'm not afraid of what I expect. It can't be as bad as you make it out to be."

He turned away in frustration. "It would be easier for me if I hadn't fallen in love with you."

"You are sweet." She leans over and kisses him again. Several agains.

"I can't let you do it, Oriel, I just can—" Suddenly, he rolls away and sits up. "Wait a second. Wait just one single imploding second!"

He turned and began rummaging through the drawer of a little night table. Tossing paper and film spools aside, he finally comes up with a thick document and a pen. He starts scribbling furiously.

She sits up and looks interestedly from the wad of paper to Dave's intent face.

"What are you up to now?"

He continues writing furiously, occasionally shifting to a new page. A last note, and he pauses, not looking up.

"There. It's not as thorough as I'd like, but it doesn't take much. I'm making this into a special, short-term contract. With an 'escape clause,' so to speak. It's not ironclad. But in the event of a sudden, radical modification in any of your shows, it'll protect you against just about anything extreme the director and writer can dream up for you."

Another thought and he returns to the contract for another last-minute adjustment. After a last survey of his handiwork, he hands it to her.

"There! Give this to whichever headsman presides over the symbolic shackling tomorrow. Chances are no one will read it until it's signed and too late. No one'll be expecting any changes."

She takes it gently and puts it aside without so much as a quick glance. Her arms curl around his shoulders.

"Oriel..."

"Ummmm?"

"Oriel?..."

"Ummm?"

"You talk too much."

The room is moderately crowded. A party atmosphere prevails, and some of the costumes worn by the women seem indeed better suited to an evening out. They are closely rivaled, sartorially, by the men-folk. Several kinds of smoke of varying degrees of potency and pungency make question-mark shapes in the air, despite the best efforts of the purifiers.

One woman outshines them all.

Two gentlemen occupy her perimeter. One is bald and fading to fat. Familiar fat. It is Uncle Don Texas. The other is much younger, tall, devil-bearded and saturnine of visage. He doesn't talk, but he smiles a lot. Oriel is magnificent in gems, silverdust, and rain-fur. Her pixie face is the same, but there is something else there. Several somethings, and they are not the result of cosmetics. She is a star now, and pulses.

David enters via the far door and looks around hopefully. Uncle Don spots him first.

"David, my boy! Over here, lad!"

Dave acknowledges his uncle's bellow from across the room.

"Hello, Uncle Don. Johansson."

Oriel is a bit flustered to see him but recovers nicely.

"David, dahling. How delightful to see you here! You didn't say anything."

"I flew in from Nice just a few hours ago. They told me you'd be here."

"Well, they were right, weren't they?" she offers gaily. "Dear David, how are you?"

"I'm not too sure, anymore."

He takes her by the arm and steers her away from the others. Don harrumphs softly and Johansson smiles.

"This is the first chance I've had to see you since that night," he whispered. "Did you get through the contract session all right?"

"Contract session?"

"Don't you remember that contract I prepared for you? You must have signed already. You took it."

She giggles. "Oh, *that*! David, the most marvelous thing happened! I took it with me to the session like you said. Your Uncle Don—really, he is a dear—and that nice Mr. Pelligrini gave me a much better contract. *Lots* more money, believe it or not, and *top* billing!"

"Oriel," he moans, grabbing her shoulders tightly. "Don't you have any idea what you've done? You signed away your life for the duration of that contract! Why didn't you listen to me, Oriel, why? *Why?*"

"David, you're hurting me!"

Don and the tall young man have wandered over.

"Say, what is this?" bubbles Don. "This is supposed to be a happy occasion! And you, my young nephew, look decidedly funereal."

"C'mere a minute, *Uncle*." David draws the older man aside. "Why'd you have them change her contract from the one she showed up with?"

"Have them change?...Oh, you mean that thing she brought in for us to countersign? Hell, Dave, you ought to know the boys in legal would never let anything as loose as that slip through. Especially for new talent. Double-especially for a pretty broad. I could care less, but Pelligrini and old Mooseface would boil over. Besides, all they did was give her a standard, no-cut union contract. What's eating you?"

David sighs, resignedly.

"Nothing, nothing. You just did what you thought was right, Uncle Don. And everyone and everything seems to agree with you. I just...oh, intercourse!"

"David!"

"Skip it." He walks over to the punch table.

"Listen, Oriel. We'll talk about this over dinner tonight."

"Oh, David, I *am* sorry! But I didn't expect you. Leif and I are going out this evening. He's going to be my leading man in the series, you know. The studio's throwing a big publicity party afterward."

Leif deigned to speak. "Sorry, old man."

"Aren't we all?" He turned and headed for the door.

"Extraordinary," said the leading man, sipping his punch.

"Oh, dear," murmured Oriel, "do you suppose he went away mad? I didn't intend to upset him."

Weaving slightly from more than just punch, Don observed seriously, "No, despite our damndest, I think he went away sane." He smiles at the precious girl's puzzled frown. "Another martini, my dear?"

David's desk is molting papers. It has added two things: a small calendar and a shallow glass dish. In the dish exist water, a stone, a plastic plant, and a small green turtle. They are in harmony. The beautiful metal desk shines in the subdued light. But there are more circuits in the turtle.

The little grid, an abstract jack-in-the-box, makes an appearance. It chimes.

"Yes, Miss Lee?"

"There's a young lady here to see you, Mr. Texas. Oriel Vanity."

He grins mirthlessly. "*The* Oriel Vanity?"

"Yes, sir."

"Send her—" The door bursts open.

"Well, Oriel. I haven't seen you in some months. How's the show doing?"

She looks haggard and drawn, hair disarrayed. The beauty is still there, untouched. The cancer is inside. He knows. He's seen it before.

"David, you've got to help me!"

"So?"

"The ratings have been fluctuating like crazy for weeks now! One Friday they're in the top five, the next we barely make the top fifty. But that's not what bothers me. David, they added a new co-star last week! A girl!"

"I know the girl. Very attractive."

"Her talent's in her tits. David, I'm afraid that ... they're going to replace me with her."

He stares at the turtle, thinking hard. If the tiny amphibian has any suggestions, it keeps them to itself. Oriel sniffles. Hysteria is just around the corner.

He reaches across the desk and takes both hands gently in his.

"I'll do everything I can, Oriel."

She lets the tears come and falls into his arms. They embrace, but not as before, no, not as before.

The turtle blinks at the sudden change of light.

There are a hundred and sixty floors in the great building and fifteen sub-levels, not counting parking. Decision makers occupy a portion of them, power-wielders considerably less. David talks to most of them. He pleads. He argues and cajols. He threatens and promises.

He gets a lot of head-shakes, all horizontal.

Eventually, he ends up in an office more familiar than the others. He has been speaking impassioned words for some time, without hope. This is realistic.

"But *why*, Don, why? Why can't you do something? You know what will happen if those ratings don't firm up?"

Don has listened to his nephew with considerable patience. He has taken much from David that would have been suicide for any other lesser employee. He is sympathetic, but firm.

"Out of the question, David. It's not only because she's the lead. You can't touch a contract like that. It would shake the whole foundation of the industry.

Precedent, you understand. If I could do anything, believe me, I would. But I'm not ready for a martyr's chair yet." He shrugs.

"Then there's no hope?" sighs David, slumping back in the chair.

"Look, it's not as bad as all that!" begins his uncle on a hopeful note. "Sure, they're adding another broad to the show. They do that all the time. If the viewers register favorably in Oriel's voting situations the next couple of weeks, why, she'll be home free for the rest of the season. Just take it easy and don't worry so much. Christ, kid! People are starving. There's other things to grumble over."

David's apartment is comfortably furnished, although not on a scale reflecting his considerable income. The living room is mostly natural woods and wood-plastics, indirectly lit. At the moment, Dave is conversing with a young man about his own age and the woman seated with him. She is half-pretty and a little shy, even with Dave. The man happens to notice his chronometer.

"Say-y-y." He looks at his wife. "We'd better get going, hon. It's past the kids' bedtime. And I have to be in Madrid tomorrow." He moves to get up.

"Stay where you are, Nick. I'll get them." Nick relaxes as David rises and heads for another room.

The bedroom is furnished in the same style as the living room, with warmer colors. The twins, seven-year-old Jamie and Jodie, are locked onto the tri-vee screen.

David pauses, notices the large, custom-built screen. A popular kiddie cartoon is on one of the minor channels. The current superhero is busily engaged in the

102

dismemberment of the forces of evil. David walks over and touches them both on the shoulder.

"Time to go, kids."

"Awww, Uncle Davey!"

"Please let us stay a minute longer, Uncle Davey," pouts Jodie, brushing her curls from her face. "We just voted!"

"Okay," he said, checking his own watch. "But just a minute." They return their attention avidly to the set.

The multi-plane camera lingers lovingly over the gory remains of the evil alien's castle. The superhero, his trusty dog flying effortlessly at his side, soars into the horizon to the heroic strains of some cornflake manufacturer's personal anthem. The credits begin.

"Okay ... "

" ... Uncle Davey!"

They scramble or flow off the bed and run to the living room. David follows, thoughtful.

Nick and Willa are waiting at the iris doorway, coats already donned. The children fuss as their own jackets are adjusted.

"Good night, Nick," offers David as the two shake hands. "And bon voyage. Good luck in Madrid. If you run into a sportscaster name of Hector Rodriguiz at the BCE, say hi to him for me."

"Will do, Dave. We had a lovely evening."

"Any time, Nick. You and Willa should stop by more often."

"We will, I promise. 'Night."

"Good night, Dave." Willa smiles. They kiss.

"Night, sis." He bends and kisses each of the children.

They depart down the hall, the kids waving and yelling bye-byes.

The auto-chef in the kitchen dispenses a tall glass

of cold beer and some rather fancy sandwiches under his careful programming. These in hand, he heads for the bedroom.

The food goes onto a night table. He switches the tri-vee back on and begins to remove his clothes. Once in the bed he takes a long sip from the frosted glass and flips channels.

He tries several, stops, and backs up slowly until the set locks on one he has already passed. A kicking, screaming, half-naked girl is being dragged down wet stone stairs by two gentlemen who are far removed from the well groomed. It is Oriel.

He stops sipping the beer.

She is strapped down to a long table in a dungeonlike room filled with medieval torture instruments. The camera lingers lovingly over each while one of the men helpfully expounds on their history and uses from off-screen. The angle changes to reveal a brawny individual clad only in jeweled loincloth. He is standing next to a glowing brazier, stirring the coals with a short iron rod. Oriel's writhings and squirmings are very convincing.

A pert young brunette suddenly appears on the screen.

"Well, tri-vee viewers! Isn't this exciting? As we have seen thus far tonight, secret agent Jade Green has refused to divulge the secret location of the resistance fighter's headquarters to the evil Dictator Generalissimo Bohr. It is up to you, dear viewers, to decide her fate! Will agent Mark Craig and the guerrillas arrive in time to save the beauteous Jade from a horrible fate?"

A closeup of Oriel's tear-streaked face is helpfully inserted.

"Or will the evil Dictator and his men succeed in extracting the information from her?"

"If you wish the lovely Jade to be rescued, please press the first button on your kinovoter; that's button one, the red. On the other hand, if you wish Generalissimo Bohr and his men to succeed in their nefarious activity, press the green button, number two. The choice is yours, afficionados!" She does a dramatic turn to face the wall map.

David stares unwaveringly at the screen. The glow throws his features into sharp highlight. His expression is unfathomable.

His hand moves slowly to the side of the bed. A small pink box is set there, firmly attached to the frame. It is featureless, except for two small buttons projecting outwards, one red, one green.

His hand hovers over the buttons. He has plenty of time...

Gift of a Useless Man

What do you give when you've nothing left to give? When you've naught left to offer friends to whom you feel indebted? When you're busted, in more than one sense?

We spend a fortune in this country sweeping away the byproducts of ourselves, ridding ourselves of personal waste. But how do you define "waste"? Might not what we consider waste be considered valuable by someone else? Sometimes values are so hard to define they escape analysis.

When you come right down to it, my body, your body, every *body* is nothing more than a wondrously efficient and complex chemical plant, one that even DuPont can't duplicate. Better living through chemistry.

And most of the time, we're not even aware

of the fact that this irreplaceable plant is producing all the time...

———

Both Pearson and the ship were rotted out.

He hadn't known that when he'd rented it (having no intention of returning it and not worrying about that since both the credslip he'd used to pay for it and his corresponding identification were fakes), but he'd been in too much of a hurry to care.

The ship had made the Jump in one piece; but when he'd come out into normal space again, he'd found several small but critical components that had come out in many pieces.

All that was left of it now was a pillar of smoke and vaporized metal climbing into a pale blue sky. He could not bring himself to curse it. He knew the feeling. And it had ejected him, though somewhat less than safely. He was alive, and that wasn't much. All he felt now was an overwhelming tiredness, a fatigue of the spirit. A numbness of the soul.

Surprisingly, there was no pain. Inside, Pearson continued to function. Outside, he could move his eyes and lips, twitch his nose, and—with enormous effort—raise his right arm off the flat, sandy ground. His face was no longer merely a small part of an expressive self: it was all that remained. What the rest of his body, encased in the remnants of his flight suit, looked like, he could only imagine. He did not wish to imagine. He knew his right arm was intact, because he could move it. Beyond that, all was morbid speculation.

If he was lucky, very lucky, he might be able to use

the arm to turn himself onto his side. He did not bother to make the effort. There were no more illusions, at last no more illusions, circling languidly in Pearson's consciousness. On the eve of death, he had become a realist.

It was a tiny world he'd inflicted himself upon, no more than a very large asteroid, really. Silently, he apologized to it for any damage his crash might have caused. He was always apologizing for doing damage.

He was breathing, so the thin atmosphere was less tenuous than it looked. No one would find him here. Even the police who'd been chasing him would leave off searching. Pearson was a most insignificant criminal. Not even a criminal, really. To qualify for that label you had to do something modestly harmful. "Criminal" implied someone dangerous, threatening. Pearson was merely irritating to society, like a minor itch.

Well, he'd finally gone and scratched himself, he thought, and was surprised to discover he had the strength and ability left to laugh.

It made him black out, however.

When he regained his senses, it was just beginning to grow light. He had no idea how long this minuscule world's day was. Therefore he had no idea how long he'd been unconscious. He might've been out a day or a week, human time. Though he no longer thought of himself as human. Complete muscular paralysis, save for his face and one arm, had left him a living corpse. He was unable to move about, nor reach the concentrates in the battered survival pack that might or might not still be attached to the leg of his suit, or do more than breathe in the feeble atmosphere that was temporarily keeping him alive. He rather wished he'd blown up with the ship.

He would not starve, however. He would die of

thirst first. Living corpse, Pearson. Brain in a bottle.
It gave him plenty of time to reflect on his life.

Actually, he'd been something of a living corpse all
along. He'd never felt for anyone or anything, and not
very strongly for himself. Never doing anyone any
good and not having the capability to do anyone serious
evil, he'd just sort of muddled along, taking up space
and other people's air.

I'd have made a better tree, he mused tiredly. Pearson wondered if he'd have made a very good tree.
Certainly he couldn't have been a worse tree than he
had a man. He saw himself as a youth, cocky in a
sniveling sort of way. Saw himself toadying up to the
smoother, more professional criminals in hopes of
worming his way into their company, their society,
their friendship.

Naw, he hadn't even made a very good boot-licker.
Nor could he go straight, the couple of times he'd tried.
The real, legal world had regarded him with the same
resigned contempt as the less virtuous. So he'd lived
in a tenebrous, mucousy vacuum of his own invention,
not quite functioning efficiently in the mental sense
and only barely in the physical.

If only... but no, he stopped himself sharply. He
was going to die. Might as well be honest for a change,
if only with himself. The misfortunes he'd suffered
were his own doing, always his own doing, not the
fault of others as he'd forever been telling himself.
There had been a few pitying ones who'd tried to help
him. Somehow he always managed to screw things up.
If nothing else, perhaps he could die being honest with
his own thoughts.

He had heard that dying of thirst was not pleasant.

The sun went down, and no moon came up. Naturally not, for a world this small could not afford the

luxury of a moon. It was a wonder it held onto a breathable atmosphere. Pearson wondered idly if there was life existing on the fine, flat soil around him. Plants, maybe. He'd come down too fast and messily to spend time on such details. Since he was unable to turn his head, he could do no more than wonder.

Air rippled across him, a cool night breeze, pleasant after the mild, hazy heat of day. He felt it keenly on his face. The rest of his body's external receptors were dead. It was possible he'd suffered severe burns. If so, he couldn't react to them. In that respect the paralysis was a blessing. He knew that other parts of his body were functioning, though, He could smell himself.

When the sun rose again he was still wide awake. He estimated this world's day at three to four hours, followed by a night of equal duration. The information was of no practical use, but such speculation helped keep his mind busy. He was slowly adjusting to his situation. It's said the human mind can adjust to anything.

After a while he discovered the thought of death no longer bothered him. It would be a relief of sorts. No more running; from others, from his pitiful self. No one would grieve over him. No one would miss him. By his absence he would spare others the infection of his presence. The first hints of thirst, faint but unmistakable, took possession of his throat.

Short days passed and a few clouds appeared. He'd never paid any attention to clouds and little to the weather. Now he had time and reason to study both. He could see nothing else. It occurred to him he might be able to use his one functioning arm to turn his head and thus vary his line of sight. But when he tried, he found the arm would not respond sufficiently to carry out the complex maneuver.

Odd, the emotions. He discovered that the chance his one working limb might be becoming paralyzed frightened him more than the certain onslaught of death.

Clouds continued to gather above him. He regarded them indifferently. Rain might prolong his life a few earthly days, but eventually he'd starve. The concentrates in his suit pack could keep him alive for months, probably longer considering his lack of activity. But they might as well have been vaporized with the ship. He couldn't reach them.

His mind speculated on possible methods of suicide. If his arm would respond and there was a sharp piece of metal nearby, a scrap of ship, he might cut his throat. If . . . if . . .

It did rain. Gently and steadily, for an entire half day. His open mouth caught enough to sate him. The clouds passed and shattered, and the distant sun returned. He felt it drying his face, assumed it was doing so to the rest of his body. He formed a new appreciation for the miracle of rain and the process by which it's transformed into blood and lymph and cells. Amazing, astonishing accomplishment; and he'd spent a short lifetime taking it for granted. He deserved to die.

I am growing philosophical, he thought. Or delirious.

Short days gave way to brief nights. He had completely lost track of time when the first bug found him.

Pearson felt it long before he saw it. It crawled up his cheek. Maddeningly, he was unable to scratch at it or brush it away. It traversed his face, stopped, and peered into his right eye.

He blinked.

The tickle returned. He hadn't caught it, then. It was on his forehead now. After pausing there, it walked down across his left cheek, retracing its first approach.

111

Out of the corner of his left eye he saw it as it dropped to his shoulder. It was blue-black and too small for him to discern individual details. It definitely looked like an insect.

It stopped on his shoulder, considering its surroundings.

Maybe it would be better this way, he thought. It would be faster if the bugs devoured him. When he'd bled enough, he would die. If they started below his head, he might never feel any pain before he passed out.

Silently, he encouraged the insect. Go on, buddy. Bring back your aunts and uncles and cousins and have yourselves a feast, courtesy of Pearson. It'll be a blessing.

"No, we cannot do that."

I'm delirious, he mused distantly, adding in reflex, "Why not?"

"You are a wonderment. We could not eat a wonderment. We are not deserving enough."

"I'm no wonder," he thought insistently. "I'm a wastrel, a failure, a thorough mistake of nature. Not only that," he concluded, "I am lying here conversing telepathically with a bug."

"I am Yirn, one of the People," the soft thought informed him. "I am not what a bug is. Tell me, wonderment, how can something so huge be alive?"

So Pearson told him. He told the bug his name, and about mankind, and about his sick, sad existence that was soon to come to an end, and about his paralysis.

"I am saddened for you," Yirn of the People finally said. "We can do nothing to help you. We are a poor tribe among many and are not permitted by the Laws to reproduce much. Nor do I begin to understand these strange things you tell me of space and time and size.

I find it hard enough to believe that this mountain you lie within once moved. Yet you say that is so, and I must believe."

Pearson had a sudden, disturbing thought. "Hey, look, Yirn. Don't get the idea I'm any sort of god or anything. I'm just bigger, that's all. I'm really less than you. I couldn't even make a good pimp."

"The concept does not translate." Yirn gave the impression of straining. "You are the most wonderful thing in all creation."

"Bullshit. Say . . . how can I 'talk' with you when you're so much smaller?"

"Among our People we have a saying that it is the size of the intellect that is important, not the size of the size."

"Yeah, I guess. Look, I'm sorry you've got such a poor tribe, Yirn; and I appreciate your being sorry for me. No one's ever been sorry for me before except me. Even a bug's sympathy's an improvement." He lay quietly for a while, regarding the bug, which preened minute antennae.

"I . . . I wish I could do something for you and your tribe," he finally said, "but I can't even help myself. I'm going to die of hunger soon."

"We would help if we could," came the thought. Pearson had a feeling of sadness all out of proportion to the creature's size. "But all we could gather would not feed you properly for a day."

"Yeah. There's food in my suit pack, but . . ." He fell silent. Then, "Yirn, tell me if there are shiny metal coverings on my lower body."

Moments passed while the insect made a hike to the promontory of a knuckle and returned. "There are what you describe, Pearson."

"How many People in your tribe?"

"What do you have in your mind, Pearson?"

Pearson told him and Yirn of the People replied. "Enough."

It took days, local days, for the tribe of Yirn to open the catches on the suit packs. When it became apparent the People could digest human food, a great mental rejoicing filled Pearson's brain; and he was glad.

It was a truly humble Yirn who later came to communicate with him. "For the first time in many, many generations, my tribe has enough to eat. We can multiply beyond the restrictions the Laws impose upon those bereft of food. One of the great blocks you call concentrates can feed the tribe for a long while. We have not tried the natural foods you say are contained in the greater pack beneath you, but we will.

"Now we can become a real tribe and not fear those tribes that prey on the poor. All because of you, great Pearson."

"Just 'Pearson,' you understand? You call me 'great' again and I'll..." He paused. "No. I won't do anything. Even if I could. I'm finished with threatening. Just plain Pearson, if you will. And I haven't done a goddamn thing for you. Your people got at the food all by themselves. First time I ever thought anything of concentrates."

"We have a surprise for you, Pearson."

Something was crawling with infinite slowness up his cheek. It had a little weight, more than the People. He saw it edge into his vision. A small brown block. Dozens of tiny blue-black forms surrounded it. He could hear their effort in his mind.

The block reached his lips and he opened them. Some of the People were terrified at the nearness of that bottomless dark chasm. They turned and fled. Yirn and other leaders of the tribe took their places.

The block passed over his lower lip. The People exerted a last, monumental effort. Some of them expired from it. The block fell into the chasm.

Pearson felt saliva flowing, but hesitated. "I don't know what good it'll do in the long run, Yirn, but . . . thanks. You'd better herd your folks off my face, though. There's going to be an earthqua . . . no, a Pearsonquake, in a moment."

When they were safely clear, he began to chew.

It rained the next morning. The raindrops were the size of raindrops on Earth. They posed a terrifying threat to the tribe, if they were caught out in the open. A few drops could kill someone the size of Yirn. But the entire tribe had plenty of shelter beneath the overhang of Pearson's right arm.

Many weeks later, Yirn sat on Pearson's nose, staring down into oceanic eyes. "The concentrates will not last forever, and the real foods we've found in your 'pack' beneath you will last less so."

"Never mind that. I don't want you to eat those. I think there's a couple of carrots, and on an old sandwich, there should be tomato slices, lettuce, and, I think, mushrooms. Also pocya, a small kind of nut. The meat and bread you can eat, but save some of the bread. Maybe you can eat the mold."

"I do not understand, Pearson."

"How do you find food, Yirn? You're gatherers, aren't you?"

"That is so."

"Then I want you to take the carrots, and the tomato, and the others—I'll describe them to you—and also samples of every local plant your people eat."

"And do what with them, Pearson?"

"Gather the elders of the tribe. We'll start with the concept of irrigation. . . ."

Pearson was no agriculturist. But he knew, in his primitive way, that if you plant and water and weed, certain foods will grow. The People were fast learners. It was the concept of staying in one place and planting that was new to them.

A catch basin was dug, at the cost of hundreds of tiny lives. But the concentrates gave the People great energy. Tiny rivulets began to snake outward from the basin, away from the protective bulk of Pearson. When it ceased raining, the basin and the thread-thin canals were full, and the minute dams came into good use. Another basin was dug, and then another.

Some of the human food took and grew, and some of the local foods took and grew. The People prospered. Pearson explained the idea of building permanent structures. The People had never considered it because they could not imagine an artificial construct which would shed rain. Pearson told them about A-frames.

There came the day when the concentrates ran out. Pearson had been anticipating it and was not dismayed by the news. He'd done far, far more than he'd dreamed of being able to do those first empty days alone on the sand, after the crash. He'd helped, and been rewarded with the first real friendship of his life.

"It doesn't matter, Yirn. I'm just glad I was able to be of some use to you and your people."

"Yirn is dead," said the bug. "I am Yurn, one of his offspring, given the honor of talking to you."

"Yirn's dead? It hadn't been that long . . . has it?" Pearson's sense of time was hazy. But then, the life-span of the People was far shorter than man's. "No matter. At least the tribe has enough to eat now."

"It does matter, to us," replied Yurn. "Open your mouth, Pearson."

Something was crawling up his cheek. It moved at a fairly rapid pace. Tiny wooden pulleys helped it along, and over the pulleys were slung long cables made from Pearson's hair. A path for it was cut through his beard by dozens of the People using their sharp jaws.

It fell into his mouth. It was leafy and vaguely familiar. A piece of spinach.

"Eat, Pearson. The remnants of your ancient 'sandwich' have given birth . . ."

Soon after the third harvest, a trio of elders visited Pearson. They sat carefully on the tip of his nose and regarded him somberly.

"The crops are not doing well," said one.

"Describe them to me." They did so, and he strained the hidden places of his brain for long-unused schoolboy knowledge. "If they're getting enough water, then it can only be one thing, if they're all being affected. The soil here is getting worn out. You'll have to plant elsewhere."

"Many are the leagues between here and the farthest farm," one of the elders told him. "There have been raids. Other tribes are grown jealous of us. Our People are afraid to plant too far from you. Your presence gives them confidence."

"Then there's one other possibility." He licked his lips. The People had found salt for him. "What have you been doing with the wastes from my body?"

"They have been steadily removed and buried, as you directed," said one, "and fresh earth and sand brought constantly to replace the region beneath you, where you dampen the ground."

"The soil here is growing tired," he told them. "It requires the addition of something we call fertilizer. Here is what the People must do . . ."

Many years later, a new council came to visit Pearson. This was after the great battle. Several large, powerful tribes had combined to attack the People. They'd driven them back to the fortress mountain of Pearson. As the battle raged around him, the leaders of the three attacking tribes had led a forceful charge to take possession of the living god-mountain, as Pearson had come to be known to the other tribes.

Straining every remaining functional nerve in his body, Pearson had raised his one good arm and in one blow slain the leaders of the onslaught and all their general staff, and hundreds of others besides. Taking advantage of the confusion this engendered in the enemy's ranks, the People had counterattacked. The invaders were repulsed with heavy losses, and the land of the People was not troubled after that.

Many crops were destroyed. But with liberal doses of fertilizer supplied by Pearson, the next crop matured healthier than ever.

Now the new council sat in the place of honor atop Pearson's nose and gazed into fathomless, immense eyes. Yeen, eighth son-in-line from Yirn the Legendary, held the center.

"We have a present for you, Pearson. You had told us months ago of an event you call a 'birthday,' and rambled much about its meaning and the customs that surround it. We cast our thoughts for a suitable gift."

"I'm afraid I can't open it if it's wrapped," he quipped weakly. "You'll have to show me. I wish I could offer you one in return. You've kept me alive."

"You have given us much more than life. Look to your left, Pearson."

He moved his eyes. A creaking, grinding noise began, continued as he watched empty sky and waited. The feeling-thoughts of thousands of the People reached him.

An object slowly rose into view. It was a circle, set atop a perfect girderwork of tiny wooden beams. It was old and scratched in places, but still shiny: a hand mirror, gleaned from God knew what section of his backpack or suit pockets. It was inclined at an angle across his chest, and down.

For the first time in many years he could see the ground. Before he could express his thanks for the wonderful, incredible gift of the mounted old mirror his thoughts were blanked by what he could see.

Tiny rows of cultivated fields stretched to the horizon. Clusters of small houses dotted the fields, many gathered together into semblances of towns. A suspension bridge made of his hair and threads from his suit crossed a tiny stream in three places. On the other side of the People-sized river were the beginnings of a small city.

The mirror crew, through an ingenious system of pulleys and cords, turned the reflector. Nearby was the factory where, he was told, wooden beams and articles were manufactured from local plants. Among the tools used to shape the beams were sharp bits of Pearson's fingernails. Huge tents housed other factories, tents made from the treated skin which peeled regularly off Pearson's suntanned body. Tools moved smoothly, and pulleys and wheels carried people to and from, lubricated in part with wax taken from Pearson's ears.

"Offer us something in return, Pearson?" said Yeen rhetorically. "You have given us the greatest gift of all: yourself. Every day we find new uses for the information you give us. Every day we find new uses for what you produce.

"Other tribes that once we fought with have joined

with us, so that all may benefit from you. We are becoming what you once called a nation."

"Watch... watch out," Pearson mumbled mentally, overcome by Yeen's words and the sweeping vistas provided by the mirror. "A nation means the onset of politicians."

"What is that?" asked one of the council suddenly, pointing downward.

"A new gift," came his neighbor's thought, also staring down the great slope of Pearson's nose. "What is it good for, Pearson?"

"Nothin'. I learned a long time ago, friends," he said, "that tears ain't good for nothing..."

Yusec, hundred and twelfth son-in-line from Yirn the Legendary, was resting on Pearson's chest, enjoying the shade provided by the forest of hair there. Pearson had just finished a bit of a wonderful new fruit the People had grown on a far farm and brought in especially for him. Pearson could see Yusec via one of the many mirrors mounted around his face, all inclined to offer him a different view of his surroundings.

A party of young was touring his pelvic region and another was making its way around the base of his ear. Others came and went from him on crude escalators or one of the many huge stairways that mounted him on all sides. Groups of archivists stood nearby, ready to record any stray thought Pearson might produce. They even monitored his dreams.

"Yusec, the new food was very good."

"The farmers of that region will be pleased."

There was a pause before Pearson spoke again. "Yusec, I'm dying."

Startled, the insect rose to his feet, stared up at the

120

massif of Pearson's chin. "What is this? Pearson cannot die."

"Bullshit, Yusec. What color is my hair?"

"White, Pearson. It has been so for many decades."

"Are the canyons of my face deep?"

"Yes, but no deeper than in my great-grandfather's time."

"Then they were deep then. I am dying, Yusec. I don't know how old I am because I long ago lost track of my time, and I never troubled to compare it to your time. It never mattered. It still doesn't. But I am dying.

"I'll die happier than I once thought I would, though. I've done more moving since I've been paralyzed than I did when I was mobile. I feel good about that."

"You cannot die, Pearson." Yusec repeated his insistence while sending out an emergency call for the hospital team set up many years ago solely to serve Pearson's needs.

"I can and will and am," came the reply, and a frightened Yusec heard the death coming over Pearson's thoughts like a shadow. He could not imagine a time without Pearson. "The hospital people are good. They've learned a lot about me on their own. But there's nothin' they can do. I'm gonna die."

"But... what shall we do without you?"

"Everything you do is done without me, Yusec. I've only given you advice, but the People have done all the actual work. You won't miss me."

"We will miss you, Pearson." Yusec was resigning himself to the massive inevitability of Pearson's passing. "I am saddened."

"Yeah, me too. Funny, I was almost coming to enjoy this life. Oh, well." His thoughts were very weak now, receding like the sun around the world.

"Just a last idea, Yusec."

"Yes, Pearson?"

"I thought you'd use my body, the skin and bones and organs, after I'd gone. But you've gone beyond that. Those last bronzes you showed me were real good. You don't need the Pearson factory anymore. Silly idea, but . . ."

Yusec barely caught the last Pearson thought before his presence left the People forever . . .

"They're people, sir! I know they're no bigger than an eyelash, but they've got roads and farms and factories and schools and I don't know what else. Our first non-human intelligent race, sir!"

"Easy, Hanforth," said the Captain. "I can see that." He was standing outside the lander. They'd set down in a large lake to avoid smashing the intricate metropolis which appeared to cover the entire planetoid. "Incredible's the word for it. Anything on that wreck site?"

"No sir. It's ancient. Hundreds of years at least. Detectors found only fragments of the original ship. "The native delegation, sir?"

"Yeah?"

"They have something they want us to see. They say some of their major roadways are wide enough for us to travel safely, and they've cleared all traffic."

"I guess we'd better be courteous, though I'd feel safer doing our studies from out here, where we can't hurt anybody."

They walked for several hours. Gradually they reached an area near the site of the crater produced by the impact of an archaic ship. They'd seen the object rise over the sharp horizon, believed in it less as they drew nearer.

Now they stood at its base. It was a metal spire that

towered fifty meters into the watery blue sky, tapering to a distant, sharp point.

"I can guess why they wanted us to see this." The Captain was incredulous. "If they wanted to impress us, they've done so. A piece of engineering like this, for people of their size...it's beyond belief." He frowned, shrugged.

"What is it, sir?" Hanforth's head was back as he stared toward the crest of the impossible spire.

"Funny...it reminds me of something I've seen before."

"What's that, sir?"

"A grave marker..."

Surfeit

For many years I lived near the Santa Monica Pier, in greater Los Angeles. The Santa Monica Pier is the one you've seen in dozens of movies and television shows, the one with the old merry-go-round built on its shoreside end. (Remember it from the movie *The Sting*?)

Below the pier young men and women fake hara-kiri every day by surfing between the barnacle-encrusted pilings. This is called shooting the gap or shooting the pier. It goes on every day and you have to be nuts to try it.

Less daring, I rode the waves well clear of the dangerous pilings. Now I live in Arizona, where the big waves are more than scarce. But the memories linger, of salt on your lips and sand under your wetsuit, of the stormy days when the Big Ones would come rolling in all the way from Japan and only the skilled and/

or foolhardy would chance the angry water. And as with all memories of early pleasures, sometimes those waves rise a little higher with each retelling...

The Monster was all mouth and no body, and you would hear it before you could see it.

Joao Acorizal knew of it without having to employ sight or sound. He knew of it through story and legends, which are far more descriptive than simple senses could be. He'd studied the history of the Monster, its whims and habits, colors and moods.

From the time he'd been a boy on Thalia Major and had first heard of the Monsters of Dis he knew someday he would confront and do battle with them. It was preordained.

His parents and friends had listened to his somber daydreaming and had laughed at him. If by some chance he one day managed to raise enough money to travel to far Dis he would cower fearfully before the Monster, too weak to confront it. One or two friends had actually seen tapes of the Monster and assured Joao it was too much for any man of Thalia to handle. Better to forget it and aim for the attainable.

Kirsi had been his wife for twenty years and hadn't been able to make him forget the dream.

She spoke as she paced the floor of their living room, her sandals clacking intermittently on the floor as she alternately crossed thick throw rugs and smooth terratone tiles.

"I fail to understand you, Joao." She was waving her hands at him, as full of animated little gestures as the noisy macaques which roamed the trees in the garden behind the house. "You've worked hard all your life. So have I." She stopped, indicated the tastefully furnished, comfortable room.

"We'll never be rich, you and I, but we'll never go begging either. We've a good life. We've two fine children who are just old enough now to realize that their father is crazy. Everything we've worked for, all that we've built up together, you want to throw away to satisfy a childhood infatuation." She shook her head pityingly, her long black hair swirling against the back of the white print dress. "Husband of my life, I don't understand you."

Joao sighed and looked away from her, out the broad window which overlooked the beach. The sun was rising over the Atlantic. Tranquil waves broke like eggs against the sand. Thalia's sun, slightly yellower and smaller than Sol, turned the water to topaz. Thalia Minor, the twin world, was out of sight, hiding on the other side of the globe.

"We have more than enough money. The trip will not inconvenience us save for a little while."

"Money? You think I give a damn about money?" She came up behind him, locked her arms possessively around his waist, and leaned her head on his back. Her warmth sent a shiver through him, as it had on that first night twenty years ago.

"Money is nothing, husband. You are everything." She turned him around and gazed hard into his face, searching, trying to find the key to whatever drove him so she could somehow pull it from his mind and cast it into the sea. "I do not want you dead, Joao."

He smiled, though she couldn't see it. "Neither do I, Kirsi."

She pulled away sharply. "Then why are you in such

a hurry to throw life aside? God knows you're no antique, but you're not a professional athlete either."

He turned and bent to kiss her gently. She made a fuss of flinching. "And that, my love, is precisely why I must go to Dis now, before it is too late..."

Conversation and Kirsi seemed so far away now. He was on Dis at last, and soon he would confront the Monster and its relatives. For thirty years he'd dreamed of the challenge to come. Thirty years of practice, thirty years of honing his skills, thirty years of dreaming, about to become reality.

That is, if he could muster one day's worth of great courage.

His eyes tried to penetrate the salt mist as he and his companion challengers made their way across the damp, barren rocks. A few low scrubs clung tenaciously to the surface. Sea crustaceans crawled fitfully from crack to crevice.

There were twenty-four competitors in the group. Eighteen men and six women, ranging in age from eighteen to forty-two. Joao was grateful he was not the oldest. Only second oldest.

But not in spirit, he told himself firmly, and not in heart.

Salt spray drifted foglike around them. The raucous complaining of seabirds mixed with the sibilant hissing of ichthyorniths filled the moist air of morning.

The walk was a ritual part of the contest. No spectators were allowed to join the competitors on the walk, no judges or media reporters. The first confrontation with the Monster would be made by the entire group. Then they would return to the assembly and departure station to make final preparations for their individual, intimate meetings.

Conversation was by way of whispered shouts; whispers out of respect for their opponent, shouts so they could be heard above the periodic roars of the Monster. They were now very near the end of the peninsula, and the bellowing from up ahead shook the solid granite, sending a subtle warning tremor through the contestants' bare feet. They could not see the Monster yet, but it was hissing at them through the rock.

"First time?"

"What?" Joao wiped spray drip from his forehead and eyes and looked to the source of the query.

"I asked if it was your first time." The man who spoke was very short and extremely muscular. It was not the well-defined muscularity of the body builder but the squat, thick build of the truly strong. He had bright blue eyes and his hair was cut bristle short, a blond brush that gave him a falsely belligerent look. His swim briefs were blue and red checks in front, solid red behind.

"Yes." Joao stepped over a dull mustard-colored crab-thing armed with quadruple pincers. It flinched back but did not flee from him. "Is it that obvious?"

"Not really. But if you've been through it before you can tell." They walked on.

"How many times for you?" Joao asked curiously.

"This'll be my third." The man grinned. "It's hard, since the contest is held only every three years. Would be my fourth, but I broke my leg the last time."

"You don't have to warn me. I've read about this every year for the last thirty."

The man laughed. "I didn't break it during the contest. Two days before time I slipped on my front porch and snap, that was it for the next three years. Spent the whole contest watching."

Joao managed to laugh with him. They walked on

silently for several minutes. The sea mist thickened, was partly countered by the rise of a stiff breeze. The rest of the contestants kept pace nearby.

"Name's Janwin." The man put out a hand. Joao shook it. It was not wrinkled as he expected but smooth. The grasp was firm, controlled. "I'm local."

"Joao Acorizal, from Thalia Major. I'm a builder, mostly private homes."

"Circulatory surgeon, Dis Central Hospital Complex. Pleased to meet you. The important thing is to have confidence in yourself. Be alert, keep an eye on your path and the other alert for the predators. Don't be afraid to use your balpole, and if you're going over or under, use your rockets and get the hell out. Everyone does. Risk taking impresses the judges, but points don't mean a damn to dead pulp.

"You get three chances during the contest but only one life. There's nothing to be ashamed about if you bail out. My first contest there were only fifteen rides out of forty-five attempts, and no completes. I've never had a complete ride and seen damn few." He went quiet, studied Joao professionally. Ahead of them they could hear the rock-shattering groan of the Monster, very near now.

"You've got good legs, real good. Any tears or pulls in the past six months? This isn't something you go into if you're even slightly damaged."

Joao shook his head. "I know that. I've done thirty years of homework and as much practice for this day. I've never been in better shape."

"That's what your mind tells you. Well, I ought to shut up. I'm no fledgling either. Experience counts for a lot." He looked ahead. "Almost to the Point. I'm sure you've seen tapes of it. It's a little different in person, up close. Remember, watch out for predators and try to relax."

"That sounds like a contradiction, but I'll try. Thanks for the advice." He added impulsively, "If I don't win, I hope you do."

Janwin shrugged. "I've never placed higher than seventh. But that doesn't matter. What matters is that I'm still here. With all my parts. Keep that in mind when you're out there and tempted to push your luck a little. All the points in the world won't make up for the loss of an arm or an eye." He looked a little uncertain, finally asked, "You have a family?" Joao nodded. "Are they here?"

"No. I wouldn't let them come."

The surgeon nodded approvingly. "Good. If anything happens I'll see that the details are properly taken care of. You can do the same for me, though I have friends here."

"Agreed!" Joao had to scream it out because they were at the slight rise at the end of the promontory that marked the tip of the narrow peninsula.

Then they were slowing, everyone crowding unconsciously close together, and he could see the Monster.

High overhead, hanging like dark eyes in a pale blue sky misted with sea spray, were Cerberus, Charon, and Pluto, three of the four large moons that circle the planet Dis. Grouped together like that they occupied much of the morning sky. Dis's sun was just above the horizon, below the moons. The three satellites were also rising, their perambulating orbits bringing them into alignment in this manner only once every three years. Soon the sun would be behind them, and for a while daylight would touch land in surreal confusion.

Below was the Monster they helped to raise.

The wave was larger than any Joao had ever seen, but he expected that. He studied it calmly, analytically, and did not shake. The wave lifted heavenward, still far out at sea. White foam like broken teeth began to appear on its crest. It surged hungrily toward the high promontory. It started to break.

The curl appeared, began to retreat steadily southward, and the roar came to those who watched. It was a roar that stirred the blood and primeval thoughts. All the dark dreams of childhood, all the terror of drowning and smothering under a great weight, were wrapped up in that single monstrous, relentless wave.

And still it rose as it broke to the south, an immense gray-green blanket suffocating the horizon, the thunder of its sharp curl wiping out all other sounds. From the safety of the salt-swept point the contestants watched the curl and wave as it fled away from them, ducking only when the trailing backside of the wave smashed its green hammerhead against the rock to drench them all.

Out at sea, visible through the mist, making good use of the peculiar slope of the seabottom, Dis's lighter gravity, and the tidal confluence of the sun and three fat moons, the next Monster was growing.

The contestants stood, chattering loudly in order to be heard, all eyes appraising the water.

"About eighty feet," said Janwin thoughtfully. "Normal runs fifty, storm-drive pulses sixty to seventy. We only get these really big ones when the three moons line up every three years and add their pull to everything else. It should be an interesting couple of days."

Three contestants withdrew on the way back to the assembly area. No one taunted or chided them. The

131

inmates have no right to make fun of the sane. The judges calmly marked the dropouts off the list.

Assistants were available to help in preparation. Acorizal turned their eager faces away. He'd lived with his board for five years. He'd broken it in, broken it for real, had repaired it lovingly with his own hands. He knew every inch of it, every contortion in the grain. He needed no help. But he made sure to work alongside the helpful Janwin and watched him make ready so that he could ask questions.

Once one of the contest supervisors approached the surgeon, whispered something to him before moving on to the next contestant. Janwin had listened, nodded, then ambled over to where Acorizal was checking the release pulls on his backpack and making certain the solid fuel boosters were clean and full.

"Weather report just in. Scattered clouds, winds five to ten out of the southwest. That shouldn't affect balance or crests. There's a tropical cyclonic storm weaving around out there. We shouldn't get any bad winds, but you know what that'll do to the swells. On top of everything else." There was a twinkle in his eye.

"I've never had a chance to ride a hundred-footer. If a proper swell comes in on us, get out of my way."

"I'll race you for it," Acorizal replied with a grin. Janwin moved away and the builder turned back to readying himself. He dismissed the thought of a hundred-foot wave. It could no more be comprehended than the distance between two stars, or the gulf that was the number billion. It was a physical abstract only, one without counterpart in reality. For himself he wished only an uncomplicated wave. That, and to survive.

His board was formed of honeycomb tripoxy resins. It was fifteen feet long by four wide and light enough for one man to carry. Twin shark-fin stabilizers protruded downward from the front third of the board, another pair from near the blunt stern. Above the stern were twin air stabilizers joined by an adjustable airfoil.

Studs set into the upper surface of the board were connected to thin duralloy control wires running to the four stabilizers and the airfoil. You could not touch the studs with your hands, only with your feet.

He picked up his balpole. It was made of the same material as the board except for the twin spiked knobs that ballooned from either end. The pole could be used for balancing or for fighting off any carnivores who might frequent the turbulence of a great wave. Several such were indigenous to Dis. No energy weapons or devices of any kind were permitted save for the tiny solid-fuel backpacks.

The pack was your life. A rider who was thrown or who lost control of a wave had several options. You could dive into the body of the wave and hope to swim out through the backside. You could shrink into a fetal ball and hope to ride the wave out. Or you could fire your pack with either of two releasing shoulder pulls and soar above the wave, to drop freely behind it into the water. Whenever possible, it was best to use the pack.

He checked his wet suit for leaks. Pressure or impact of a certain degree would automatically cause the heavy rubberized suit to inflate, hopefully to send a helpless rider bobbing to the surface. The suit would also protect against bruises and scrapes. It would not always save your life. Joao pulled the hood over his head, wiggled his toes. Only his face was exposed. His suit was bright orange with red striping.

A hand tapped him on the shoulder. Janwin was

there, not smiling now. His face beamed from a suit hood of electric orange. "Ready? Time to go."

Acorizal nodded, hefted his board. There was nothing more to be done but to do it.

Another rider backed out as they were boarding the skimmers. Acorizal watched her, sitting forlornly on her board, as the skimmer he was in lifted. He waved understandingly, but she did not wave back. The Monster had beaten her already, as it had beaten several others. There was no shame in that.

Acorizal had not even thought of withdrawing. Not yet, anyway. At least he was going to get wet.

The skimmer rose, turning in formation with two others. Cheering was continuous from the assembled spectators who'd gathered to watch the contestants prepare. Tridee pickups turned smoothly to follow the skimmers as they hummed westward.

Acorizal wondered if tonight, incredibly far away, Kirsi and the children would be watching. Kirsi had told him prior to his departure that under no circumstances would she watch the broadcast or allow the children to, but he wasn't so sure.

Picking up speed, the skimmers left the staging area. Soon the cliffs that fringed the western coast of Dis's largest continent fell away below. Lines of color marked the places on the cliffs where the spectators were strung out like opaque glass beads.

A wave was passing below. Its aspect was very different when viewed from high overhead instead of face on. The white crest reminded him not of teeth now but of lace lining the flowing, rippling hem of a woman's skirt. The lace drew a smooth line southward as the curl broke steadily toward distant Scratch Bay. Acorizal watched until the curl faded from sight.

Soon the skimmers' engines also began to fade and

the little craft dropped surfaceward. Out here on the broad open ocean the waves were merely cocoons from which the Monsters would hatch. The Monster now had a back as well as a face, and the skimmers set down on its undulating spine. Engines raced as the craft settled into the water. Riders and boards dropped over the sides, to pepper the dark green surface.

Acorizal felt stronger the instant he tumbled in. He floated easily, his board attached to his ankle by a breakaway cord. He ducked his head and swam beneath it. The water was chilly out over the deeps. It shocked his eyes open and dissolved the cobwebs of uncertainty in his brain.

All around him, riders were mounting their boards. The brightly hued wet suits looked like confetti scattered across the water.

Acorizal felt something lift him, heave him skyward. He went up, up, along with his board and companions, ten, twenty feet, only to be gently lowered again. A wave had just passed beneath them, full of power and incipient threat.

It left him feeling not fearful but exhilarated. There, he thought. That alone was worth it. If I do nothing else, if I can't make a wave, it was worth coming all this way just to feel that swell.

A board was coming toward him, light as a feather on the surface. Janwin stopped paddling, looked over at him. "Save your legs and mount up, man."

Acorizal spat salt water. "It feels good."

"Sure it does, but don't waste your energy. Your adrenaline's all pumped up. Get on your board, relax, and let it go down."

Acorizal decided to take the advice, clambered onto his board with the ease of long practice, and sat there, his face drying in the rising sun. "When do we start?"

He was watching the monitoring skimmer, bobbing nearby.

"We've already started." Janwin grinned at the other man's expression of surprise. "Some can't stand to wait. Two took off on that last swell." He shook his head. "There's no advantage to going first, but you'll never convince some people of that."

"I never saw them go," Acorizal murmured. "So soon. Isn't it better to wait for a wave that feels right?"

Janwin shrugged. "To some I guess the first wave feels like the right wave."

"Well, I'm taking my time. I'm in no hurry. I've come a long way for this, and I'll be damned if I'm going to rush it."

"Good for you." Janwin nodded approvingly. "You don't get many chances. I prefer to wait too."

Hours passed. One by one the riders took off, to disappear southward. Once something large, white, and full of teeth appeared, to be driven off by a shot from the monitor skimmer's lookout. Reports on the progress of vanished riders were broadcast to those who remained, amplified by the skimmer's sound system.

"Meswith Brookings . . . four hours, twenty minutes. Bailout clean. Harlkit Romm . . . three hours, forty-five minutes. Swimout, exhaustion, but otherwise clean." Acorizal knew Romm would score higher than Brookings for bailing out without using his backpack.

"Eryl-cith al Hazram . . . four hours, thirty-two minutes." There was a pause, then the voice from the speaker added softly, "Bailout failure; wipeout. Body not yet recovered." There was silence for a while, then the voice continued mechanically. "El Tolst, five hours, fifty-six minutes. Swimout, collapsed lung, neck sprain, otherwise clean. Jewel Parquella, five hours, ten minutes . . ."

During the waiting another pair of riders withdrew, were helped silently aboard the monitoring skimmer. The sun rose higher while beneath it three moons jostled for pulling position. Janwin and Acorizal discussed water.

"Normally we could expect double sets," the surgeon was saying, giving the swell lifting them a critical eye. "Three large waves followed by three small. The storm's changed that. We're getting three large, three small, and three or four storm waves larger still but highly variant." He glanced over at his companion.

"Naturally you'd like to catch one of the latter, but they can be tricky. You might get a double wave, one crest on top of another, and that would force an early bailout. You'd get a ride, but too short to score many points."

The sound of an arriving skimmer interrupted their conversation. Besides the surgeon and Acorizal two other riders still waited for a wave. One went away with the swell that rolled under them as the skimmer touched down.

A board appeared on its flank, went over the side followed by a rider. The man mounted, paddled over to join the remaining three contestants. It was Brookings. He was lean, much younger than Janwin or Acorizal. His face was flushed and scoured clean, but he was not panting very hard and his strokes were smooth and sure.

"Hello, Brookings. Back for your second?" Janwin inquired. The younger man nodded, looked understandably pleased with himself.

"Caught a seventy-five-footer," he told them. He leaned back on his board, hyperventilating. "The first couple of hours were easy enough. After that you start to feel it in the legs. Then your eyes get snaky. I decided to bail out when I found myself seeing a double tube behind me."

"Smart move," said Janwin. "We got your report. You had a good ride on a good wave. Have they found al Hazram yet?"

Brookings looked past them, toward the invisible coast. "Not yet. They're afraid his suit might've failed. They told me he caught a storm wave at least a hundred feet five. He was apparently doing fine until he got too fancy. Got too low on the wave and too close to the curl. The wind from the collapsing tube blew him off his board."

"What about his pack?" Acorizal asked.

"Ignited okay but he was so low the crest caught him. He didn't clear it and it broke right over him. If his suit failed they'll never find him." He went quiet for a moment, then sat up straight on his board and began paddling. They were rising toward the sky.

"I like this one . . . see you." Then the swell had him in its grasp and he was gone.

"We'd better get going," Acorizal observed. "If he's on his second wave . . ."

Janwin shook his head. "Competition comes second, remember. Survival's first. You've got to feel comfortable with the wave you choose or you might as well turn in your corpse right now."

So they continued waiting. Janwin took off fifteen minutes later. That left Acorizal and the last rider. Swells came and went as they sat on their boards.

Kirsi . . . I'm glad you're not here and I wish, oh how I wish that you were! His face was getting hot from the midday sun.

The sound of a returning skimmer drifted down to the two waiting riders. He squinted, made out the prong noses of two boards projecting from the racks on one side of the little craft. Two more successful riders returning for their second waves. He couldn't wait much longer or it would be too late to try for the required three rides. There was only tonight and tomorrow. He did not want to have to make two rides tomorrow, and not even a saint would try to ride the Monster at night.

Then he saw the swell. It loomed high behind him over his right shoulder, so green it was almost black. It was a huge one, wide as the sky and rising like a bubble breathed out from something vast and patient. But he was not alone and there was courtesy to observe.

He looked anxiously across at the other waiting rider, saw that the man also saw the nearing swell. It continued to rise steadily, bearing down on them like a runaway starship. Acorizal had to force himself to wait.

Abruptly the other rider let out an agonized cry of despair and started paddling for the monitor skimmer, taking himself out of competition for the swell, out of the day, out of the contest. Acorizal turned his head eastward and began paddling furiously, his balpole clipped lengthwise beneath his knees.

He was afraid he'd waited too long. For a long moment he hung suspended atop the swell. Then he was moving forward with less and less effort. He stopped paddling, continued to move, picking up speed and beginning to slide slightly downward. The swell continued to build and a giant green-black hand boosted him toward the sky. Now he could pick out the faint, far line of cliffs that marked the land.

He climbed to his knees from his belly, accelerating steadily. His toes tensed on the slightly resilient surface of the board. He stood, edged back on his rear leg an inch, then moved his front leg to match. The fingers of his left hand tightened on the ignition cord of the backpack.

He felt fine. The ride was smooth and easy, the board responding instantly to his subtly shifting weight and gentle toe-touches on the control studs. The balpole he held tightly in his right hand. He stopped rising, hung suspended in midair.

Then he looked down. His fingers tensed further on the loop of the backpack release as instinct almost betrayed him.

Far, far below was the surface of the water, flat and shining like steel in the rising sun. Air ripped at his face; salt stung his eyes. Wind whistled around him. His mind was momentarily numbed by the hundred-foot drop he overhung, but twenty years of practice took over, shifted his body.

Then he was screaming down the face of the gigantic wave, ten, twenty, thirty feet. He leveled off, keeping his weight back but centered, adjusting the airfoil to slow the precipitous drop. The stabilizers kept him level as the front four feet of his board hung over emptiness and sliced through the air.

An incredible rush went through him, an indescribable combination of sheer terror and pure ecstasy. To his right was a moving green cliff that towered over his head, thousands of tons of living water. To his left was nothingness.

He grew conscious of the steady, unvarying roar of the Monster, only now it was not terrifying but simply awesome. He was set on the board, had become part of it. He risked a look backward.

Behind him tons of water cascaded endlessly from thirty feet overhead to smash into the withdrawing waters seventy feet below. It formed a vast glassy green tunnel which rising sunlight turned into an elongated emerald: the tube. Wind blew out of it as curling water forced air ahead of the collapsing arc. It sounded a special, higher note in the overall thunder of the Monster.

He held tight to the balpole with both hands, letting loose of the pack release, and adjusted his balance. Then he thought to check his suit chronometer.

He'd been on the wave thirty minutes.

Moving slightly backward he luxuriated in the feel of the matchless ride, always watching the curl and the crest high above to make sure no surprises were about to tumble down to crush him. The waves held their shape with remarkable consistency, but occasionally one could collapse unexpectedly, the curl vanishing as the unwary, too-confident rider found himself buried under a million tons of water.

But Acorizal's wave rolled on and on, machinelike, the curl trailing behind his board like a friend urging him onward.

Gradually his confidence grew. He let himself feel out the wave, slipping his board high up on the green wall only to plunge dizzyingly back down when it seemed sure he'd burst through the crest, dropping low almost into the bottom of the curl to stare up at eighty feet of liquid cliff high above.

When he felt secure enough, and he'd been three hours on the wave, he let himself slide backward, back into the tube. It was almost peaceful inside, so numbing was the roar of the breaking curl. The tunnel he rode in was high and wide, the wind powerful behind him. He had to be careful. He did not want to be blown off the board by a collapsing tube, to be swallowed by the tumbling crest.

Something materialized in front of his face, just out-

141

side the curl. He frowned, then let the board edge outward. The apparition multiplied into many.

He'd been told of the Trintaglias. They floated just ahead of him, their blue eyes bulging curiously at the strange figure that appeared in their midst. Their air sacs were fully inflated, the taut yellow-pink skin stretched thin as paper. They varied in size from several inches to a foot in diameter, riding the air current that preceded the tube on long, thin fins that doubled as wings.

Occasionally one would dip down to snatch something edible from the water. Some would collapse their sacs and vanish into the wall of the wave; others would drift higher or lower according to internal pressures. Once he reached out and touched one. It jerked away from him, turned to float sideways in the air and regard him wide-eyed and reproachful.

He checked his time. Five hours and thirty-five minutes. He had already managed the second-longest ride of the day. His legs were throbbing, and the gastrocenemius of the left was starting to cramp. His eyes were red from the salt spray, while his mouth, paradoxically, was dry from lack of water.

Off to his left, as he moved cautiously out of the tube, he could see the high, running ridge of the continental edge. Ahead, as always, there was only the endless, thundering curve of water.

Another thirty minutes, he promised himself. Another thirty minutes and I'll have the longest ride of the day. He couldn't bring himself to bail out yet, though his legs threatened to fail him and his arms felt like limp weeds. Everything had gone so well. The wave still had size and power and exhibited no signs of weakening. How far did they run, he wondered? He hadn't researched it much, not thinking he'd ever be in a position to care. Could you ride one all the way around the continent? Or perhaps from pole to pole?

Another thirty minutes. Another thirty minutes of wet hell and he could bail out.

The Vaxials almost got him.

Only the fact that one mistook the end of the balpole for part of the rider saved Acorizal. The narrow, eellike head reached out of the wave wall and snapped at it viciously, teeth grinding on the sharp metal. All six longitudinal fins were extended for balance, and the dark red gill slits back of the jaws were pulsing with excitement. An eye the size of his hand stared malevolently out of the wave at the startled Acorizal.

Somehow he kept his balance on the board, but it was a near thing as he instinctively leaned away from those thin, needle-sharp teeth.

The reaction helped him. The Vaxial let loose of the inedible balpole and snapped at the air where Acorizal's shoulder had been an instant earlier. The weight shift caused the board to shoot upward along the wave face. The crest of the Monster came closer with shocking speed.

Acorizal left his feet and threw himself forward. Down, damn you, get your nose *down*!

The board responded, dipping to slide rapidly downward. It had been a close thing. Acorizal had nearly shot out through the crest. At best he would have flown into the air on the other side of the wave, a good ride completed and the Vaxials circling to pick him off the board. At worst he would have caught the crest with the nose of the board and gone over backward, to fall helplessly head over heels until the entire immense weight of the wave pulped him against the water below.

He continued to race down the front of the wave. Behind him, a pair of blunt, toothy snouts attached to twenty-foot-long snakelike bodies glided through the wave in pursuit. Eventually the Vaxials would catch up to him. They lived in the waves and had no worries about balance.

He readied the balpole as he pushed back into a kneeling position, tried to judge how he was going to strike out without losing his balance and board.

An ugly head emerged from the water. Acorizal leaned, slashed down and sideways with the spiked end of the pole. It made contact with a flat, glassy eye, and blood spurted. The Vaxial vanished instantly.

Lucky blow, Acorizal told himself grimly. He was so tired his hands shook. He scanned the green wall for signs of the other carnivore. Maybe, he thought, it's gone to help the other. Maybe they're mates. He stared, locating wave fish and other creatures but no hint of the Vaxial.

Then there was awful pressure on his back and a ripping sound.

He fell forward, desperately trying to keep his balance on the board despite the weight on his back. He could feel those long, needlelike teeth on his neck, piercing the tough material of the suit and his skin and his spine. He screamed in terror.

Then the pressure was gone. He hadn't seen the Vaxial attack and did not see it go, but it did not reappear. Which was no wonder, if the backpack had gone down its throat.

He held the balpole weakly with one shaky hand as he lay prone on the board and felt at his back with the other. The pack was definitely gone, wrenched from its clips on the suit by those powerful jaws. His eyes frantically scanned the water all around the board, but the creature did not show itself again. After a while the Trintaglias returned, in ones and twos, and he took their presence for a good sign.

He no longer could isolate individual bruises and sores. His body was one continuous ache as he studied the wave. With his backpack gone there was no easy bailout. He could rise to the crest and hope to break cleanly through to the other side, or he could dive into the wall, swim like mad, and then inflate his suit to bob to the surface . . . if the Vaxial hadn't torn the suit's air chambers as well.

If he misjudged either attempt he would very likely drown. If he wasn't battered to death inside the wave.

One thing he was certain of: he could not get back on his feet. His legs were too far gone. He let the balpole slip away and hugged the board with both arms, not caring if some swimming predator beneath chose to make a meal of his clutching fingers.

He'd had a good ride, one of the best of the day. Somehow his anguished muscles would have to hold him tightly to the board until someone on shore realized the danger and sent out a skimmer to rescue him.

Please God, let that be soon, because I have no strength left in me.

He willed himself to stay conscious. If he went to sleep on the board it would all be over in seconds. The board would rise up into the crest as his weight slipped backward, and he would go over the falls, to be thrown a hundred feet downward. At least that would be quick. There would be no drowning. Just a single quick, irresistible weight and then unconsciousness and death.

He shook himself, pulled himself forward on the board. He'd been daydreaming and had risen to within ten feet of the crest. Now he numbly nosed the board downward again, back into the safety of the middle part of the wave. The sonorous boom of the curl followed patiently on his heels.

God, I'm tired, so tired, he thought. Let it be over. I've done what I came for and more. Now I just want it to be over. Where the hell was the rescue skimmer? Couldn't they see he was on the verge?

He would have to do something, he knew. He could not hang onto the board much longer, let alone guide it properly. Both his brain and body were worn out. Only sheer stubbornness had held him together this long.

Diving into the wave was out. He didn't have enough strength left to swim two feet, let alone drive his body through the water. It would have to be a crest break, then.

He started to let the board slip upward. One hand felt down the slick side of the wet suit until it touched on the inflation knob. Once he broke through the crest he'd inflate the suit, hoping the monitoring skimmers would pick him up before the next wave came by. He hoped he could stay conscious enough of his surroundings to inflate the suit at the proper instant.

Everything was a wet blur before his salt-encrusted eyes. Sky and water merged into one. Was he at the crest yet? If he waited too long he'd go over the falls.

Then white washed over him and he coughed weakly. The wave had not waited for him to make a decision. He remembered Janwin's warning about the uncertain actions of storm-generated waves.

The curl disappeared, subsumed in a single endless break as the wave lost its shape and collapsed atop him.

It was dark and wet and his board was gone. Dimly, he pressed at the inflate switch on his suit side, knowing it would only allow the wave to pound him repeatedly against the surface or the sandy bottom. But at least this way they might locate his body.

I'm sorry, Kirsi. Good-bye.

Then he was up again, bobbing in the air, his arms and legs unable to move for the air that enveloped them. Too soon, it was too soon. He twisted, turning on his belly-balloon.

Two men were coming toward him. That surprised him. The second, bigger surprise was that they were not swimming. They were wading. Dazed, Acorizal tried to focus burning eyes. There was a hissing sound. One of the men was deflating his suit. He tried to yell at the man, but his mouth wasn't working any better than his brain. He thought he could hear people yelling.

Then the air had drained from the suit and he was in the water once more. Only there was no supportive salt water this time but instead the arms of the two men holding him up. They had to. He didn't have the strength to stand.

"What . . . ?" Tongue and jaw wouldn't work together. "What . . . ?"

One of the men, young and tall, was looking at him with a mixture of wonder and admiration. "You don't know?"

"Don't know . . . anything," Acorizal mumbled, coughing.

"This is Scratch Bay. This is where the waves die, rider." The man pronounced the last word with emphasis. "You rode your wave all the way in. All the way."

"How . . . how big when I went over?"

"Oh, that? We all thought that was a last-minute flair to impress the judges. It wasn't?"

"Judges can go to hell. No . . . flair. How big?"

147

"About ten feet," said the other man, who had Acorizal's right arm across his shoulders. "You just rolled over." He gestured forward with a nod of his head. "Your board's safe, up on the beach."

"Ten feet." Acorizal's mouth twisted.

A familiar face was waiting to greet him as they stumbled into the shallows. It peered concernedly into Acorizal's as the rider was laid out on a suspension mattress on the beach. Cheers filled the air, drunken parodies of true speech to Acorizal's mind. They were mixed with the admonitions of officials who kept the near-hysterical crowd at bay.

"Hello, Joao," said Janwin as he checked his friend's heartbeat. "How are you?"

Acorizal squinted through the salt at his friend. "Chewed up," he gasped softly. "Chewed up and spit out like an old wad of gum." He saw that a bandage was draped across the surgeon's head and suspension straps supported his plastisealed left arm, and he framed a question with his eyes.

"Oh, this?" Janwin smiled, moved his sealed arm. "I went into mine, tried to swim out. Too late to use my pack. Tore the shoulder ligaments. I'm afraid my riding's over for this year. What the hell happened to your pack?"

"Vaxial," Acorizal explained. He spent a few moments choking before he could continue. "It was trying to eat me. I hope it suffocates. How long was I up? I can't see too well."

"Eight hours and five minutes. The last hour spent glued to your board, I'm told. You lost a stabilizer. They're fixing it now."

"That's nice."

"First complete ride in twelve years," Janwin continued admiringly. "Except for Nuotuan in 'twenty-four, and she was dead by the time they got to her. You're not dead."

"No, I'm not."

Janwin hesitated. "I guess I ought to let you rest, but I have to know." He leaned closer, away from the probing reporters. "How was it?"

But Acorizal was already unconscious.

He got points for riding the tube. He got points for fighting off the Vaxials. He got points for style and points for length. Brookings had more cumulative time but fewer style points. On the basis of the one ride Acorizal was declared winner. They told him about it two days later, when he regained consciousness.

One of the honorary judges, a media star from Terra, was present to hand over the trophy and prize money. Media reporters flocked around the man who'd never swum more than a hundred yards at any one time in his life. The man was very tall and handsome and not a very bad actor. His voice was rich and deep, well suited to making presentations.

But they couldn't find Acorizal. He wasn't in his hotel room and he wasn't anywhere to be found in Scratch Bay Towne. They searched for him on the beach, expecting to find him bathing in the rapturous stares of his admirers, but he wasn't there either.

Who they finally found was Janwin, sitting at the board works helping a younger rider align his newly fitted stabilizers.

"I'm busy and I'm due back at the hospital tonight," the surgeon told the anxious cluster of reporters and officials.

"Just tell us, do you know where he is?"

"Yeah, I know where he is."

The media star looked very distressed. "I'm on contract here." He checked his bejeweled chronometer.

"I'll give this another ten minutes, and then I've got to catch the shuttle out to my ship."

"Then you'll have to miss him," said Janwin.

"Where the hell is he?" wondered one of the more irritated honorary officials, a man with much money and little else.

Janwin shook his head. "Where do you think he'd be?" He pointed northwestward. "He took a skimmer and follow crew with him."

"Crazy," muttered the official. "Doesn't he want his trophy and money?"

"I expect he does," said the surgeon thoughtfully. "But he told me he has to go home tomorrow. I'm sure he'll be grateful to accept the prize and cash.

"But first he has to catch another wave . . ."

The Dark Light Girl

There are two sensible ways to drive across the desolate American Southwest. You can take US 10, which parallels the Mexican border all the way to central Texas, or you can try the northern route through mountainous upstate Arizona and New Mexico.

Only locals travel the north-south routes. If you slip off these truncated interstates onto state highways, the pavement starts to wind through steep mountain gorges and over broad stretches of empty highlands little disturbed since the time of the first settlers. The local Indians quit hawking epoxied turquoise and put more time in souping up their Ford pickups. Time seems to slow in conjunction with the speed limit.

Get a little farther off the main arteries and you find yourself cutting through small towns where the passing of a strange car is enough to inspire an evening's conversation. Folks thereabouts value their privacy. That's why they live where they do. And most of them were born and raised in those parts.

It's interesting to note that near some of these neglected byways the future was born...

Wells didn't want to lose the tire. But he'd argued with rough road and, as usual, the road had won. Now one-fourth of his car's support was a dead rubber doughnut baking in the sun outside the old Chevron station. A thin young man coated with grease, blue jeans, and fading acne was rotating the tire in a tank of water. The dark grease on his arms gleamed in the failing New Mexico light.

"It's all torn up, mister. Not just a puncture. See?" Wells noted the bubbles gurgling from the submerged tread.

"I see. So, what would you suggest?"

The youth rose. He'd been genuinely sympathetic ever since Wells had limped in. Friendly, small-town mechanic. At least I know he's not trying to shaft me, Wells thought. The hole in the tire was big enough to drive a rat through. He wondered what kind of transmission you'd put in a rat.

Damn but it's hot, this country. Even at five.

"I can get you a new one out of Carrizozo tomorrow," was the helpful reply. "I'd go now, but it's getting on closing time and I'm the only one here. Mr. Ordway's gone up to Santa Fe to visit his sister."

"Then it looks like I'll be spending the night here." Wells couldn't afford the towing charge all the way into Carrizozo, even if he could find a truck willing to undertake the round trip this late on a Friday.

He studied the cluster of small homes and shops whose outlines rippled in the setting sun. That unrelenting antagonist was at last beginning to fall behind the broken teeth of the Malpais peaks.

"Is there a motel in town?"

"Yes, sir." The mechanic turned, self-consciously wiping his hands on a rag greasier than his palms. He pointed northward. "Go up the highway a block . . . it's a short block," he added, mindful perhaps of Wells's city accent, "and turn right on B Street. The Mescalero's two blocks east. Cafe of the same name right next to it."

"That a good place to eat?"

"That's the only place to eat, unless you feel like hiking a mile south to the Stuckey's."

"Thanks. I guess that's it, then." Wells made a face, aimed a desultory kick at the hapless tire. "What time tomorrow?"

The mechanic shrugged. "Can't say for sure. Depends on when Mr. Ordway gets back. I can't close the station."

"Yeah. I understand. Get me a Goodrich if you can. And thanks." He turned away from the mechanic's polite, "You're welcome," and started up the blacktop.

The last edge of the receding sun had turned bloody when he made the turn off the highway. B Street was paved, flanked with neat little houses. Tile roofs and stucco walls, cactus in the front yard, separate garage in back. There were no fences. Wells revised his accident-inspired opinion of the nowhere town slightly upward. He'd spent time in far worse places.

Of course, you *had* to deviate from the Interstate, he reminded himself gloomily. L.A.–Dallas isn't a long enough drive, you had to make it longer. You wanted to explore the back country, visit the unseen and untouched.

There were reasons why Agua Caliente was unseen and untouched. It had nothing to boast of except isolation, a common commodity in the American West. He wondered where the hot springs were that must have given the town its name. There were always hot springs.

A tarantula scuttled across his path, advancing in fits and starts like an advertising accountant in rush hour traffic. It paused briefly to confront him, raising up on its hind legs and threatening with those in front. Wells detoured carefully around it. There were no tarantulas in West Los Angeles. The hirsute arachnid was as alien to him as a visitor from Pluto. The spider raised no cry of victory at its minor triumph, simply turned and resumed its patrol.

The Mescalero Motel was a train of individual cottages paralleling the small creek that separated town from hillside. At the head of the train was a somewhat larger building.

CAFE. BUD. EATS. Cafebudeats. An old Afrikaans term, he told himself, applied to the simpler cuisine of the American road by a visiting semanticist from Cape Town U. Which I am not.

What I am is hungry. Wells let the screen door clatter shut behind him.

There were two booths and three tables and all were empty. A couple of local monuments, both ancient, one bearded, sat chattering to each other at the counter. Wells told himself they doubtless rendezvoused here every day, were as much a part of the decor as the naugahyde upholstery and the stained mirror over the coffee and milkshake mixers. Only a retired man in a small western town could nurse a single cup of coffee through an eight-hour day.

He slid into one of the booths, picked up the menu sandwiched between the salt and pepper shakers and the sugar bowl. Mexican special-special-special $3.95 with chips, it proclaimed to an indifferent world. That he would ignore. On the off chance the patty melt might once have passed close by a steer he ordered it from the moon-faced waitress.

"Thank you, sir." Big smile, genuine. Small towns, he told himself. Sirs and thank yous. Fresh air and faces.

The coffee fossilizers ignored him, and the waitress disappeared through the swinging door into the distant kitchen. Wells was left to stare out the window.

Like the motel cabins the cafe snuggled up against the creek and foothills. Rushes, weeds, and would-be cottonwoods marked the course of meandering melt water. As Wells watched, a mother skunk and four young materialized from the brush to drink. Wells had never seen a skunk outside of a zoo or bad cartoons. The mother watched while the kittens drank. Then they filtered back into the brush.

The patty melt was a pleasant surprise, the beef apparently devoid of soy, that omnipresent despoiler of the American fast food dream. He enjoyed it, and the french fries, and the iced tea that was brewed from tea leaves instead of reconstituted rust.

The elderly lady who managed the motel smilingly accepted his American Express, plastic peonage having penetrated even to this biblically obscure hamlet. She showed him to his cabin.

"You'll have plenty of privacy, Mr. Wells," she assured him. "You're all by yourself. We don't get many

155

visitors this time of year." She peered meaningfully behind him. "Do you have a car?"

"Blew a tire on my way in. It's at the Chevron station. They have to fetch a replacement from Carrizozo."

"Oh yes. Michael is all by himself now, since Harry Ordway went up to Santa Fe to see his sister. She's not well, you know. Michael's a good boy, Mr. Wells. He'll bring your new tire first thing in the morning."

The double bed was clean, the sheets smelling of lemon. There was soap in the bathroom. With the back window open he could hear the faint song of the creek.

"Good night, Mr. Wells. Sleep tight."

"Thank you, Mrs. Appleton. See you in the morning."

He lay awake out of habit, gazing at the black and white TV. The offerings of the single channel soon paled, but he couldn't fall asleep. It was too quiet. The creek tried, but it was no match for the traffic that flowed past his Santa Monica apartment.

Something else made a noise outside the window. Gravel disturbed, bushes irritated. Too large for a skunk, he thought. He swung his naked legs off the bed and crept toward the window. With luck he might see a peccary, or even a cougar come down out of the hills to drink. That would be worth seeing. The moon was half full. It painted the rocks a weak silver.

The sound was repeated, mixed this time with laughter. Wells grimaced and turned for the bed. Of course, he reminded himself, it's Friday night. The local kids can stay up late. If they made too much noise he could always report it to the manager. He didn't want to wake the nice Mrs. Appleton, though.

Something caught his eye. He turned back to the window, and got very cold. A girl was running along the dry, opposite bank of the creek bed. Occasionally she would glance back over her shoulder and try to stifle a giggle. She was wearing a simple white dress and sandals. Her blonde curls fluttered with each little jump she took. Her complexion was pale as incoming fog. She was truly beautiful, not *Vogue* fake or *Cosmo* creepy, but as beautiful and pale as the white gypsum sands of the national monument to the south.

And she glowed like a torch.

It was an ethereal greenish-yellow, sunlight stained with tincture of lime, at once insubstantial and powerfully real. It did not emanate from her clothing or some powerful compact lantern concealed in a pocket. It radiated forth from her cheeks, her exposed legs and ankles, from the tips of her fingers, even from her hair.

Not a ghost, Wells tried to reassure himself with frightening calm. Not a ghost, no, no, not in sandals and polyester, not here between Oscura and Carrizozo just off New Mexico State Highway 54. His chest hurt, reminding him to breathe.

He leaned into the window screen, the mesh scratching his nose as he strained to follow the running apparition's progress. His heart pounded and his fingers dug hurtfully into the sill. He wanted that vision. Oh, how he wanted her!

Then she was gone beyond the turn in the creek, her giggling mixing with its watery own. A faint glow showed above the rocks after the image had passed. It rose and dipped like a searchlight. Then it, too, had vanished.

Slowly he returned to the bed. He squeezed his eyes tight until tears came. He was not dreaming, not asleep. His name was Haskell Wells. He was twenty-eight, on his way from Los Angeles to Dallas to switch to the *Times* subsidiary paper there. He'd just blown a tire, eaten a patty melt, seen a tarantula, a skunk, and a ghost. Around three o'clock fatigue finally overpowered incredulity and he fell asleep.

In the morning certitude cracked. But not completely. He was a reporter, a trained observer. Too much remained clear in his memory. The glow, the beauty, the pulsing desire that had nearly overwhelmed him lingered as his fork did over breakfast.

Something in his expression brought forth concern from the waitress. "Something wrong, mister?"

"Umm?" He looked up from his eggs. They were getting cold. Around him, other locals were finishing their meals. Small town, early risers, he told himself. "It's nothing. I think." He grinned, forked egg into his mouth. "I think I saw a ghost last night."

"A ghost?" She smiled, but it seemed to require a conscious effort. Wells picked up on it instantly. "Here? In Agua Cal?"

He nodded. "Right out back of my cabin. A girl. She was wearing sandals and a white dress and had shoulder-length blonde hair and she glowed like St. Elmo's Fire. A ghost."

The waitress's smile petrified. Wells moved food around on his plate and tried not to appear interested.

"We don't have any ghosts around here, mister," she told him too quickly. "If we did, they'd most likely be Apaches. It's their souls that're layin' all over these mountains."

"This was no Apache." He nibbled his toast. "Cheerleader, maybe. I don't think blondes were common among the Mescaleros."

"Then you didn't see nothing, like as not," she said with finality. "Eggs okay, then?"

"Perfect. Thanks."

She nodded. "You want anything else, you ask."

She left him to take an order from a newly arrived couple seated at the table nearest the counter. Wells decided it must have been quite an order, because she talked to them for a long time. After she left, the middle-aged woman at the table glanced hurriedly toward Wells's booth, looked away fast when he chose to glance back.

There seemed to be a lot of interest in Agua Cal in something that wasn't. Wells was a good reporter. Had the ol' nose for news, as they said. What tickled his senses in the little dining room wasn't Chanel No. 5.

"Pretty here," he told the mechanic later. "Take your time with that tire. I've got a long way to go and I'm kind of enjoying the rest, even it it wasn't planned. I think I'll take the day off and leave tomorrow morning. It's supposed to be cooler tomorrow anyway."

"That's what the weatherman on Channel Six said last night," the mechanic agreed. "Glad you're having a nice time." He watched for a while as Wells walked back toward the motel.

Wells went through the motions of a man preparing for bed. He undressed, brushed his teeth, took a shower, watched the sun go down, spent a couple of hours eying the icons of the tube, then rolled over and turned out the light. He lay motionless for two hours, until ten P.M. It was Saturday night.

At ten he slipped from beneath the covers and dressed on the floor. Then he leaned close to the open back window and settled down to wait. He waited and watched until his eyelids drooped. Midnight. The witching hour, but neither witches nor ghosts materialized. He saw a snake and mother skunk with her brood. Once an owl skimmed low over the creek bed, struck and failed, soared away hooting disappointment at the moon over a near mice miss.

But no wondrous dryad came floating along the water's edge.

At two o'clock he made a decision. The old screen moved aside easily, quietly. He slipped over the window's edge and dropped to the gravel behind the cabin.

The ghost had moved from south to north. He started south, using the brush for cover and crossing the meter-wide rivulet in a single leap. Jump-ups and stick-me-tights and grass burrs decorated the hems of his pants' legs, pricked him through his socks. He fought them with terse, soft curses but did not stop to pick them off.

He walked for at least an hour. No one confronted him. The sole confrontation took place in his own, increasingly confused mind. He *was* on a long drive, alone. It was very hot, the landscape monotonous, dulling. The only thing that kept him going was the certain knowledge that had his imaginative brain chosen to conjure up a spirit it would not have taken the oh-so-prosaic form of an exquisite teenage blonde wearing a dress from Sears Roebuck.

He stopped to check his watch. Four in the morning. Soon the sun would be up and he'd have nothing to show for his nocturnal excursion save a wasted night's sleep. That would mean he'd have to catch up by staying over yet another day. All because of a momentary aberration.

Well, screw it. Spirits, however lovely, were not a part of real life. Getting to work on time in Dallas was. He kicked angrily at the gravel because he couldn't kick himself and started back toward the motel. He had a long hike ahead.

That's when he heard the music.

It was barely audible at first, rising and falling in regular cadence. It did not come from town. Turning a slow circle, he hunted with his ears, trying to pinpoint it. Kangaroo rats watched his pirouette without comment.

The music came from the east, from above. He started climbing.

The steep hill gave him no trouble, nor did the higher one beyond it. All those hours spent in the frenzied organized combat of the racquetball club were paying dividends. He neared the crest of the second hill. The music was much louder. He found he was sweating, not entirely from the climb. Then he was staring over the johnson grass and low scrub that fringed the ridge.

Below and beyond lay a depression with a flat floor of crushed rock. Most of the fragments were the size of his fist. The pulverized stone crawled up the far side of the little valley. A dark gap showed in the side of the mountain where the material ended. It looked like something had cut into the slope with a giant meat cleaver.

And *she* was there. The boy she danced wildly with had red hair cropped close, big ears and freckles. He wore jeans and sneakers and a sweatshirt and glowed like a giant screen television against the red and gray rocks.

They whirled 'round each other, twisting like flames in the hand of a Samoan fire-knife twirler, two pale green suns revolving about a common center, a bipedal binary. The bright, pulsating glow was especially intense where they held hands.

Five other couples cavorted atop the rocky stage, an insipid if somehow threatening setting for so spectacular a display of the unnatural. All twelve radiated that brilliant green-yellow glow. They formed a living Fourth-of-July pinwheel in the starry night, a vortex of light and youthful laughter.

Twelve of them, Wells thought. Twelve ghosts dancing not on the head of a pin (or was that angels?) but a scalped hillside. His throat was as dry as the nearby Tularosa Basin. He made no notes, uttered no sound louder than the beat of his heart, simply stared and tried to believe.

They seemed so real, these playful young supernaturals. They were too alive, too lovely to be phosphorescent zombies, dervishing about a rockpile not a hundred miles from Albuquerque. Yet his eyes registered and his brain interpreted.

There was not an unattractive one among the celebrants, though none matched the preternatural beauty of his delicate blonde. Six Aphrodites partnered with half a dozen young Apollos. They radiated health and vitality and attractiveness as they glowed green-yellow bright. Wells found himself leaning through the brush. His gaze was locked unbreakably on the spinning siren, the carnal blonde of the green fire. He could feel her burning body against his own, taste her half-parted lips, see himself drowning in the essence of her.

And yet there was something wrong with the bacchanale. It was the music they danced to. The music did not fit such a gathering, did not seem appropriate for a coven of mystical celebrants.

The music of the moment was the Rolling Stones doing "I Can't Get No Satisfaction." When that song ended the same group segued into "Brown Sugar." Wells recognized the tape, though he couldn't see where the machine was sitting. His feverish brain shunted aside the relentlessly electric music. There was nothing, nothing here, nothing for him save those pale thighs and that taunting, teasing face, drawing him toward her, pulling him irresistibly downward.

162

"We don't want to hurt you, mister. We just want to talk to you."

Something hard and unyielding was pressed against Wells's spine. He turned.

Three men stood behind him. Two looked to be in their early forties. The third was considerably older. His expression was sorrowful in the moonlight.

"I'm Charlie Zimmer," said the man holding the shotgun against Wells's back. "I really wouldn't want to have to shoot you, mister." The gun moved significantly. "A twelve-gauge can make an awful mess of somebody at this range. Ain't no reason for it, if you'll just take a moment to listen."

"I will be sensible." Wells spoke with conviction. But he was still trying to watch the dancers. They had not vanished into the nether regions with the arrival of the other men. The newcomers could surely see them, yet they displayed no surprise at the eerie, luminous presences whirling to the music on the rocks below.

The second man wore a western hat and picked at an ear as he spoke to the elder. "Where you want to do this, Doc?"

"Motel's fine. Nobody'll bother us with questions. Reena knows, I suspect." He turned to the reporter, extended a hand. "My name's Sal Withers. Town doctor." Wells shook hands. The shotgun had not strayed.

"Wish I could say I was pleased to meet you, Doctor."

The older man grinned pleasantly. "Maybe we can remedy that."

Wells looked back down at the ghosts. They continued their dancing, remained in his sight. The blonde was especially close now, her legs flaring, her hair alive with light. She was unquestionably the most exquisite, most desirable creature he'd ever imagined. His desire blotted out everything else; the unreality of the moment, the three quiet men, the shotgun. He found himself reaching out for her, reaching out for the light, wanting, wanting...

"Watch it, Charlie! He's going over!"

Wells stumbled down the slope toward the dancers. As he neared them his vision blurred with the closeness of the beauty that had to be his, that cried out for him to possess. *She* turned to face him, gaped. The dancing stopped, though the raucous Stones continued to howl in his ears.

The blonde's partner stepped protectively in front of her, glowing brightly against the rock. Wells raised a fist to strike wildly at the Adonis.

Then he recognized the pimply face of the mechanic Michael beneath the flickering, compelling glow; and the shock slowed him. Something dented the back of his skull...

He awoke in bed in his cabin. The three men sat at a table nearby. They were playing cards. A fourth voice announced, "He's awake again." Wells stared as the manager moved away from the side of his bed and spoke to the elder. "I'll leave you now, Doc."

"Thanks, Reena." She closed the door behind her as the three men put down their cards and moved toward the bed. One traded three deuces and a pair of jacks for the twelve-gauge, cradled it loosely under an arm. Not loosely enough, Wells quickly decided. Besides, his car was still back at the garage.

He put a hand to the back of his head. There was a damp washcloth resting there, clammy and cold. No hole, though. And he couldn't recall the echo of a shot.

The doctor gestured at the man cradling the gun.

"Charlie caught up to you before you reached Jolene." He sounded apologetic. "He tried not to hit you too hard."

"Jolene...the ghost?" Wells remembered the vision that had danced before him on the rocks, the desire that had overwhelmed him, the mad charge down the slope.

The third man shook his head. "Nope. Jolene's m' daughter."

Wells raised himself slowly, rested his back against the iron bedstead. "That's crazy. If ever I saw a ghost, she was it. And she was dancing with eleven cousins." He frowned, suddenly remembering the young mechanic.

The men listened, exchanged looks. "He means Mike Billings, Jim Billings's boy," said the one called Charlie.

The oldster sat down on the end of the bed. "They are not ghosts, Mr. Wells. They're luciferites."

Wells's gaze traveled to the implied threat of the shotgun. He remembered stories he'd read and discarded as tripe; small towns filled with isolated cults and populated by religious fanatics who look just like Uncle Ed and Aunt Erma. Relatives of Rosemary's Baby. Any second now they'd calmly be explaining to him why they needed his heart for the monthly sacrifice. He debated whether he ought to try jumping the man holding the gun.

They reacted to the sudden expression of fear that came over his face. It was not, however, the kind of reaction he expected. They were laughing at him. Charlie extended a cigarette.

"Now, Charlie, you know I don't approve of that," said the doctor.

"Aw hell, Doc. This poor fella's had a night of it. Give him a break."

Wells's hesitation faded. He accepted the cigarette and matches gratefully. "Yeah, gimme a break. And an explanation. I saw twelve ghosts. You say they're not." He broke three matches before getting the cigarette lit.

Doc Withers gathered his thoughts. "Do you know where you are?"

Wells frowned. "Agua Caliente, New Mexico."

"Near where?"

"I don't see what? . . ."

"You want explanations?" Wells nodded. "Near where," the doctor repeated patiently.

Wells tried to remember the road map. "Oscura and Carrizozo, State Highway Fifty-Four. White Sands National Monument. Alamogordo. Rubirosa. Interstate Forty to the north, Ten to the south."

Withers nodded slowly. "White Sands. Alamogordo. Those mean anything to you?"

"Yeah. National Monument and . . ." His voice trailed away.

The doctor smiled grimly up at his companions. "I think this may be okay. He's educated." He turned his attention back to Wells. "Have you ever heard of luciferin?"

The reporter shook his head. White Sands. Alamorgodo. 1945. Glowing. His brain was racing, trying to catch up, two steps behind information and implication.

Withers rose, paced as he continued talking. His gray hair was peeling back from his forehead. Outside, the June sun was shining brightly. He did not strike Wells as a man concealing a sinister secret.

"I've lived here most of my life. Set up practice here

after the end of the war. I like being a country doctor, the easy pace, the people. I didn't know about the tests until the fifties. Nobody did who wasn't directly involved with the project. But I learned later on, like the rest of the folks in this region did. We're isolated here, but we're not hicks.

"Tillis's boy Jeremy was the first." The man standing next to Charlie nodded once. "Jeremy's twenty-three now. He's the oldest. The others showed up in turn."

"Others." Wells was staring at the somber-faced Tillis. "Other luciferites."

"That's what we call 'em." The doctor glanced back at his companions. "See, I told you he was smart."

Not too smart for my own good, I hope, Wells told himself worriedly. But he was starting to relax slightly, despite the presence of the shotgun. These men weren't acting or talking like devotees of Satan.

"What the hell is a luciferite?"

"Everyone has a certain amount of luciferin in their body," Withers explained. "Usually minute amounts. Not enough to amount to anything. And even smaller amounts of luciferase. A few creatures have substantial amounts in their bodies. Especially fireflies."

Cause and effect came crashing together in Wells's mind.

"Bombs weren't the only things they were testing back in '45," Withers went on. "There was also a lot of talk about how nuclear medicine was going to revolutionize treatment of everything from cancer to warts. Took them a while to learn that trying to cure ancient diseases by dumping a load of isotopes on them might do more harm than good.

"Remember that rocky flat you saw the kids dancing on?" Wells nodded. "That's an old chemical dump site.

Hundreds of them around the country. This one's sort of unique, I expect, because it received more than your usual loads of PCBs and insecticides. The folks at Alamorgordo were playing around with some interesting chemical combinations pretty much free of supervision, until the government closed them down after the war." He shook his head slowly. "What some folks won't do to try and hide their mistakes. Not to mention dirty linen.

"That dump lies above the river that feeds the town reservoir. Over the years, stuff's been seeping into the town water supply a little at a time. Nobody noticed anything at first. It took three generations before the build-up reached the point where it began to affect children's body chemistry.

"It doesn't show up until puberty, reaches full strength by the age of sixteen. I try, but I haven't the facilities for isolating the enzymatic combination that's responsible. It doesn't seem to have any overt harmful effects, only interesting side effects. I'm sure the change in the chemicals released into the body at puberty has something to do with activating it."

Wells was no longer frightened, only fascinated. "To do with what? What effects are you talking about?"

"Hugely increased production of luciferin in the body, matched by a corresponding increase in the amount of luciferase. The latter's an enzyme itself. When it's present it permits oxidization of the luciferin, and you get..."

"Fireflies," Wells whispered wonderingly. He thought a moment, then spoke sharply to the doctor. "Why haven't you reported this? Why hasn't anyone been?..."

"'Scuse me, mister." Charlie smiled dolefully down at him. "It's our kids." His expression was taut, his words a plea for understanding. "Doc here says there's no signs of anything really harmful in them. No...no cancer or anything like that."

"Except for the luciferite effect they're perfectly normal adolescents," agreed Withers.

"See," Charlie continued, his fingers moving nervously, "we love our kids. Doc here says that if news of what's happened to them got out, well, the government might take 'em away from Agua Cal. Take 'em away from us. To study 'em."

"Our children like it here," Withers went on. "They don't want to be studied. They've all been to school or go there now. They know the fate of bugs under microscopes.

"They can control the effect, conceal it from outsiders. Usually they keep to their special places, where they can show off for each other in safety. It was bad luck you happened to see Jolene Lytton that night. We'd hoped you might forget it."

"You're only a country GP," Wells said evenly. "The effect *could* be harmful. There could be side effects."

"If any one of the kids shows any signs of ill effect, we'll have to submit them to hospital care and take our chances," said Withers. "But so far that hasn't been necessary. I check them regularly. I've taught them how to check themselves. They understand. They like what they've become, Mr. Wells. They don't want to be cured.

"And there's another reason for keeping their ability hidden from outsiders. We here in Agua Caliente have a hard enough time dealing with it. We leave them alone, don't go up to watch their games and dances. We don't go watch them, because if you do, you can lose control of yourself."

"You ought to know about that by now, mister," said Tillis.

Wells thought back to last night, to the sight of the spinning, flashing beauty and the effect she had upon him. He remembered his intense, overpowering urge to possess her, to take her to him. Lose control, yes, and he'd lose it again if given the chance.

"I know what you're feeling," Withers told him. "I'm no more immune to the effect than you are. In order to cope with it you have to understand it for what it is." He moved toward the door. "Jolene, you can come in now."

Wells tensed, his gaze shifting to the doorway. His loins throbbed in expectation, his muscles contorted. A girl came in. *The* girl. The vision, except...

Except she was not the vision, though she was undeniably the girl. His desire vanished instantly. She smiled shyly at him, a pretty but in no way extraordinary nineteen-year-old. Same hair, same dress, but something missing. The power, the compulsion, was gone along with the light.

"Thank you, Jolene. You can leave now."

"Yes, Doc." As she exited, a faint, brief flash of green-yellow light emanated from her body. Wells blinked. Then she was gone. He turned a dazed expression to Withers.

"I know, son. You see, it's the luciferite effect, the special light, that makes them all seem so beautiful. It's a dangerous thing, one they're just learning to keep under cover. For their own good." For a second his kindly demeanor seemed swamped by something unpleasant and primal. He shook it off, was once again the kindly country physician.

"That's why our children's secret must be kept, Mr. Wells. That's why they have to keep their lights hidden from the rest of the world. Not even the most jaded scientist, the most dedicated researcher, could resist it. The beauty they can surround themselves with could mean their deaths. There is such a thing as being able to make yourself *too* attractive." He started for the door. Tillis and Charlie joined him.

"I think you understand, young man," Withers said in parting. "I think you'll keep our little secret. You see, it's not the ability to generate the glow that's dangerous; it's the passion, the arousal it can produce in others. Why do you think certain insects generate such a light, Mr. Wells? We think we're so advanced, so above the rest of nature. We're not.

"That glow, it's a kind of visual pheromone. We're none of us immune to it, any more than the insects are. I'm seventy-one years old, sir, but when I see that glow . . . well, I don't feel seventy any more. I don't feel anything except one thing, and that's what's so dangerous.

"The kids have been changed. They can handle it, deal with it. But not the rest of us. Not us unsuspecting innocents. It's too powerful for our systems.

"So you think about it, Mr. Wells. Think about the thing that rose up out of your brain last night on the hill and took control of you. The primitive part of your brain. Think about what could happen to those kids if that effect was magnified by a couple of hundred attentive scientists, male and female both." He smiled somberly a last time as he prepared to close the door on his way out.

"We're all fireflies, Mr. Wells."

The door shut firmly. Wells was alone in the room. He sat motionless on the bed and considered what the old doctor had said.

Crazy, he told himself, crazy and silly and foolish.

I can control my emotions as well as anybody. Sure I can. He remembered the morning on the mountainside, the glow, the overwhelming throbbing in his loins and the mindless, blind desire that had taken complete command of him. All because of a little light, a peculiarly attractive glow.

He got up from the bed and hastily began gathering his things. Because he couldn't fool himself any more than he'd been able to fool his own body. Because that light destroyed common sense and careful thought.

No, he wouldn't reveal the secret of the luciferite effect. Not to his new bosses in Dallas, not to anyone. Because if it became known, people might come to the little town to drink the water in hopes of gaining the ability for themselves. Well-meaning researchers might synthesize the necessary compounds and spread the talent to everyone.

Wells was a sensible, happy man. He did not want to see civilization destroy itself through nuclear holocaust. Far less did he want to see reason and civilization ruined in a sexual one...

Instant with Loud Voices

Some insist science and religion don't mix.
Me, I'm not sure they've ever been separated.
You need a little faith to believe in things
like quarks and such concepts as color.

But we prefer to separate and categorize,
compartmentalize our observations and our
knowledge for easier access. Relegate each new
discovery to its proper slot.

As we drift closer and closer to the great
central mysteries of existence, it may be that
matters of science and religion will converge
instead of moving farther apart. Doesn't each
new discovery bring with it not assurance but
a dozen brand-new questions begging to be
answered?

How the devil was he going to tell Hank Strevelle that his life's work wouldn't work? As he hurried down the brightly lit white corridor, Ken Jerome tried to compose the right words as well as himself.

The remote unit via which he'd run the final check hung loosely from his right hand. His lab coat fluttered from his shoulders. The corridor was a football field of eggshell white, the remote unit a rectangular ball, and he was running, running hard and uncertainly toward the wrong goal.

There was nothing wrong with the concept of the question. It was the figuring that troubled Jerome. That, and the fact that no one knew if a machine could be mentally overstressed.

He'd spent a last hectic week reprocessing, rechecking. Wilson at MIT had confirmed his calculations, but at this late stage even Wilson's prestige might not be enough to get the question aborted.

He rounded the last bend in the main corridor. The guard smiled as he held up a restraining hand. Jerome had to wait impatiently while his identity tag was checked against the records. He was panting heavily. Forty-nine unathletic years old, and it was a long time since he'd run this far with anything heavier than a new equation.

The guard was smiling at him with maddening politeness. He was a handsome young man, probably a moonlighting theater arts student waiting for some visiting producer or director to stumble over his cleft chin.

"Nice day, sir. You should slow down. You look a little flushed."

Wait till you hit the archaic side of forty, Jerome thought. But all he said as he retrieved his ident card was, "I expect I do." The guard stood aside as the diminutive engineer hurried through the double doors.

Down another corridor, this one narrower and underpopulated. Through another check station, four glass doors strong enough to have defeated Dillinger, and into The Room. The Room was the only one in the building. It *was* the building. It had been built to house a single important entity and its attendants. Jerome was one of the attendants. The entity was DISRA—Direct Information Systematic Retrieval and Analysis.

The Room was a modest three stories high and roughly the length and width of a football field (I must be going through male menopause, Jerome thought idly, to account for all these sports metaphors here lately). As human constructions went, it was not especially awesome. Nor was the physical appearance of DISRA overwhelming. What it represented was.

The flat sides of the three-story machine were transparent, allowing inspection of the exterior components. Yellow and white monitoring lights winked on and off, giving the epidermis of the machine the aspect of a captured night sky. They indicated to any knowledgeable onlooker that the computer was powered up and working on only minor problems.

If a similar machine had been built back in the 1950s it would have covered most of North America and still been inferior in capability to DISRA. Twenty years of effort, money, and intelligence had gone into its construction. Jerome had been involved with the project for the last ten of those years.

Each year new techniques, new knowledge, were acquired and immediately integrated into the design of the machine. Its architect, Henry Strevelle, was no dogmatic, blind believer in his own omnipotence. He was as flexible as his creation and eager to adapt the best ideas of others into its framework.

If only he'll be flexible now, Jerome thought worriedly.

DISRA had been in operation for the past six years, answering questions, pondering hypotheses, dispensing immensely valuable opinions on everything from Keynesian versus Marxist economics to particle physics. When the Secondary Matrix was linked with the DISRA Prime two years ago, Catastrophe Theory had for the first time taken on the aspect of a real science. DISRA had shown itself capable of predicting major earthquakes as well as fish population stocks. Space probes of many nations and consortiums were now programmed with previously unimaginable accuracy.

Six months ago construction on DISRA Prime itself had concluded. After a month of testing, Hank Strevelle had begun the task of programming the complex for a single question.

And, Jerome knew, DISRA was too valuable to mankind for that question to be asked.

He found Strevelle conversing with two technicians. The world's greatest computer scientist was six-four, thin as an oxygen tank, and nearly as pale as the enclosing walls. His hair was brushed straight back and gave him the look of a man always walking into the wind. Jerome envied him the hair as much as the brain beneath. We are all frail, he thought.

Strevelle looked away from the techs as Jerome came over. He smiled tolerantly. He knew what was coming. Jerome had been badgering him with it for weeks.

"Now, Ken," he said, "you're not going to hit me with your pet peeve again, are you? Now, of all times?" He glanced at his wrist. "Five minutes to startup. Give me a break, will you?"

Jerome conducted his words by waving the remote. "I've spent all night and most of the morning hooked up with the Eastern Nexus. Everything confirms what I've been telling you since the fourth of the month. You put this question to DISRA and we're liable to lose the whole works. A computer *can* be overstressed. Not a normal computer, but nothing about DISRA is normal."

"You're a good man, Ken. Best theoretical engineer I ever worked with. You'll probably be chosen to run DISRA operations when I retire."

"I can't run what isn't there."

Strevelle let out a resigned sigh. "Look, there are two and a half decades of my life and most of my reputation in this cube of circuits and bubbles and agitated electrons." He jerked a thumb back at the softly humming machine. "D'you really think I'd risk all that if I believed there was the slightest chance of losing capacity, let alone more serious damage?

"The machine runs twenty hours each day, four down for repair and recheck. Half the world depends on it to make decisions, or at least to offer opinions. Even the Soviets want it kept functional. They haven't experienced a single wheat or corn failure in the ten years they've been relying on DISRA's predictions."

"Wilson confirms my calculations."

For a moment the great man appeared uncertain. "Kenji Wilson, at MIT?" Jerome nodded. Strevelle mulled that over, then his paternal smile and eternal optimism reasserted themselves.

"Wilson's the best alive, Ken. I won't deny that. But he bases his calculus on DISRA's own information and DISRA doesn't seem disinclined to try the question. Besides which, he doesn't know DISRA the way I do."

"Nobody alive does, Hank. You know that." He desperately tried another tack. "Look, if I can't get you to call this off, at least postpone it so I can refine the figures." He held up the remote, touched tiny buttons. A series of equations flashed across the small screen, hieroglyphs of a physics so advanced that fewer than a hundred minds in the world could comprehend it.

Strevelle shook his head. "I've seen your work for weeks, Ken. I don't buy it." He gestured toward the control booth, led Jerome toward it. "There are five senators there plus representatives from all over Europe and Asia. I can't put them off." His eyes gleamed from under brows tufted with fleece.

"You know what that group of senators promised me? That if we derive any kind of sensible answer to the question, anything at all, they're going to try and put through appropriations to double DISRA's capacity. *Double* it. I won't be around to see that happen, but I don't care. It'll be my legacy, the first computer that doesn't just approximate the ability of a human brain but equals or surpasses it."

"Run this program," Jerome said, "and you're liable not to *have* any legacy, Hank." I'm not saying it right, he told himself frustratedly. I'm not making my point strongly enough, emotionally enough. I'm a bland personality and I live with a calculator. Damn to the hundredth power! He's going to go through with it.

The equations weren't solid enough, he knew. Though given the glow of the great man's expression, Jerome wasn't sure the solidest math in the universe could have dissuaded him today. He resigned himself to the asking of the question.

Five senators. Jerome tried to tell himself that he was wrong, that Wilson was wrong. They could be.

Certainly Strevelle knew what he was doing. They'd said DISRA couldn't be built and Strevelle had built it. He'd proven everyone wrong. Among his early detractors had been the youthful, brilliant theoretician named Kenneth Jerome.

I hope to God he proves me wrong again.

There were quiet greetings and introductions, idle conversation to cover nervousness. Only a couple of reporters had been allowed in, one from the New York *Times*, the other from *Der Spiegel*. Friends of Strevelle from the early days of derision and doubt. Now they would receive recompense for that early support. Strevelle never forgot a circuit, or a friend.

He folded himself into a chair next to the master control board, touched instrumentation, murmured to his ready associates. Jerome stood back among the curious. He was Strevelle's backup in case the great man had a stroke or forgot some item of programming. But Strevelle had the body of a man half his age and the mind of several. He would not collapse either physically or mentally.

"Quiet, please," a technician requested. The multilingual muttering in the booth faded to silence.

Strevelle thumbed a switch. "Condition?"

"Ready," replied a tech.

"Secondary Matrix?"

"On-line," came the quiet announcement.

Strevelle was too prosaic to construct a dramatic gesture. He just touched the button.

Banks of monitors sang in unison behind the watchers. Beyond the angled glass, out in The Room, thousands of tiny indicator lights suddenly flared green, red, blue. The inspiration was wholly mechanical, but it had the look of a hundred Christmas trees suddenly winking to life simultaneously, and provoked appreciative murmurs of admiration from the non-scientists in the group.

There were eight DISRA-2's emplaced in major cities across the United States, four more in Europe, four again in Japan. The Japanese were not involved in the question because of time-sharing conflicts and other problems. Together, the sixteen constituted the Secondary Matrix. They would combine to ask the question which DISRA Prime would attempt to answer.

Six massive communications satellites were temporarily taken out of commercial service to shunt the constituents of the question to DISRA, shutting down half the communications of Europe and the continental United States for fully eight minutes. It was dark outside The Room and still not morning in London. The timing had been carefully planned to cause minimal disruption to the world's commerce.

Five months of laborious pre-programming now spewed in an electronic torrent from two continents into the waiting storage banks of DISRA Prime, filling them to capacity.

The eight minutes passed in tense silence. Jerome found that his palms were damp.

The digital clock on the wall marked time silently, continued past the eight minute mark as the technician on Strevelle's right said calmly, "Programing received."

In The Room DISRA glowed like some ponderous deep-sea monster, awaiting instructions. It's not human, Jerome reminded himself firmly. It's different, and in its limited way superior, but it's not human. Even Strevelle agrees to that.

Strevelle touched the button beneath the plate which read, "Process question," then sat back and lit a small, feminine cigar. The onlookers shuffled uneasily. A red light came on beneath another readout and the single word everyone was waiting for appeared there: WORKING.

Someone made a bad joke in French. A few people laughed softly. Everything was functioning properly. It was the import of the question that had been put to DISRA which was making them nervous, not any fear of mechanical failure.

DISRA worked on the question, digesting at incredible speed the immense volume of programing it had been fed. Normally, the most complicated inquiry took less than three minutes to solve. The digital on the wall counted.

Half an hour passed. The readout on the console glowed steadily red. WORKING. The lights behind the transparent panels of the machine flashed rapidly, efficiently. While they waited, the onlookers discussed science, politics, their personal travails and problems.

The power requirements for such processing were enormous, another reason for running the program at night. Demand in the city was way down. As it was, there was still barely enough power to meet the demand, but the local utilities had been notified well in advance and were prepared to deal with any possible blackouts. Extra power had been purchased from out-of-state utilities to help cope with the temporary drain.

Forty minutes. Jerome considered. Better that he be proven wrong, much better. Of course, even if he and Wilson were correct, nothing might happen. When it was all over he intended to be the first to congratulate Strevelle. Despite their disagreement in this, they were anything but rivals.

For the first time in several weeks his concern gave

way to curiosity. After all, he was as interested as anyone else in the machine's answer.

To support DISRA's pondering, everything known or theorized about the Big Bang had been programmed into it. That included just about the entire body of physics, chemistry, astronomy, and a number of other physical sciences, not to mention all of philosophy and more. All in support of one question.

When was the Big Bang and what, precisely, did it consist of?

An equation for the Creation, Jerome mused. There were a few who'd argued against asking the question, but they were in the minority and outvoted. Many prominent theologians had helped with the programming. They were as anxious for a reply as the astronomers. DISRA would answer first in figures, then in words.

Forty-five minutes. One of the technicians on Strevelle's right leaned suddenly forward but did not take his eye from the console. "Sir?"

Strevelle glanced down at him. He'd gone through four of the small cigars and was on his fifth. "Trouble?"

"Maybe. I'm not sure. We're running at least two cyclings now, maybe more."

Jerome joined Strevelle at the technician's station. Cycling occurred when a component of a question could not be either solved or disregarded. Yet the machine was programmed to answer. Its design demanded an answer. If not shut down or if the programming was not canceled, the same information would be run over and over, at greater strength and drawing on greater reserves. It was a rare occurrence.

"Four sections cycling now, sir. If the figures are right." He looked anxiously up at Strevelle.

"Cancel it, Hank," Jerome urged him quietly. "While there's still time."

"Eight sections, sir." The technician no longer tried to hide his nervousness. "Ten. Twelve."

There were forty sections comprising DISRA Prime. Forty sections devoted to Direct Information Systematic Retrieval and Analysis. Strevelle said nothing, stared stolidly down at the console, then out at the working machine.

"We've still plenty of capacity. Let it cycle."

"Come on, Hank," Jerome muttered intensely. "It's not going to work. You've reached beyond the machine's capacity. I told you."

"Nothing's beyond DISRA's capacity. We've asked it a perfectly logical question and supplied it with sufficient information to answer. I expect an answer." He put both hands on the console and leaned forward, his nose nearly touching the slanting glass.

"Twenty sections," muttered the technician. All the other technicians were watching his station now. "Thirty...thirty-five..." Behind them something was buzzing, louder than the crowd.

"Forty...all sections cycling, sir." The technician's voice had turned hoarse.

Out in The Room there was no sign anything out of the ordinary was taking place. On the console WORK-ING continued to glow its steady red.

Then someone turned a spotlight on Jerome's face and just as quickly turned it out...

The glass had missed him. So had most of the flying scrap. One of the support beams had not.

Still, he was one of the first out of the hospital, and the arm was healing nicely. He didn't need it for a while anyway, since there was nothing to work on for at least a month. Strevelle was already drawing up his new plans, dictating them from his hospital bed.

The roof was mostly gone, blown skyward to fall back in or to dust the campus, but the reinforced concrete walls had held. They'd been designed to withstand Richter scale nine earthquakes and near nuclear explosions. A little internal blowup had strained but not shattered them.

In the remnants of The Room workmen were cleaning up the last of the debris while technicians were already discussing where to begin rebuilding. DISRA resembled a cake that had fallen in on itself. About seventy percent of the machine was completely gone, scattered across the surrounding community in tiny pieces or else vaporized during the overload. So rapid was the final cycling even the safeties had been overloaded. The city-wide blackout had lasted two hours.

Jerome strolled around The Room, picking his way carefully over the remaining debris, chatting with those technicians he knew. There was no air of depression about The Room. An experiment had failed, that was all. Time to rebuild and try it again.

A slight figure near one of the walls was neither workman nor tech. Jerome squinted, thought he recognized the man, and made his way across to him.

"Hello. Hernandez, isn't it? From the *Times*? You were in the booth with us when she blew."

The man turned away from his examination of the concrete, smiled from beneath an afterthought of a mustache and extended a hand. "Yes. You're Dr. Jerome, aren't you? I understand the old man's already planning DISRA Prime Two."

For some reason Jerome felt embarrassed. "Yes. He's incorrigible. But we have to have a DISRA. The

Secondary Matrix can only handle so many of the lesser inquiries. The world needs its questions answered."

"But not today's." Hernandez chuckled. "The astronomers will have to wait at least another generation."

"For that question? I don't think the government will let them try it again. Too much money for too little return."

"Oh?" The reporter was jotting notes down on a small pad. He's old-fashioned, Jerome mused. An odd trait to find in a science reporter.

Hernandez noticed his stare. "Tape recorders aren't right for every situation. There are people working here and I don't want to bother them. You're not bothered?"

"No. Just sore. It could've been a lot worse. Ninety-five percent of the energy seemed to go skyward instead of sideways."

"I know. I put that in my article."

"So I heard. Thanks for your kindness. We're going to need all the help we can get, despite the need for a new DISRA. Our public image isn't exactly at its most polished right now."

"Doesn't matter. As you say, the world needs a DISRA, and the public hardly suffered." He waved his pen at the wall. "A few people thought DISRA was the mechanical equivalent of a human being."

"A few people believe in astrology, too. DISRA was a brilliant machine, but that's all. Its superiority was limited to a few specific areas."

"Of course." Hernandez made some more notations, then indicated the wall. His voice lost some of its usual reportorial smoothness.

"Have you noticed the lines and markings on the concrete?"

Jerome had not paid much attention to the scorching. His attention had been centered on the ruined machine in the middle of The Room. But the source of the marks was obvious enough.

"You remember that most of DISRA's exterior paneling was transparent," Jerome said. "When she blew, the intense light was slightly masked by dark circuitry." He tapped the wall. "So we got these negative images seared into the walls, sort of a flash blueprint."

"That's what I thought." Hernandez nodded slowly. "I've seen such things before, only the outline was human and not mechanical."

"Oh, you mean the Hiroshima silhouettes," Jerome said, "the outlines burnt into the streets and walls of people close to the bomb when it was dropped?"

"I wasn't thinking of them," the reporter murmured. He traced some of the circuit patterns with his pen. "These are much more detailed, more delicately shaded than just a plain outline."

"That's explainable." Jerome wondered what the reporter was driving at.

"You know," said Hernandez quietly, "there's intelligence, and there's intelligence. There are representations of man and representations of man. Sometimes you can ask too much of a man just as you can of a machine. It's taken us a long time to reach the stage where we could make a machine suffer like a man."

"If it suffered," said Jerome chidingly, "it didn't suffer like a man."

"I wonder," said the reporter.

"You said you've seen such markings before." Jerome tried to bring the conversation back to a sensible tack. "If not the Hiroshima markings, then where?"

Hernandez turned, sat down on a broken conduit and regarded the remnants of the machine the bulk of whose substance had vanished.

"On an old shroud, in Italy, in Turin..."

Communication

It's a bit frightening to think that all our early television communications are still drifting through the immensity of the universe, and that we may in the end be judged not by our great achievements in art and science but by whatever our first alien visitors chance upon in the course of monitoring random signals, be it Toscanini with the NBC Symphony or Ward Cleaver laying down the law to the Beaver.

That's silly, though. Surely any race intelligent enough to cross the gulfs between the stars will take a careful, thoughtful look at any such transmissions it picks up. If nothing else, quantity as well as quality will prove a measure of value.

Wonder what the aliens will make of the quantity of air time devoted to some of our more widely used products?

"It's big, Sattersly, but not very big. Not as big as I expected."

"That's only the shuttle, the landing craft, Mr. President. Their main ship is still in orbit."

"Oh." The President of the United States went quiet. He had a lot on his mind.

His executive assistant leaned back and squinted skyward. It was a cloudy day and the heavens were the color of tarnished silver. The colorful canvas windbreaks that had been emplaced to keep the scalpel breath of the wind off the backs of the attending dignitaries stood out like dabs of oil paint against the greensward of Salisbury Plain.

A different flag cracked and snapped from the crest of each temporary shelter. Looking like picnic ants awaiting the first falling olive, long lines of black limousines filled the nearby highway. None of the dignitaries had arrived via helicopter. Their use would have shortened the time out from London or Heathrow airport, but the brisk winds and occasional rain made their employment chancy.

The limousines were more dependable. No leader wanted to arrive late because of something as mundane as a mechanical failure. Not when he or she might be the one the aliens would choose to negotiate with.

The descending craft was a pale yellow ellipsoid. There were no visible wings, nor projections or windows or means of support. A steady whistle reached the ground from the alien ship, incongruously like that of a train calling out through the night. It reminded the

President of the night freights he'd listened to while resting sleepless on the sill of his own bedroom window, as a boy back in Indiana.

He lowered his gaze momentarily from the slowly dropping vessel to glance into the shelter set up alongside that of the U.S. Standing out in the wind before it was a stubby, balding old man in a severe dark suit. He reminded the President of Mr. Walters, the toy store manager back in Evansville.

He did not act much like Mr. Walters, however, for all his chubby-cheeked countenance. His name was Victor Buzukoi and he was the Premier of the Union of Soviet Socialist Republics and the second most powerful man in the world. I wonder, Buzukoi, did you lean out your window at night as a child and listen to the wail of passing trains?

The alien ship was touching down on the crest of the grassy knoll around which the crescent of shelters had been arranged. The President turned his attention away from his counterpart.

The aliens' appearance was no shock. They'd thoughtfully beamed self-descriptions along with their initial greetings several weeks ago, when their interruption of international television programming had shocked a complacent humanity into the realization that it was no longer alone in the universe.

They had proposed the time and site for this first, crucial meeting, given a few details of their own home, and a short description of their intention in visiting Earth. They were technologically advanced, though not omnipotently so; had been studying mankind via its storm of electronic transmissions for a number of years now, and were desirous of opening friendly relations with the people of Earth.

The one surprise was their height. Their initial

broadcast had made no mention of it and there were no human reference points on the alien ship. There were three of them, each between two and three meters tall.

They paused outside their ship, looking around and apparently discussing something among themselves. Then they turned and strode straight for the American shelter. Or was it the USSR's? Clearly their studies, albeit performed at long range, had provided them with some knowledge of the Earth's political map. The visiting leaders of the other nations quickly put aside their disappointment at having not been chosen and watched anxiously to see what the aliens would do next.

Oddly enough, the President was reminded of the day he had to deliver the oral section of his master's thesis at Ohio State. A nonsensical analogy, he told himself forcefully. You're not on trial here. Relax. Greet them as a leader, equal in stature if not knowledge. Smile at them. Perhaps their examination of our television broadcasts has given them some familiarity with our facial expressions.

The alien ambassadors halted several meters away. They were standing on a line directly between the leaders of the world's two dominant powers, studying both shelters with apparent interest.

Up close the President noted that they were bipedal, smoothly proportioned beneath their shiny blue suits. Round, sad eyes flanked noses that were slightly prehensile, like those of a tapir. Their external ears were short and stubby, set on top of the head instead of at the sides. A brush of silver fuzz ran from their foreheads to disappear down the backs of their suits. Their hands were six-fingered and graceful and they spoke through wide, lipless mouths when they conversed in their own language.

Each alien wore a thin mask over its nostrils. This was attached by a narrow tube to a tank at the waist. Trace gases vital to their health but not present in sufficient quantities in our atmosphere, the President thought, considering one of the briefings he'd received from his science advisers. Or maybe they're just having a smoke.

The aliens stood there until the humans facing them began to fidget. Finally the tallest of the three ambassadors stepped a little closer, moving with a wonderfully loose-limbed action of its long legs, and spoke to both the President and the Premier.

"As you know," it said in passable English (a boost for our side, thought the President as he silently enjoyed the scowl that came over Buzukoi's face), "we are here to extend our greetings to the peoples of the Earth on behalf of the Central Federation, to invite you to join with the family of civilized worlds and to participate in the Great UnRaveling."

"We welcome you to our world on behalf of the people of the United States of America," said the President.

"And for the peoples of the Soviet Union, Earth's most diverse nation and most gracious hosts," added Buzukoi in English as fluid as the President's.

"We thank you both," replied the alien noncommittally. It continued to look past both men, as though missing something. "As we explained via our transmission, we hoped to meet here today the leaders of all your most powerful and experienced social groupings, to continue with a single representative of your species all future negotiations and discussions."

Now it was Buzukoi's turn to smile. President Andress was in the middle of his second term, but Buzukoi had been Premier for ten years. If the aliens made their selection according to experience . . .

"We have prepared for this important decision by careful examining of your numerous radio, and more recently, television broadcasts, attempting to utilize them to settle upon this vital personage."

That made it a toss-up between him and Buzukoi, the President thought. Buzukoi had been in power longer, but Andress had been on far more broadcasts because of the greater American television presence. Which one would the aliens perceive as being the more experienced, the longest in power?

He did not have long to wait. "We have learned from these broadcasts of one who dominates your communications, whose longevity and evident popularity with the people far exceeds that of any other," the alien continued. Its nose set to wriggling and the President wondered what the gesture signified.

"However, we do not see him present among you. Therefore we must wait until he arrives, for we have determined that it is he with whom we shall discuss the future of all relations between the Central Federation and the peoples of Earth."

Andress looked around in bewilderment, trying to see which many-termed senior statesman might not yet have arrived. Quick to take advantage of the lull, Buzukoi stepped toward the alien.

"I have been a regular figure on the transmissions of the People's Government for far longer than any other important leader here." He smiled pleasantly across at Andress.

"Propaganda broadcasts do not qualify as a measure of true popularity, do not indicate the real affection of the people," said the President firmly, matching the Premier's step forward with one of his own.

"That is true enough," commented the distracted alien, still searching among the shelters. Andress beamed at this concurrence, hoping the small army of cameramen and photographers were recording his moment of triumph.

"Yet the individual we seek to deal with is manifestly not here," the alien repeated. Andress's smile flattened as he stared at the alien. So did Buzukoi's.

It continued to ignore them, stare beyond into the recesses of the shelters. Its confusion and disappointment shone through its alienness.

"Where *is* Johnny Carson?..."

The Last Run

Often a science fiction story will be based on actual developments in science, or on current events. Familiar subjects used as springboards for science fiction stories include up-to-date developments in space exploration, medicine, entertainment, and so on.

Much rarer is a fantasy story based on current events. Or at least, such stories used to be scarce. The genre is changing, moving away from elves and trolls and the inspiration of middle-European folk tales to more intimate and familiar hallucinations. Stephen King and Fritz Leiber extract fantasies dark and discomfiting from our own urban mental garbage.

The hobby described in this tale is real enough, as are the people who practice it. As to its morality, it's not for me to render judgment.

Others might be less reluctant to do so, however...

Banzai Runner ain't got no home
Empty highway is where he roam
Gas in his bloodstream
Oil on the brain
Make for a man who drives insane

Everyone knew Bill Switch didn't give a damn about
death. People who indulged in the special type of
street racing Bill enjoyed couldn't afford to think
about it. Not that he and his competitors were *really*
crazy. Just indifferent.

When he was fifteen, Switch took an old Willys
Jeep belonging to his father and turned it into a
passable street racer. Now, to fully appreciate what
that means, you have to know something about the
structure of a Willys Jeep. Bill's accomplishment
was comparable to transforming a Mexican plaster
pot into something out of Benvenuto Cellini.

When they sent him to Nam they had the rare
good sense to assign him to a motor pool. Bill spent
a perfectly happy war toying with armored personnel carriers and trucks. He turbocharged a tank long
before pentagon researchers and the Chrysler Cor-
poration decided that would be a good idea.

When he came back he opened his own little
garage. Specialty work. It could have made him rich.
God knows how many professional racing teams
wanted the wizard of San Bernardino prepping their
Formula Ones.

Bill always turned them down. That wasn't his style. He got his satisfaction from tricking up street cars and then beating their owners with his own machines. The streets of Southern California became his racetrack, the freeway system his Indianapolis 500.

There were a few others who felt the way Bill did about street racing. Most of them knew Bill, or of him. If they didn't know him they found out fast enough when the quiet big man beat the crap out of them some night on the freeway.

See, Bill Switch and these few others, they weren't your usual street racer. They didn't match hopped-up Fords on Kester in the Valley or low-riding Chevys on the East Side. To this little group, getting a street car up to a hundred fifty wasn't worth the gas it burnt.

They did their racing on the freeways that encircle greater Los Angeles, in the early morning dark when few other cars were on the road and when the Highway Patrol would look the other way in search of stranded campers and groping adolescents.

A race could cover twenty miles to a hundred or more. The men and women who matched up this way were usually very rich. They had to be, to afford the cars they used. You couldn't call them hot rodders, or street racers.

Even the police called them banzai runners.

Banzai Runner, you better watch out
Check your real-view mirror
Got Smokey in a dither
Gonna try and getcha whether
You're ready or not

I knew Bill because once in a while he deigned to work on my Corvette, a pretty but unmuscular '69 with side pipes but little else. Nice little commuter car, suitable for old ladies and men with delusions of grandeur. Bill's shop was in San Berdoo, and I'd unknowingly dropped by there one day in hopes of getting one of the custom mufflers replaced.

Well, Bill took pity on me and repaired the muffler. He also did something unseen under the hood which took five years and fifty thousand miles off that 'vette's life. In the unpredictable manner of events, we became friends. Not real close. Just Hi, howareya, smile and wave. That sort of thing. Bill liked to pick my brain, which I willingly gave him access to. In turn, he'd usually let me know on what night he'd have a little match race set up.

I'll never forget that particular night. Sultry Southern California September midnight, all gray outlines clad in tropical overtones. There were two challenging Bill. It's unusual for more than one at a time to take on a competitor. Bill relished the opportunity.

One of them was a prominent actor. You'd recognize the name, so I better keep my mouth shut, just in case. I'm not the litigious type.

He drove a Ferrari Boxer. Decent car, smooth of line and painted fire-engine red as a whore's nail polish. The actor shammied it lovingly, boasting to anyone who'd listen how he was going to cream the Wisp's ass. That was Bill's nickname. The Wisp, as in Will-o'-the.

In his enthusiasm the actor forgot about the other driver. He shut up a little when the rest of the competition drove up.

The man who climbed out of the driver's seat

wasn't much over five feet in height. He was a plastic surgeon who'd driven all the way out from Beverly Hills just for the race. What you could interpret through the single-piece beige driving suit had about as much fat on it as a culotte steak, despite the body's sixty years.

His car was a Lambourghini Countach, silver, tricked up with special front and rear spoilers, special flare work, and a suspension low enough to decapitate any caterpillar that didn't duck. When he revved that engine it sounded like one of the turbines at Hoover Dam, where I once spent an awed summer day.

The actor paled a little, but then his resolve stiffened and he climbed back into his own car. The Ferrari was tuned perfectly. Its driver might be intimidated but the Boxer was not.

Then Bill arrived. The starting point was just past the Kaiser Steel plant in Fontana. The race would be a short one, just a few miles to the Highland off-ramp. The surgeon and the actor had their first look at Bill's famous Wisp car. They started to laugh, thought better of it, and ended up by looking plain confused.

Bill drove what appeared to be a stock Plymouth station wagon, painted powder blue, with blue curtains on the windows. Except for the low front shocks and oversized tires it would not have looked out of place carrying groceries from a supermarket.

The actor and the surgeon put their confusion aside and turned serious. Each of them, Bill included, had put up ten thousand, winner take all. The three cars eased out onto the freeway. This early in the morning the little-used stretch of concrete was empty.

The starter fired his pistol. The Lambourghini bellowed and the Ferrari rumbled. You could hardly hear Bill's engine among them.

There was a soft, rising growl from the three cars as they accelerated. I waited with a couple of others at the halfway point, our own cars parked inconspicuously on the shoulder.

As they neared we could see that the Countach was slightly in the lead, the Boxer close but seemingly losing ground, with Bill bringing up the rear. I was trying to watch the surgeon's face through my night binoculars. At that moment he didn't wear the expression of a man I'd want slicing into my guts.

Suddenly above the steady roar a new tone sounded, a deep-throated barrooommm like a five-hundred-pound bomb going off. The Wisp materialized from the darkness. I clocked the Countach at two hundred and thirty miles per as they passed us. The Wisp went by it like a Harley passing a training bike. I wish I could've seen what the surgeon was thinking.

There was a real explosion soon after, as the Countach's straining engine blew. We rushed out and helped the doctor from his car. Somebody put a fire extinguisher on it. Fifty thousand bucks, up in pouf.

The actor lasted a minute or so longer, but slow and steady wasn't going to win this race. He pulled off the freeway too fast to slow down in time, lost control. The Boxer ended up among the heavily taxed grape vines. He came out shaken, more concerned for his face than the car.

Ready or not don't worry Wisp none
Over two hundred he's just havin' fun

The Last Run

Lambourghini blown its engine
Ferrari in the ditch
Ain't a one can catch that Wisp,
Bill Switch

I was the only one to drive out to meet Bill. He'd pulled off onto Highland, the street as deserted as the freeway. He was lying on a crawly under the car, using a light. He barely fit. Bill Switch was six five, weighed two forty, and couldn't look nasty-mean if he had to.

"Hi," he called out to my feet. "How're the others?"

"Okay. The surgeon had guts. He gave it everything he had."

"Yeah," echoed Bill's voice from beneath the station wagon. "You put some of these respectable citizen types in a real vehicle, they go from Jekyll to Hyde in seconds."

Bill had a 454 Chevy under the hood of the wagon. But that was for casual racing, for going to the market. It only powered the front wheels. Taking up most of the back of the wagon and connected to the rear drive train was a 900-hp Pratt and Whitney aircraft engine, built to go into small racing planes, the kind that zip and snort around the checkered pylons. Bill would use the 454 to toy with his opponents and then he'd kick in that hibernating airplane plant. With turbocharging, that boosted his total horsepower *way* up over a thousand. That station wagon looked stock, but it had more bracing inside than the Brooklyn Bridge.

But Bill wasn't satisfied. He told me that someday he wanted to put a jet engine into a van, if he could figure out a way to stabilize the damn thing.

We were all alone, with the grapevines and crickets. The others were still helping to tow the doctor's

Countach off the freeway and pull the Boxer from the vineyard, when the stranger drove up.

It eased out from the dark hole beneath the overpass and pulled up behind the Wisp wagon. It was painted the blackest black I'd ever seen, so black it was almost purple. Must've been thirty coats of lacquer on it. The headlights burned red because of the special rock shields over them.

I didn't recognize the car, but, then, I was hardly an expert. It wasn't any Indy type, not formula. It didn't look like a Lotus or the custom Mazda. It hardly had any lines at all. The windshield was barely six inches high.

The driver who stepped out was dressed in matching black, a fashion affected by many runners (Bill preferred jeans and a sweatshirt). He was as tall as Bill but much thinner. I guessed him to be in his forties and wondered what he did for a living. The occupations of banzai runners were often as interesting as their cars.

He leaned against the wagon and waited patiently, smiling unpleasantly at me while he waited for Bill to emerge. The crawly squeeked. Bill saw the newcomer, rose, wiped his hands. His gaze flicked past him to the ebony car behind.

"I hear you like racing," said the stranger. He nodded toward the freeway. "You just proved that you could. How'd you like to race me?"

> *Banzai Runner got a challenge now*
> *Funny sort o' guy*
> *Has fire in his eye*
> *Talks funny, kinda wry*
> *And his car ... oh, wow!*

Bill rubbed his nose. "I don't know. Don't know your car. That's something of a first for me."

The stranger's grin widened. "It's an import. Not Italian, not French."

"Israeli? I hear they're doing some interesting things over there."

The man shook his head. "Not Japanese, either. It's kind of a hybrid of my own design. Does that matter?"

"Nope. Not to me. Just curious."

"They say you're the best."

Now it was Bill's turn to smile. "They're right."

"I've got five hundred thousand here. In unmarked hundred dollar bills. That'd buy you the jet engine you want and plenty of time to play with it. You'd never have to work on another old lady's car."

Bill eyed the money. "I can't match that, not even if I threw in my shop in the bargain."

"I wouldn't have any use for your shop," said the stranger.

"Then what'll I bet?"

The stranger put his arm around Bill's shoulders and the two of them walked out into the grapevines. My skin was beginning to crawl and I was having cold chills despite the heat of the night. I didn't like this guy. I didn't like his smile, his attitude, the funny moan his idling black stiletto of a car made.

None of it seemed to trouble Bill. They strolled back toward the road and I could see them shaking hands. I felt bad about it, but it wasn't my decision to make.

"To be fair we should test endurance as well as speed," the stranger was saying. "Of the drivers as well as the cars."

"I'm agreeable," said Bill thoughtfully. "How

about from Indio to the border? First one across the bridge is the winner."

> The Wisp never turned a challenge down
> No black-clad stranger's about to make
>   him frown
> San Berdoo to the River
> Only two hundred mile
> "It's a race," said the stranger,
>   with a terrible smile

"Sounds exciting," said the other driver.

Bill nodded toward the black car. "You run on alcohol?"

The stranger shook his head. "Something not nearly so exotic. I propose next Monday night, at two A.M."

"Good enough."

Bill never worked as hard as he did that following week. I saw him in his shop on Thursday and he barely glanced up long enough to acknowledge my presence. I knew he was seeing that half million and the jet engine van he'd dreamed of.

I asked Mario, one of his mechanics, what Bill was up to in the stern of the powder-blue wagon.

"Beats the hell out of me, man. He's puttin' in some kind of overdrive or somethin'. Tryin' to drag another five hundred horse out of it."

I shook my head. "He's crazy. He'll blow himself up, over that distance."

"It's not for the whole race, I think." The mechanic spat on the oil-stained concrete. "If anybody can do it, the Wisp can."

I was waiting across the bridge Monday night morning. Not too many people knew about the race.

Those who did were spread out along the length of the chosen route. A big crowd would tip off the Highway Patrol that something unusual was up. We all had CBs and hf monitors, both to keep track of the Man and warn off the truckers.

I didn't see the start, of course, but we could follow the progress over the CBs.

They started out near even. By the time they passed Desert Center, Bill had pulled slightly ahead. The four fifty-four and the Pratt and Whitney were doing their job, meshing efficiently, burning up fuel and distance with incredible precision. Later we learned that the noise was so loud the people in Desert Center woke up and badgered Civil Defense, wanting to know if the munitions depot outside Barstow had gone up.

> *Banzai Runner on Interstate Ten*
> *Doin' two hundred twenty-five*
> *Hardly a man alive*
> *Could match that drive*
> *Only somethin' far past human ken*

Outside Blythe, coming up on the last leg of the race, the stranger made his move. The spectators assembled there said the black car didn't roar or rumble, just gave out a kind of rising shriek that steadily intensified, until it finally drowned out even the Pratt and Whitney.

Someone with binocs said she got a look at Bill's face as he went by and that it was taut and sweaty. No fear, though. Not in Bill Switch.

We had our first glimpse of them as they roared through town. Sirens began to sound all over the place as the Highway Patrol's patience finally ran out. But there wasn't much they could do except watch until the runners burned themselves out. No patrol car could catch a banzai runner.

The black car was in the lead. We could make out those flaming headlights clearly from our position on the bluff across the Colorado.

Then there sounded a distinct explosion, like a plummeting jumbo jet. Lights were winking on all over the sleeping town as the citizens awoke to something unnatural in their midst.

> That black demon car was pulling ahead
> Watchers 'cross the River thought the
>   Wisp was dead
> The Wisp looked down
> Kicked the overdrive in
> Came up on that demon near enough
>   to win

The explosion was the sound of Bill kicking in his special trick overdrive. Through our scopes and binoculars we could clearly see the pale station wagon pulling up, making ground on the black racer. They were barely a mile from the California side of the bridge. First one across would win. Then they were even, and then, unbelievably, Bill was ahead!

Those monster engines were making too much noise for us to hear the tire blow. At nearly three hundred miles an hour Bill's car swerved left. He fought to straighten out, brought it momentarily back on line before it squealed rightward. It went through the flimsy guard rail, hit a bump, and soared gracefully into the air, describing an arc like a dying pelican as it fell. Even this far south the breadth of the

Colorado was substantial. The Wisp didn't make much of a splash. There was no explosion. It must've gone straight to the bottom.

> *Banzai Runner you've gone too fast*
> *At two ninety-six*
> *The accelerator sticks*
> *Flesh and rock don't mix*
> *Road and bridge you've passed*

I never saw a car going that fast brake as rapidly as did that black bullet. The driver went only a mile or two into Arizona before slowing enough to turn around and rush back toward us. He parked and climbed out, and you could see that he'd been in a race. His formerly icy demeanor was shattered, and that unshakable self-confidence I'd seen in him that night in San Bernardino was missing. He'd won, but barely. If Bill hadn't lost that tire it might've been a different story, and the stranger knew it.

He gazed respectfully down at the limpid sheet of gray that was the Colorado. I was nearest to him. Most of the others had scrambled down the bluff, and a few were already swimming out to where Bill's wagon had sunk. I knew they wouldn't find a thing. So did the stranger standing next to me. I moved a couple of steps away from him.

> *The Devil slowed down and got*
> *   outta his car*
> *That was powered by souls*
> *   who'd fallen too far*
> *Eyed the wreck in the River*
> *That held Bill Switch*
> *Said, "You nearly beat me, boy,*
> *   I'm sorry 'bout the hitch."*

"Tell me," I asked hesitantly, "if the tire had held, *could* he have beaten you?"

The stranger considered. "I don't honestly know." He smiled down at me. "Of course, you can't believe anything I say, can you?" I noticed now that his eyes were yellow, and it wasn't due to contact lenses. Funny that I hadn't picked up on that before. Or maybe I hadn't wanted to.

I'm not an especially brave man, but I have an unreasonable disregard for death. So I said, "I think he had you beat cleanly."

Those awful pupils brightened ever so slightly, just enough to make me tremble a little. But I had made no bet with this banzai runner, and he knew it.

> *Banzai Runner, you've lost your soul*
> *Now the Devil take you home*
> *On his hot roads to roam*
> *Cars of fire, not of chrome*
> *No more chance to rock n' roll.*

"Could be he had. He was the best I've ever raced against. He was better than his machine, which is unusual in a man. Very unusual. But he lost." He turned and started back toward his car. I heard him mumbling to himself.

"Maybe some of the forfeit is salvageable. We'll see."

I never saw that black car or its driver again, and I never hope to. I no longer go out in the dark hours of early morning to watch the banzai runners race. I just stick to my papers and pen advertising jingles.

Oh, and I never exceed the speed limit. Someone might think to challenge me to a race.

The Last Run

Now the Devil knows a good thing
*   whenever he sees it*
Gave the Wisp a uniform and
*   driver's work kit*
So the next bus you board
Better listen to the bell
Might be the Devil's chauffeur
Wisp drivin' you down to
*   Hell...*

Wu-Ling's Folly

Our den is done in a Western motif. A second-floor landing runs above the floor. My wife's father was a rancher in West Texas, one Lewis Oxley by name, and the remnants and reminders of his working days fill our den walls: spurs, branding irons, barbed wire, and tools with strange names and stranger uses.

But there's not much you can do with a second-floor landing once it passes the only second-floor door. What results is a sort of second-story, oversized what-not shelf. It calls for oversized what-nots, I imagine, but of what shape and kind?

Walking past and below this unused space one day, I commented to my wife, JoAnn, that maybe we needed something like a stuffed bear up there.

"Why not a dragon?" she countered.

"Don't be silly," I said. "There were no dragons in the Old West."

"How do *you* know?" she shot back.

And people ask where story ideas come from...

———————————————————————————

Hunt and MacLeish had worked for the Butterfield Line for six and seven years, respectively. They'd fought Indians, and been through growler storms that swept down like a cold dream out of the eastern Rockies, and seen rattlers as big around the middle as a horse's leg. All that, they could cope with; they'd seen it all before. The dragon, though, was something new. You couldn't blame 'em much for panicking a little when the dragon hit the stagecoach.

"I'm tellin' ya," Hunt was declaring to the Butterfield agent in Cheyenne, "it were the biggest, ugliest, scariest-lookin' dang bird you ever saw, Mr. Fraser, sir!" He glanced back at his driver for confirmation.

"Yep. S'truth." Archie MacLeish was a man of few words and much tobacco juice. He was tough as pemmican and as hard to handle, but the incident had turned a few more of the brown-stained whiskers in his copious beard gray as an old Confederate uniform.

"It come down on us, Mr. Fraser, sir," Hunt continued emphatically, "like some great winged devil raised up by an angry Boston Temperance marcher, a-screamin' and a-hollerin' and a-blowin' fire out of a mouth filled with ugly, snaggled teeth. 'Twere a sight fit t'raise the departed. I gave it both barrels of Evangeline." He indicated the trusty ten-gauge resting in a corner of the office. "And it ne'er even blinked. Ain't that right, Archie?"

"Yep," confirmed the driver, firing accurately into the bronze-inlaid pewter spittoon set at a corner of the big walnut desk.

"I see." The Butterfield agent was a pleasant, sympathetic gentleman in his early fifties. Delicate muttonchop whiskers compensated somewhat for the glow the sun brought forth from his naked forehead. His trousers were supported by overloaded suspenders which made dark tracks across an otherwise immaculate white shirt. "And then what happened?"

"Well, both Archie and me was ready t'meet our maker. You got to understand, Mr. Fraser, sir, this varmint were bigger than coach and team together. Why, them poor horses like t'die afore we coaxed and sweet-talked 'em into town. They're bedded down in the company stable right now, still shakin' at the knees.

"Anyways, this ugly bird just reached down with one claw the size o' my Aunt Molly's Sunday dress and plucked the strongbox right off the top, snappin' the guy ropes like they was made o' straw. Then it flew off, still a-screechin' and a-brayin' like the grandfather of jackasses toward the Medicine Bow Mountains."

"God's Truth," said the driver.

"This is all most interesting," Fraser mumbled. Now, while known as a sympathetic man, the Butterfield agent would have been somewhat disinclined to believe the tale to which his two employees were swearing, save for the fact that MacLeish and Hunt were still standing in front of his desk rather than cavorting drunk and debauched in the fleshpots of Denver, spending free and easy the ten thousand in gold which the missing strongbox had contained.

And, of course, there was also the confirmation afforded by the stage's three passengers, a reputable Mormon rancher from Salt Lake and two of his wives. At the moment, the ladies were under the care of a local physician who was treating them for shock.

"Couldn't it have been a williwaw?" he asked hopefully.

"Nope," said MacLeish, striking with unerring accuracy into the spittoon a second time. "'Tweren't the likes o' no wind or beastie I ever seed nor heard tell of, Mr. Fraser. I kinna say more than the truth." He squinted hard at the agent. "D'ye doubt our word?"

"No, no, certainly not. It's only that I have no idea how I am to report the nature of this loss to the Company. If you'd been held up, that they would understand. But this... you must understand my position, gentlemen. There will be questions."

"And *you* should've been in ours, Mr. Fraser, sir," Hunt told him fervently.

The agent was not by his nature an imaginative man, but he thought for a moment, and his slim store of inventiveness came to his rescue. "I'll put it down as a storm-caused loss," he said brightly.

MacLeish said nothing, though he made a face around his wad of fossil tobacco. Hunt was less restrained. He gaped at the agent and said, "But there weren't no storm where we was comin' through, Mr...."

Fraser favored him with a grave look. Hunt began to nod slowly. Meanwhile, MacLeish had walked to the corner and picked up the ten-gauge. He handed it to his partner. The two of them started for the door. And that was the end of that.

For about a week.

* * *

"Another month, boys, and I think we can call it quits." A bulbous nose made a show of sniffing the air. "Snow's in the wind already."

"Damned if you ain't right, there, Emery," said one of the other men.

There were four of them gathered around the rough-hewn table which dominated the center of the cabin. They were spooning up pork, beans, jerky, dark bread, and some fresh fowl. It was a veritable feast compared to their normal cold meals, but they had reason to celebrate.

Johnny Sutter was an eighteen-year-old from Chicago who'd matured ten years in the twelve-month past. "I," he announced, "am goin' to get me a room in the finest whorehouse in Denver and stay stinkin' drunk for a whole month!"

Loud guffaws came from the rest of the men. "Hell, Johnny," said one of them, "if'n yer goin' t'do that, don't waste your time doin' it in a fancy place. Do it in the streets and let me have your room."

"Dang right," said another. "You'll get yourself too stiff t'do what you'll want t'be doin'."

"Not stiff enough, mos' likely," corrected the mulatto, One-Thumb Washington. He laughed louder than any of them, showing a dark gap where his front teeth ought to have been. He'd lost those two teeth and four fingers of his left hand at Shiloh, and never regretted it. Two teeth and four fingers were a fair enough trade for a lifetime of freedom.

Wonder Charlie, the oldest of the four, made quieting motions with his hands. His head was cocked to one side, and he was listening intently with his best ear.

214

"What's wrong with you, old man?" asked Johnny, grinning at all the good-natured ribbing he was taking. "Ain't you got no suggestions for how a man's to spend his money?"

"It ain't thet, Johnny. I think somethin's after the mules."

"Well, hellfire!" Emery Shanks was up from his chair and reaching for his rifle. "If them thievin' Utes think they can sneak in here the day afore we're set t'—"

Wonder Charlie cut him off sharply. "'Tain't Utes. Ol' Com-it-tan promised me personal two springs ago when I sighted out this creekbed thet we wouldn't have no trouble with his people, and Com-it-tan's a man o' his word. Must be grizzly. Listen."

The men did. In truth, the mules did sound unnaturally hoarse instead of skittish as they would if it were only strange men prowling about the camp. It if were a grizzly, it sure would explain the fear in their throats. A big male could carry off a mule alive.

The miners poured out the cabin door, hastily donning boots and pulling up suspenders over their dirty long-johns. One-Thumb and Emery fanned out to search the forest behind the hitch-and-rail corral. The moon was swollen near to full and they could see a fair piece into the trees. There was no sign or sound of a marauding grizzly. One-Thumb kept an eye on the dark palisade of pines as he moved to the corral and tried to calm the lead mule. The poor creature was rolling its eyes and stamping nervously at the ground.

"Whoa, dere, General Grant! Take it easy, mule... Wonder what the blazes got into dese mu—"

He broke off as the mule gave a convulsive jerk and pulled away from him. There was something between

215

the camp and the moon. It wasn't a storm cloud, and it certainly wasn't a grizzly. It had huge, curving wings like those of a bat, and wild, glowing red eyes, and a tail like a lizard's. Thin tendrils protruded from its lips and head, and curved teeth flashed like Arapaho ponies running through a moonlit meadow.

"Sweet Lord," Johnny Sutter murmured softly, "wouldja look at that?"

The massive yet elegant shape dropped closer. The mules went into a frenzy. Wonder Charlie, who'd been at Bull Run as well as Shiloh and had emerged from those man-made infernos with his skin intact, didn't hesitate. He fired at that toothy, alien face, a rifle *ka-booming* through the still mountain air.

The aerial damnation didn't so much as blink. It settled down on wings the size of clipper ship toproyals and began digging with pitchfork-size claws at the watering trough just inside the corral. The mules pawed at the earth, at each other, at the railing in a frantic desire to crowd as far away from the intruder as possible.

One-Thumb ducked under the sweep of a great translucent wing and shouted in sudden realization, "Curse me for a massa, I think the monster's after our gold!"

Sure enough, several moments of excavation turned up a small wooden box. Inside lay the labor of four men sweating out the riches of a mountain for a year and a half, a glittering horde of dust and nuggets large enough to ensure each of them comfort for the rest of his life.

Monster bird or no, they'd worked too damn hard for any of them to give up so easily that pile they'd wrested from the icy river. They fired and fired, and when it was clear to see that guns weren't doing any good, they went after the intruder with picks and shovels.

When it was all over, a somber moon beamed down on a scene of theft and carnage. The gold was gone, and so were the bodies of young Johnny Sutter and One-Thumb Washington and a mule named General Grant...

There were not many physicians residing in Cheyenne at the time, and fewer still who knew anything about medicine, so it was not entirely coincidental that the one who treated the Mormon rancher's wives would also become conversant with the story related by the unfortunate survivors of the Willow Creek claim. He brought the information to the attention of Mr. Fraser, the local Butterfield Line agent who had seen to the care of the distraught passengers. Now these two comparatively learned men discussed the events of the week past over sherry in the dining room of the Hotel Paris.

"I am at a loss as to what to do now, Dr. Waxman," the agent confessed. "My superiors in Denver accepted the report I sent to them which described the loss of the strongbox on a mountain road during a violent, freak storm, but I suspect they are not without lingering suspicions. My worry is what to do if this should occur a second time. Not only would the cargo be lost, I should be lost as well. I have a wife and children, doctor. I have no desire to be sent to a prison...or to an asylum. You are the only other educated citizen who has been apprised of this peculiar situation. I believe it is incumbent upon the two of us to do something to rectify the problem. I feel a certain responsibility, as an important member of the community, to do something to ensure the safety of my fellow citizens, and I am sure you feel similarly."

"I agree. Something must be done."

"Well, then. You are positive these two men you treated yesterday were confronted by the same phenomenon?"

"There seems to be no doubt of that." The doctor sipped at his sherry as he peered over thick spectacles at the agent. "With two of their companions carried off by this creature, I should ordinarily have suspected some sort of foul play, were it not for the unique nature of their wounds. Also, they are Christians, and swore the truth of their story quite vociferously to the farmer who found them wandering dazed and bleeding in the mountains, invoking the name of the savior repeatedly."

The agent folded his hands on the clean tablecloth. "More than citizen safety is at stake in this. There is a growing economy to consider. It is clear that this creature has an affinity, nay, a fondness for gold. Why, I cannot imagine. What matters is that next time it may strike at a bank in Cheyenne, or some smaller community, when there are women and children on the streets.

"But how are we to combat it? We do not even know what we face, save that it surely is not some creature native to this land. I suspect a manifestation of the Devil. Perhaps it would be efficacious for me to have a talk with Pastor Hunnicutt of the—"

The doctor waved the suggestion down. "I think we must seek remedies of a more earthly nature before we proceed to the final and uncertain decision of throwing ourselves on the mercy of the Creator. God helps those who help themselves, whether the Devil is involved or not.

"I have had occasion in my work, sir, to deal with certain individuals whose business it is to travel extensively in this still-wild country. Certain acquaintances sometimes impress themselves most forcefully on these bucolic travelers, who are usually common-sensible if not always hygienic.

"In connection with unusual occurrences and happenings, with unexplained incidents and strange manifestations, one name recurs several times and is uttered with respect by everyone from simple farmers to soldiers to educated citizens such as ourselves. I have been reliably informed that this person, a certain Amos Malone, is presently in the Cheyenne region. I believe we should seek his counsel in this matter."

The Butterfield agent stared across at the doctor, who, having finished his sherry, was tamping tobacco into a battered old pipe. "Amos Malone? Mad Amos Malone? I have heard tell of him. He is a relic, a throwback to the heyday of the mountain man and the beaver hat. Besides which, he is rumored to be quite insane."

"So is half of Congress," replied the doctor imperturbably. "Yet I believe we need him."

The agent let out a long sigh. "I shall defer to your judgment in this matter, sir, but I confess that I am less than sanguine as to its eventual outcome."

"I am not too hopeful myself," the physician admitted, "but we have to try."

"Very well. How are we to get in touch with him? These mountain men do not subscribe to civilized means of communication, nor do they usually remain in one place long enough for contact to be made."

"As to that, I am not concerned." The doctor lit his pipe. "We will put out the word that we require his

219

presence and that it involves a matter of great urgency and most unusual circumstance. I believe he will come. As to precisely how he will learn of our need, I leave that to the unknown and ungovernable means by which the breed of man to which he belongs has always learned of such things."

They waited in the doctor's office. Just before dawn, a light snow had salted the town. Now the morning sun, hesitantly glimpsed through muddy-dark clouds, threatened to melt the serenely pale flakes and turn the streets into a quagmire.

Sitting in the office next to a nickel-and-iron stove were the Butterfield Line agent and a distraught, angry, and bandaged-up Wonder Charlie. Wonder Charlie wasn't feeling too well—his splinted right arm in particular was giving him hell—but he insisted on being present, and the doctor thought the presence of an eyewitness would be vital to give verisimilitude to their story.

The clock on the high shelf chimed six-thirty.

"And that's for your mountain man," snapped Fraser. He was not in a good mood. His wife, an unforgiving woman, had badgered him relentlessly about risking an attack of colic by tramping outside so early in the morning.

Dr. Waxman gazed unconcernedly at the clock. "Give him a little time. The weather is bad."

There was a knock at the door. Waxman glanced over at the agent and smiled.

"Punctual enough," Fraser admitted reluctantly. "Unusual for these backwoodsmen."

The doctor rose from his seat and moved to open the door, admitting a man who stood in height somewhere between six feet and heaven. He was clad in dirty buckskin and wet Colorado. Two bandoliers of enormous cartridges crisscrossed his expansive chest. In his belt were secured a Bowie knife and a LeMat pistol, the latter an eccentric weapon favored for a time by Confederate cavalry officers. It fit the arrival, Fraser thought.

The man's beard was not nearly as gray-speckled as Wonder Charlie's, but there were a few white wires scattered among the black. His eyes were dark as Quantrell's heart, and what one could see of his actual flesh looked cured as tough as the goatskin boots he wore.

"Cold out there this morning," he said, striding over to the pot-bellied stove. He rubbed his hands in front of it gratefully, then turned to warm his backside.

The doctor closed the door against the cold and proceeded to make formal introductions. Fraser surrendered his uncalloused palm to that massive grip gingerly. Wonder Charlie took it firmly, his age and infirmities notwithstanding.

"Now then, gentlemens, word's out that you folk have got yourselves a little gold problem."

"Bird problem, ye mean," said Charlie promptly, before Fraser or the doctor could slip a word in. "Biggest goddamn bird ye ever saw, mister. Killed two o' my partners and stole our poke. Took off with m'best mule, too. Out o' spite, I thinks, for surely One-Thumb and Johnny would've made the beast a good enough supper."

"Easy there, old-timer," said Mad Amos gently. "It don't do to make your head hurt when the rest of you already does. Now, y'all tell me more about this gold-lovin' bird of yours. I admit to being more than a mite curious about it, or I wouldn't be here."

"And just why *are* you here, Mr. Malone?" asked

Fraser curiously. "You have no assurance we are able to pay you for your services, or even what extremes of exertion those services might entail."

"Why, I don't care much about that right now, friend." He smiled, showing more teeth than men of his profession usually possessed. "I'm here because I'm curious. Like the cat."

"Curiosity," commented Fraser, still sizing the new arrival up, "killed the cat, if you will remember."

The mountain man turned and stared at him out of eyes so black that the agent shrank a little inside. "Way I figure it, Mr. Fraser, in the long run we're *all* dead."

With the doctor and the agent nearby to assist his memory, Wonder Charlie related his story of the devil-thing which had attacked his camp and killed two of his partners. Then Fraser repeated what his set-upon driving team had told him. He and Charlie argued a little over details of the creature's appearance, picayune disagreements involving color and size, but basically they and their respective stories were in agreement.

When they'd finished, Mad Amos leaned back in the rocking chair into which he'd settled himself. It creaked with his weight as he clasped both hands around a knee. "Shoot, that ain't no bird you're describing, gentlemens. I thought it weren't when I first heard about it, but I weren't sure. Now I am. What came down on you, old-timer," he told Charlie, "and what lit into your stage, Mr. Fraser, weren't nothin' but a full-blood, gen-u-wine, honest-to-goshen member of the dragon tribe."

"Your pardon, Mr. Malone," said the doctor skeptically, "but a dragon is a mythical creature, an invention of our less enlightened ancestors. This is the nineteenth century, sir. We no longer cotton to such superstitions. I myself once had an encounter with a snake-oil salesman who guaranteed to supply me with some powdered unicorn horn. I am not unskilled in basic chemistry and was able to prove it was nothing more than powder from the common steer."

"Well, y'all better readjust your heads a mite, 'cause that's what got your gold, and those stealings ain't no myth."

"He's right, there," said Wonder Charlie sharply.

"I had thought perhaps a large eagle that normally resides only among the highest and most inaccessible peaks..." the doctor began.

"Haw!" Mad Amos slapped his knee a blow that would've felled most men. His laugh echoed around the room. "Ain't no eagle in this world big enough to carry off a full-grown mule, let alone twenty pounds of gold in a Butterfield steel strongbox! Ain't no eagle got batwings instead of feathers. Ain't no eagle colored red and yellow and blue and pink and black and everything else. No, it's a true dragon we're dealing with here, gentlemens. By Solomon's Seal it is!"

The Butterfield agent spoke up. "I cannot pretend to argue with either of you gentlemen. I have not your scientific knowledge, sir," he told the doctor, "nor your reputed experience in matters arcane, Mr. Malone. The question before us, however, is not what we are dealing with, but how we are to be rid of it. I care not what its proper name be, only that I should not have to set eyes upon it." He eyed the mountain man expectantly.

Some said Malone had once been a doctor himself. Others said he was captain of a great clipper. Still others thought he'd been a learned professor at the Sorbonne in France. General opinion, however, held to it that he was merely full of what the squirrels put away for the Colorado winter. Fraser didn't much care. All he wanted was not to have to explain away the loss of another strongbox filled with gold, and there was a shipment of coin coming up from Denver the very next week.

"That's surely the crux, ain't it? Now you tell me, old-timer," Malone said to Wonder Charlie, "how many appendages did your visitor have streamin' from his mouth? Did he spit any fire at you? Was his howling high-pitched like a band of attacking Sioux, or low like buffalo in the distance? How did he look at you...straight on, or by twisting his head from one side to the other?"

And so on into the late morning, until the old miner's head ached from the labor of recollection. But Charlie persisted. He'd liked Johnny Sutter and One-Thumb Washington, not to mention poor ole General Grant.

Canvas tents pockmarked the sides of the little canyon, their sides billowing in the wind. Piles of rails and ties were stacked neatly nearby, along with kegs of spikes, extra hammers, and other equipment. Thick smells rose from a single larger tent while others rose from the far side of the railroad camp. One indicated the kitchen, the other the end product.

The line from Denver to Cheyenne was comparatively new and in need of regular repair. The crew which had laid the original track was now working its way back down the line, repairing and cleaning up, making certain the roadbed was firm and the rails secure.

The muscular, generally diminutive men swinging the hammers and hauling the iron glanced up with interest as the towering mountain man rode into camp.

So did the beefy supervisor charged with overseeing his imported workers. Though he came from a line of prejudiced folk, he would brook no insults toward his men. They might have funny eyes and talk even funnier, but by God they'd work all day long and not complain a whit, which was more than you could say for most men.

"All right. Show's over," he growled, aware that work was slowing all along the line as more men paused to gaze at the stranger. "Get your backs into it, you happy sons of Heaven!"

The pounding of hammers resumed, echoing down the canyon, but alert dark eyes still glanced in the direction of the silent visitor.

They widened beneath the brows of one broad-shouldered worker when the stranger leaned close and whispered something to him in a melodic, singsong tongue. The man was so startled he nearly dropped his hammer on his foot. The stranger had to repeat his query more slowly before he got a reply.

"Most unusual. White Devil speaks fluently the tongue of my home. You have traveled that far, honored sir?"

"Once or twice. I'm never for sure how many. Canton's a nice little town, though the food's a bit thin for my taste. Now, how about my question?"

The man hesitated at that. Despite his size and strength, the worker seemed suddenly frightened. He looked past the visitor's horse as though someone might be watching him.

Mad Amos followed the other man's gaze, and saw only tents. "Don't worry," he said reassuringly. "I won't let the one I'm after harm you, or any of your friends or relatives back home. I will not allow him to disturb your ancestors. Will you trust me, friend?"

225

"I will," said the worker abruptly. "The one you seek is called Wu-Ling. You will find him in the third tent down." He leaned on his hammer and pointed. "Good fortune go with you, White Devil."

"Thanks." Mad Amos chucked his horse and resumed his course up the track. The men working on the line watched him intently, whispering among themselves.

Outside the indicated tent he dismounted, pausing a moment to give his horse an affectionate pat. This unique steed was part Indian pony, part Apaloosa, part Arabian, and part Shire. He was black with white patches on his rump and fetlocks, and a white ring around his right eye. This eye was unable to open completely, which affected the animal with a sour squint that helped keep teasing children and casual horse-thieves well away.

"Now you wait here, Worthless, and I'll be right back. I hope." He turned and called into the tent.

"Enter, useless supplicant of a thousand excuses," replied an imperious voice.

Seated on a mat inside the tent was a youthful Chinese clad in embroidered silk robes and cap. He wore soft slippers and several jade rings. There were flowers in the tent, and they combined with burning incense to keep out the disagreeable odors of the camp. The man's back was to the entrance and he gestured with boredom toward a lacquered bowl three-quarters filled with coins.

"Place thy pitiful offering in the usual place and then get out. I am meditating with the Forces of Darkness. Woe to any who disturb my thoughts."

"Woe to those who meddle with forces they don't understand, progenitor of a hundred bluffs."

The genuflector whirled at the sound of English,

only to find himself gaping up at a hairy, ugly, giant White Devil. It took him a moment to compose himself. Then he folded his hands (which Mad Amos thought might be shaking just a little) back into his sleeves and bowed.

Mad Amos returned the bow and said in perfect Mandarin, "Thy ministrations seem to have exceeded thy knowledge, unomnipotent one."

A hand emerged from silk to thrust demandingly at the tent entrance. "Get out of my tent, Devil. Get out! Or I will assuredly turn thee into a lowly toad, as thy face suggests!"

Mad Amos smiled and took a step forward. "Now let's just settle down, inventor of falsehoods, or you'll be the one gets done to. I can't turn you into a toad, but when I finish with you you'll look like a buffalo carcass a bunch o' Comanches just finished stripping."

The man hesitated but did not back down. He raised both hands and muttered an important-sounding invocation to the skies.

Mad Amos listened a while, then muttered right back at him.

The would-be sorcerer's eyes went wide. "How comes a White Devil to know the secret words of the Shao?"

"That's a long, nasty story. 'Course, I don't know *all* of 'em, but I know enough to know you don't know what the hell you're invoking about. I suspect that's what got you into trouble the last time. I know enough to know this is all a show to impress your hardworking kinfolk out there. You ain't no Mandarin, Wu-Ling, just as you ain't no Shao sorcerer. You're nothing but a clever amateur, a dabbler in darkness, and I think you got yourself in over your head with this dragon business."

"So that is what inflicts you upon me. That damnable beast!" He threw his cap to the floor. "May its toenails ingrow a thousand times! I knew it would bring me problems from the moment the incantation expanded beyond my ability to control the signs." He sat heavily on a cushion, no longer bold and commanding, now just a distraught young would-be lawyer whose pact with the forces of darkness had been overturned by a higher court.

Watching him thus, Mad Amos was able to conjure up a little sympathy for him, no small feat of magic in itself. "How'd you come to have to call him up, anyways?"

"I needed something with which to cow my ignorant kinsmen. There had been mutterings . . . a few had begun to question my right to claim their support, saying that I was not a true sorcerer and could not threaten them as I claimed, nor work magic back in the homeland for their relatives and friends. I required something impressive to forestall such uncertainties once and for all."

"I see. How'd the railroad feel about your brothers supporting you in luxury while they worked their tails off?"

"The White Devil bosses care nothing for civilized behavior so long as the work is accomplished on time."

"So you finally had to produce, magically speaking, or risk going to work with your own delicate fake-Mandarin hands. That about right?"

"It is as you say." He turned and assumed a prideful air. "And I did produce. A dragon of whole cloth, of ancient mien and fierce disposition did I cause to materialize within the camp one night. Since then there have been no further mutterings among my kinsmen and my support has multiplied manyfold."

Mad Amos nodded and stroked his luxuriant beard. "Yup, you got a nice little racket going here. 'Course there might be some trouble if I were to stroll outside and announce that you've got no more control over this dragon than I do over a thunderbird's eye. I think your toiling kinsfolk would be a touch unhappy."

The young man's boast quickly turned to desperate pleading. "Please, you must not tell them that, White Devil! Please . . . they would linger over my killing for weeks if they once learned that I have no power over them." His gaze sank. "I confess all this to You Who Know the Words. I have no control over this dragon. I tried to make it vanish once its purpose had been accomplished. It laughed at me and flew off toward the high mountains. I have tried to call it back, to no avail. Now it does as it pleases, threatening your own people as well. I was an overanxious fool, determined to overawe my people. I should have settled for a less dramatic materialization."

Mad Amos nodded sagely. "Now you're learning, inheritor of troubles. It's always best to make sure you've put all the parts back into a disassembled gun before you go firin' it. I kinda feel sorry for you. The main thing is, the damage this dragon's already done wasn't by your direction."

"Oh, no, Honored Devil, no! As I confess before you, I have no control over it whatsoever. It does as it desires."

"Okay, then, I'll strike you a bargain. You quit dealing off the bottom of the deck with your brothers out there. Pick up a hammer and go to work alongside them. I promise it won't kill you, and you'll gain merit in their eyes by working alongside 'em when

229

you supposedly don't have to. Tell 'em it's time for you to put aside wizardly things and exercise your body for a change. You do that, and I'll keep my mouth shut."

The young man rose to his feet, hardly daring to hope. "You would do this for me? My ancestors will bless you a hundred times."

"They'd damn well better. I'll need all the help I can gather if I'm going to do anything about this dragon you cooked up, Wu-Ling."

"But you cannot! It will surely slay you!"

"Sorry. I'm bound to try. Can't just let it wander about, ravaging the countryside. Besides which, this country of mine is a young one. It ain't quite ready to cope with dragons yet. Havin' enough trouble recoverin' from the war and the devils *it* spawned. Now, this ain't one of those types that likes to carry off women, is it?"

"It would be in keeping with its lineage if it chose to abduct and consume a virgin or two, I am afraid."

Mad Amos grunted. "Well, even so, that ain't a worry. There ain't a virgin between here and Kansas City. That means it's just this gold affinity we got to worry about. That's a new one on me, Wu-Ling. What's it want with this gold it keeps stealin'?"

"I thought one so wise as thyself would surely know, Honored Devil. Gold is a necessary ingredient in the dragon's diet."

"It eats the stuff? Well, I'll be dogged. And all this time I thought it was doin' something normal with it, like buying up spare souls or accumulatin' a memorable horde of riches or some such nonsense. Gulps it right down, you say?"

"Truly," admitted Wu-Ling.

"Huh! World's full of wonders. Well, gives me

something to think on, anyways." He gazed sternly down at Wu-Ling. The would-be sorcerer paid close attention. A baleful look from Mad Amos Malone was something not to be ignored. "Now, you mind what I told you and quit leeching off your kinsfolk out there. They're good people and they deserve your help, not your imaginary afflictions. It's tough enough gettin' by in a foreign land. I know, I've had to try it myself. I've ways of knowin' when someone gives me his word and then backs off, and I don't like it. I don't like it one bit. You follow me, son of importunate parents?"

"I follow you, Honored Devil."

Wu-Ling allowed himself a sigh of relief when the giant finally departed. He wondered by what method the dragon would slay him.

Mad Amos worked his way up into the heights of the Medicine Bows despite the signs that winter was arriving early that year. It would be bad if he were caught out on the slopes by a blizzard, but he'd weathered out bad storms before and could do so again if compelled to.

Near a fork of the Laramie River he paused and made camp, choosing an open meadow across which the river ran free and fast. To the west the crests of the mountains already slept beneath the first heavy blanket of snow.

"Well, Worthless, I guess this is as good a spot as any. Might as well get on with it. Oughta be an interesting business, unless I've figured it all wrong. In that case, you hie yourself off somewhere and have a good time. These mountains are full of herds. Find yourself some fine mares and settle down. Bet you wouldn't be all that sad to see me go, would you?"

The horse let out a noncommittal whinny, squinted at him out of his bad eye, and wandered off in search of a nice mud wallow to roll in.

Mad Amos hunted until he found a willow tree of just the right age. He cut off a green branch, shaped it, and trimmed off the leaves and sproutings. Then he sharpened the tip with his Bowie, fired it in charcoal, and used the white-hot, smoking points to etch some strange symbols in the earth around his kit. Some of the symbols were Chinese ideographs, some were Tibetan, and a few were not drawn from the lexicon of man.

Next he rummaged around in his battered old saddlebags, which some folk whispered held things it were best not to talk about. Out came an owl's head, a bottle of blue goo, several preserved dead scorpions, three eagle feathers bound together with Zuni fetishes, and similar debris. He reached in a little further and withdrew a shiny metal bar. It was five pounds of enriched tumbaga, a gold alloy made by the Quimbaya Indians of the southern continent, composed of roughly sixty-five percent gold, twenty percent copper, and the rest silver. This he set carefully down in the center of the inscribed symbols.

Lastly he pulled the rifle from its fringed and painted holster. The holster had been fashioned by one of Sacajawea's daughters. Good gal, that Sacajawea, he mused. Some day when they were both ruminating in the Happy Hunting Ground he hoped to meet her again.

The rifle had an eight-sided barrel, black walnut stock, and a breech large enough for a frightened cottontail to hide inside. It was a Sharps buffalo rifle, fifty caliber, with a sliding leaf sight adjustable to eleven hundred yards on the back. It fired a two-and-a-half-inch-long cartridge loaded with a hundred grains of black powder and could drop a full-grown bull buffalo in its tracks at six hundred yards. The bandoliers draped across Mad Amos's chest held oversized three-and-a-quarter inch shells packed with a hundred and seventy grains of black powder.

The Sharps was a single-shot. But then, if you could fire it proper without busting your shoulder, you only needed a single shot. To Mad Amos's way of thinking, such built-in caution just naturally led to a man bettering his marksmanship.

He loaded it with more care than usual this time, paying special attention to the cartridge itself, which he carefully chose from the assortment arrayed on his chest.

Then he settled down to wait.

The moon was waning and the sky had been temporarily swept clean of most clouds when he heard the wings coming toward him out of the west, out of the mountaintops. Soon he was able to see the source of the faint whistling, a streamlined shape dancing down fast out of the heavens, its long tail switching briskly from side to side as it sniffed out the location of the gold.

It landed between the river and the camp and stalked toward the lonely man on feet clad in scales of crimson. Its neck was bright blue, its body mostly yellow and gold, its wings and face striped like the contents of a big jar stuffed with assorted candies. Moonlight marched across scimitarlike teeth and its heritage burned back of its great eyes.

"Whoa up, there!" Mad Amos called out sharply in the dragon tongue, which is like no other (and which is hard to speak because it hurts the back of the throat).

The dragon halted, eyes blazing down at the human who had one foot resting possessively on the golden bar. Its tail twitched, flattening the meadow grass and foxgloves, and the tendrils bordering its skull and jaws twisted like snakes with a peculiar life of their own. Its belly ached for the cool touch of yellow metal, its blood burned for the precious golden substance which purified and helped keep it alive.

"Oh-ho!" it replied in its rasping voice. "A human who talks the mother-tongue. Admirable is your learning, man, but it will not save you your gold. Give it here to me." It leaned forward hungrily, the smell of brimstone seeping from its garishly hued lips and parted mouth.

"I think not, Brightbodyblackheart. It ain't that I resent you the gold. Everybody's got to eat. But you scared the wits out of some good people hereabouts and killed a couple of others. And I think you're liable to kill some more afore you're sated, if your appetite's as big as your belly and your desire as sharp as your teeth. I'm not fool enough to think you'll be satisfied just with this here chunk." He nudged the bar with his foot, causing the hungry dragon to salivate smoke.

"You are right, man. My hunger is as deep as the abyssal ocean where I may not go, as vast as the sky which I make my own, and as substantial as my anger when I am denied. Give me your gold! Give it over to me now and I will spare you for your learning, for though gluttonous I am not wasteful. Refuse me and I will eat you, too, for a dragon cannot live by gold alone."

Casually, Mad Amos shifted the rifle lying across his knees. "Now this here's a Sharps rifle, Deathwing. I'm sure you ain't too familiar with it. There ain't the like of it where you come from, and there never will be, so I'll explain it to you. There ain't no more powerful rifle in this world or the other. I'm going to give

234

you one chance to get back to where you come from, hungry but intact." He smiled thinly, humorlessly. "See, I ain't wasteful, neither. You git your scaly hide out of this part of the real world right now or by Nebuchadnezzar's nightshade, I'm oath-bound to put a bullet in you."

The dragon roared with amusement. Its horrible laughter cascaded off the walls of the canyon through which the Laramie runs. It trickled down the slopes and echoed through caves where hibernating animals stirred uneasily in their long sleep.

"A last gesture, last words! I claim forfeit, man, for you are not amusing! Gold *and* life must you surrender to me now, for I have not the patience to play with you longer. My belly throbs in expectation and in my heart there is no shred of sympathy or understanding for you. I will take your gold now, man, and your life in a moment." A great clawed foot reached out to scratch contemptuously at the symbols so patiently etched in the soil. "Think you that these will stop me? You do not come near knowing the right ways or words, or the words you would have uttered by now." It took another step forward. Fire began to flame around its jaws. "Your puny steel and powder cannot harm me, Worm-that-walks-upright. Fire if you wish. The insect chirps loudest just before it is squashed!"

"Remember, now, you asked for this." Quickly, Mad Amos raised the long octagonal barrel and squeezed the trigger.

There was a crash, then a longer, reverberating roar, the thunderous double *boom* that only a Sharps can produce. It almost matched the dragon's laughter.

The shot struck Brightbodyblackheart square in the chest. The monster looked down at the already-healing wound, sneered, and took another step forward. Its jaws parted further as it prepared to snap up gold and man in a single bite.

It stopped, confused. Something was happening inside it. Its eyes began to roll. Then it let out an earthshaking roar so violent that the wind of it knocked Mad Amos back off his feet. Fortunately, there was no fire in that massive exhalation.

The mountain man spat out dirt and bark and looked upward. The dragon was in the air, spinning, twisting, convulsing spasmodically, thoroughly out of control, screaming like a third-rate soprano attempting Wagner as it whirled toward the distant moon.

Mad Amos slowly picked himself off the ground, dusted off the hollow cougar skull which served him for a hat, and watched the sky until the last scream and final bellow faded from hearing, until the tiny dot fluttering against the stars had winked out of sight and out of existence.

From his wallow near the riverbank, Worthless glanced up, squinted and neighed.

Mad Amos squatted and gathered up the tumbaga bar. He paid no attention to the coterie of symbols which he'd so laboriously scratched into the earth. They'd been put there to draw the dragon's attention, which they'd done most effectively. Oh, he'd seen Brightbodyblackheart checking them out before landing! The dragon might bellow intimidatingly but, like all its kind, it was cautious. It had only taken the bait when it was certain Mad Amos owned no magic effective against it. Mere mortal weapons like guns and bullets, of course, it had had no reason to fear.

He used his tongue to pop the second bullet, the one he hadn't had to use, out of his cheek, and carefully took the huge cartridge apart. Out of the head drifted a pile of dust. He held it in his palm and then, careful not to inhale any of it, blew it away with one puff. The dust duplicated the contents of the bullet which had penetrated Brightbodyblackheart: mescaline concentrate, peyote of a certain rare type, distillate of the tears of a peculiar mushroom, coca leaves from South America, yopo—a cornucopia of powerful hallucinogens which an old Navajo had once concocted before Mad Amos's attentive gaze during a youthful sojourn in Cañon de Chelly many years before.

It was not quite magic but, then, it was not quite real, either. The dragon had been right: Mad Amos had not had the words to kill it, had not had the symbols. And it wasn't dead. But it no longer lived in the real world of men, either. In a month, when the aftereffects of the potent mixture had finally worn off and Brightbodyblackheart could think clearly once more, it might wish it *were* dead. Of one thing Mad Amos was reasonably certain: the dragon might hunger for gold, but it was not likely to come a-hunting it anywhere in the vicinity of Colorado.

Carefully he repacked that seemingly modest pair of saddlebags and prepared to break camp, casting an experienced eye toward the sky. It was starting to cloud over again. Soon it would snow, and when it started it again it wouldn't stop until April.

But not for two or three days yet, surely. He still had time to get out of the high mountains if he didn't waste it lollygaggin' and moonin' over narrow escapes.

He put his hands on his hips and shouted toward the river. "C'mon, Worthless, you lazy representative of an equine disaster! Git your tail out of that mud! North of here's that crazy steamin' land ol' Jim Bridger once told me about. I reckon it's time we had a gander at it . . . and what's under it."

Reluctant but obedient, the piebald subject of these

unfounded imprecations struggled to its feet and threw its master a nasty squint. Mad Amos eyed his four-legged companion with affection.

"Have t'do somethin' about that patch on his forehead," he mused. "That damn horn's startin' t'grow through again..."

Village of the Chosen

A good friend of mine, Bill Smythe, used to be the head rat-catcher (*i.e.*, "Rodent Control Expert") for the United Nations. He quit after spending a few years in Somalia waiting for the locals to learn the ropes of rodent extermination. When they didn't ("Allah will provide," they said, and sure enough, he did...in the form of endless foreign aid and experts like Bill), he packed it in.

Currently he's teaching the Tanzanians how to cope with their surplus of rodents, and reports with much relief that they seem much more serious about their land and its problems. It's a better duty station, and although Dar-es-Salaam isn't quite London or New York, it's a bit more sophisticated than his former duty station of Mogadishu.

You never knew what you might run into in
a place as isolated as Mogadishu...

Harley Vickers hated Mogadishu—not that he hadn't
been assigned worse duty stations. Kampala under Idi
Amin, for example, from which he'd barely escaped
with story and skin intact. Or Soweto, South Africa's
massive black slum, an ocean of misery and despair
destined someday to explode in an orgy of violence
the likes of which Africa had not seen since the time
of the Zulu wars.

No, he'd reported from worse places than Mogadishu, if not duller ones. For fresh fruit, decent cooking,
halfway reliable news broadcasts, and anything resem-
bling entertainment, you had to take a four-wheel-drive
vehicle south across the border to Nairobi. Mogadishu
was devoid of such pleasures. His only delight lay in
exploring the virgin beaches which stretched hundreds
of kilometers northward toward the Gulf of Aden. The
seacoast of Somalia was as beautifully rich as its people
were abysmally, desperately poor.

Poorer than ever because of the debilitating effects
of the seemingly endless war with their intractable and
equally poverty-stricken neighbor, Ethiopia. A human
tide of refugees washed back and forth across the dis-
puted borders of the Ogaden desert, straining to the
limits the resources of an economy that had never been
strong.

Vickers was half American, half English. He'd spent
twenty years in Africa for UPI, twenty years which
had blunted his early idealism by showing him to what
extremes man could go in defense of personal idiocies.

White or black, it was all the same. Hatred instead of understanding. Suspicion instead of conversation. He was tired.

Four months he'd spent in Mogadishu, reporting on the relief efforts and the Ogaden futility. He was ready for a change—a change to anywhere. Cairo, if he was lucky, or Nairobi, or even frenetic and always exciting Lagos. Anywhere but here, he thought as he made his way through the marketplace toward his apartment. He was sick to death of the corruption and arrogance he'd been forced to deal with in the course of writing his reports. Besides, he'd said everything there was to say about the Somalian situation. He'd been in the business long enough to know when his work was getting stale.

That's when he turned the corner by the hardware stall and nearly knocked down the green woman.

As she stumbled, her veil fell away from her face, which was as exquisite as an emerald, and as richly hued. She hurriedly fixed the shielding gauze and dashed into the crowd. A stunned Vickers could only stare after her.

Then, shoving his way through the mob of marketers, he was running in pursuit.

"Hey...hey, you, wait a minute! Wait!" He knew she heard him because more than once she glanced back to see if he was still chasing her. The crowd was thick and prevented him from closing, but it also kept her within view.

He lost her on the other side of the marketplace when she climbed not into a donkey cart or camel howdah but into a late-model Land Rover. The driver floored the accelerator and they roared along the narrow road, leaving Vickers out of breath and anxious amid the rising cloud of dust.

The image had not faded, nor had the shock. The

woman's face was vivid in his mind. It was not her exceptional beauty that transfixed him, however, as much as her extraordinary coloring. Hers wasn't the olive complexion of Aegean visitors or the coffee tone of many multiracial residents of Mogadishu. She was a bright, cheerful green—as brilliant as a St. Patrick's Day parade.

If it was due to the use of makeup or body paint, it was the most remarkable job of either he'd ever seen. When she'd blinked at him after their collision, he saw that even her eyelids were the same electric shade of green.

A blessing, a gift from Allah, a reward for his noble and virtuous life, the taxi waited for him around the block. It wasn't hard to pick up the trail of the Land Rover. The few motorized vehicles that utilized the streets of Mogadishu usually kept to the harbor front or diplomatic quarter and ignored these back streets.

The taxi driver earned his fare as they tracked the fleeing Rover through narrow brick alleys and down dirt avenues. Only when the Land Rover emerged from the city's outskirts did the driver finally concede the race.

"I am sorry, Effendi. The road go no more, I go no more." His English was broken, but to the point.

Vickers knew arguing would be futile. In truth, the driver had pushed his battered Citroen to its limit. Beyond lay a track suitable only for camels and four-wheel-drive vehicles. The taxi wouldn't last a mile on that bone-breaking path to nowhere. Vickers watched until the Land Rover sank into the evening horizon before giving the order to turn about and return to the city.

All night that glowing green face haunted him. Except for her coloring, the young woman had classic features common to this part of Africa—part black, part Arab, a delicious and exotic mix.

As far as his news assignment was concerned, Vickers had considerable discretion. So long as he filed his stories on deadline and didn't abuse his budget, he was free to go where he wished and report on the subject of his choice. His nearest superior sat behind a desk on Fleet Street.

I'll give them something interesting to print, he mused. A bright green lady—yes, that ought to perk the *Times*'s interest, as well as that of the *Daily News* and *The Star*.

It wasn't too difficult to retrace the Land Rover's progress from the point where it had fled the city. Cars outside the city limits were as rare as compassion. He was undaunted by the task he'd set for himself. Many times he'd spent weeks in the bush, living in the back of his own Land Rover.

Before leaving Mogadishu he'd packed in enough food, water, and petrol to keep him going for a month, though he didn't imagine he'd be gone that long. From what he'd seen of his quarry, she didn't appear to be nearly so extensively provisioned.

The road took him through Balad toward Johar, along the Wadi Shebelle, dry most of this time of year. The outside temperature was hellishly hot. The Rover's air conditioner hummed in protest as it fought back the searing heat.

Inquiries along the road caused him to turn toward the coast northward before reaching Johar and then on through Marek and Harardera. Even a camel track was a welcome path in the wilderness.

In Obbia an imperious army captain tried to commandeer Vickers's spare petrol. Only the waving of his UPI identification and government pass got him through to Iddan. He was nearing Migiurtinia Province without having closed on his quarry and began to wonder if he wouldn't have to drive all the way to Cape Guardafui. He was hot and tired and seriously considering whether he ought to pack it in when he saw the green woman again.

Except...it wasn't the same woman.

He saw her selling fish in one of the tiny palm-frond stalls lining the dock area of Garad, a fishing village. Her veil was off—because of the heat, Vickers surmised. Maybe she'd been beautiful once, but age and a hard life had turned her skin to parchment. She was older than the woman who had brought him this far, much older.

More intriguing still were the two bright green children he saw playing on the beach, dashing down to the water's edge in the company of other, normal-hued children, then running back to dance around the older lady's legs. Their grandmother maybe, Vickers thought as he brought the Land Rover to a stop.

The children clustered around it, touching the sides, bending to inspect the mud-caked undercarriage. Garad was an isolated community and the Land Rover was as much a novelty as the white man who drove it. As an astonished Vickers studied the two green youngsters, all thoughts of special paint and makeup were discarded. They were seven or eight years old, a bright-eyed boy and mischievous little girl, both of them green from head to toe. Only their eyes, nails, and body hair were exempt from the remarkable coloring, although the nails did have a greenish cast to them.

Vickers climbed down, made sure the door was locked, and smiled at them. They stared back at him, innocent of deception or guile. The little girl kept one finger in her mouth and stayed close to the boy. Brother and sister, most likely.

He cleared his throat and tried his Swahili, hoping it would be enough. His Arabic was tolerable, his Amharic much less so.

They understood. Vickers asked where they came from. They pointed inland. Was that their grandmother over there in the stall, selling fish? No, an aunt. He hesitated only momentarily. Why were they such an unusual color?

Because they were fortunate enough to be among the Chosen.

It was some kind of sect, then. Something interesting had come to the wastes of northern Somalia. Yet there was nothing reticent in the children's manner, no attempt to hide anything. Not that there was any need to. They were protected from the attention of the outside world by an isolation unimaginable to Londoners or even the citizens of Nairobi. Only a chance glimpse in a crowded marketplace had sent Vickers probing their sanctuary.

Inland, they said. Could they be more specific? With camel and jackass the fastest local means of transportation, Vickers knew it couldn't be very far. Surely, Mzungu, they told him. One has only to follow the Wadi Omad toward the setting sun to come to the place of the Chosen, where they lived with the rest of their village.

Not true nomadic types, then, Vickers mused. He thanked them and climbed back into the Land Rover. Laughing children followed in its wake as it rumbled forward, turned eastward beyond the last fish stall, and headed inland.

The wadi he struggled to follow was nearly dry. Only

a thin trickle cut its center like a silver thread. Antelope fled from his approach. Vickers ignored them.

It was nearly dark when he turned up out of the little canyon. Lengthening shadows revealed a gentle slope scarred by tire tracks. They led him up to the beginnings of the savanna. Thorn trees fought for the soil's moisture. Scrub brush provided homes for snakes and kangaroo rats. Towering above them all were the gleaming metal skeletons of three windmills.

No Quixote in his Land Rover, Vickers frowned as he pushed toward the cluster of mud and rock structures nestled beneath the towers. There weren't supposed to be any European outposts this far north. All the refugee centers were further inland, along the Ethiopian border, or south toward Mogadishu. Nor could he recall mention of any scientific stations or outposts in this region.

The windmills were of two types. One served to bring up water, the other two mounted windchargers for the generation of electricity. Indeed, it was unusually cool here. A steady breeze blew up the wadi from the sea. In the morning the wind probably reversed as the land heated up again.

A few lights showed inside the largest building. It was one story, cobbled together out of corrugated steel sheets, local stone, and mud. Lumber was as scarce in this part of the world as chateaubriand.

He slowed the Rover to a halt and climbed out. Set among the brush and trees, off to his left, was a sizable native village. It looked deserted. As he stood there against the oncoming African night, a peculiar susurration reached his ears. He started toward it, topped a low rise, and came to a halt.

What was probably the entire population of the village—men, women, and children—lined the crest of the next ridge. They faced the setting sun with heads back and arms outstretched. The local witch doctor or chief was leading them in a hypnotic, melodious chant.

And every one of them was stark naked and bright green.

A hand tapped the middle of his back. He whirled, sucking in his breath, his hand reaching instinctively toward the pistol at his waist. It stayed holstered as he stared. It was the woman he'd seen in Mogadishu.

Her veil was gone. So was the stifling chador. Now she wore khaki slacks, sandals, and a bush shirt. Her black hair trailed behind her. Face and exposed arms and hands were as green as those of the chanting villagers behind him.

"You are very persistent, sir," she said in heavily accented English.

His hands moved self-consciously away from the holster. "What is this place? Who are you, and who," he gestured toward the villagers, "are these people? And why does everybody here look like something out of a summer salad?"

She hesitated briefly, then laughed and hid her face for a moment. "You very funny man, sir."

A sudden thought made him say, "I hope I didn't offend you in any way."

"You did not. Come." She gestured toward the big house. "You must meet the Cobans."

For a minute he thought she'd said "Cubans" and he almost panicked. She turned to smile brilliantly at him. Her teeth were not pointed and were gratifyingly white.

"Please, sir. You will like them, the old mister and missus."

Mister and missus. That didn't sound very threatening. He moved up alongside her. Besides, he hadn't driven across hundreds of kilometers of desolation to run away at the moment of enlightenment.

"Tell me," he said as they approached the entrance to the major edifice. "Are you . . . are all these people of the 'Chosen'?"

"Oh, most assuredly so, sir. That is what the missus doctor tell us." Then she added proudly, "My name is Rala. I speak English and have read real books, so I am assistant to them. It is me they send into the city to buy things for them."

"Not only do you speak excellent English, Rala, but you are also very beautiful."

"Thank you, sir." She blushed, and her cheeks turned the most extraordinary color.

There was nothing mysterious about the room she ushered him into. The furniture appeared to be of local manufacture, handmade and comfortable. A radio/tapedeck rested on a bookcase shelf, playing unusually muted Chávez. DC-powered lamps lit the room, drawing energy from wind-charged batteries.

An elderly European lady sat on the couch, flipping the pages of a paperback book. She looked up as they entered. So did the man seated at the desk across the room. Both were in their late sixties or early seventies, Vickers decided.

The man rose to greet him. "Hello, hello. You're the first visitor Mary and I have had in some time." He smiled and extended a hand. To Vickers's relief, it was the same color as his own. "I'm Walter Coban."

"And I'm Mary," said the grandmotherly woman on the couch.

"Harley Vickers, United Press."

"A reporter. Yes, I think I've read some of your stories, Mr. Vickers," said Mrs. Coban. "You've done a lot of work about the refugee problem." Vickers nodded. "You strike me from your work as an honest, even empathetic, man."

"I write what I see," he said diffidently.

"And what do you see now?"

"Something I don't understand."

She smiled a soft, maternal smile. "You must be tired, Mr. Vickers. Thirsty and hungry as well. We haven't had company for dinner in, oh, I can't remember when. Now, since you obviously haven't come all this way to return empty-handed, we'll have to supply you with understanding, won't we? So you must also accept our hospitality."

He couldn't keep himself from grinning back at her. There was a mystery here, yes, but hardly danger. Besides, he was sick of eating out of cans.

"I bow to your demand."

"Please have a seat." She patted a cushion. "Here, next to me." Vickers joined her. Her husband vanished into a back room and reappeared a moment later, juggling three tall glasses. He gave Vickers one.

The reporter took a cautious sip, then his eyes lit up and he drank deeply. "Lemonade! With *ice*! Bless you both. Where did you get this?"

"By boat, from the south." The old man was smiling. "Rala does what she can for us in Mogadishu, but you know how limited the city's resources are. For real food you have to go farther afield. The lemons came off a trading dhow out of Malindi."

"Excepting seafood," his wife put in. "We get the most marvelous seafood here. Rala, lobsters tonight." The girl nodded, looked unhappy, and disappeared through another door.

The thought of a lobster supper already had Vickers salivating. "Really, no need to go to any expense on my account."

"Expense? My dear boy, lobsters are cheaper here than onions. Eat your fill."

The girl's sudden look of dismay had stayed with him. "When you proposed the main course, Rala made a face. Doesn't she like lobster?"

"Not particularly," said Coban. "Matter of personal taste. It's all what you're used to, you know."

"I hope I never get that blasé," Vickers told him. The cold lemonade had done wonders for his parched throat. "You promised me understanding, Mrs. Coban. For me, that means information and explanations. I sure could use some. What is this village, and why do its people refer to themselves as the Chosen? Why are they all green, and what the blazes are you two doing in this godforsaken piece of real estate?" He blinked and wiped his eyes.

Husband and wife exchanged a glance. Coban sat down in the chair opposite the couch and explained.

"Mary and I did our early work at the University of Arizona in Tucson, Mr. Vickers. Most of the time we worked at night and on our own—due to the controversial nature of our project. We tried to publish, but met only with skepticism and disparagement. That often happens in science, and it's no less pretty than in any other discipline. We persisted with our work. Eventually our funds were cut off and we had to resign our professorships.

"Our interests lie in the vital field of food research, Mr. Vickers, in particular as it applies toward relieving distress in the desert regions of the world. That is why we originally went to work in Arizona. We worked for a long time with jojoba and other native desert plants before we realized we were attacking the problem from the wrong end, as researchers have been doing for a hundred years.

"Six years after we shifted the focus of our efforts, we believed we had found a method by which most of the world's food shortages could be alleviated. We met with the same kind of cruel indifference and hostility which had greeted our earlier work. It is impossible, Mr. Vickers, to do constructive work in an atmosphere of ridicule.

"So we sought a place to work in peace and apply our theories where they might do some good. We came here, and our assistance was needed desperately. Rala and her people were starving when we stumbled upon them, Mr. Vickers. The native residents of Gala are decent human beings, but you cannot share food you do not have.

"Our project is being funded by several farseeing, wealthy Arizonans. They have let us work without interference. Great men, Mr. Vickers. I will give their names later, to use in the story you will write."

"Am I going to write a story, then?" he murmured. The old man's tale was interesting as far as it went, but he still hadn't supplied Vickers with any real answers. Were they putting him off deliberately, or was Coban simply verbose? He rubbed at his eyes again. The endless, desperately dull drive had exhausted him. He wasn't even sure he'd be able to stay awake through supper.

"Yes, you are, Mr. Vickers." Coban went on. "Both Mary and I have agreed that it is time. Your appearance here might be regarded as fate, if I believed in such things. And Mary has read your work, and respects it. That's good enough for me. You will tell the world of our little success out here in the desert. We have done what we hoped could be done."

"What's that?" Vickers asked. "Form a new religion? I saw your bare-assed villagers out there when

I drove up. Songs don't relieve the emptiness in a man's belly."

Coban smiled and his wife laughed delightedly. "Oh, Mr. Vickers, the chanting is for fun. It's not important to the process."

"What process?" Vickers mumbled. He really was tired, he realized.

"They weren't praying, Mr. Vickers." Coban told him. "They were eating."

Vickers eyed him warily. "Eating? . . . Eating what?"

"Supper, I should think. Old habits don't die easily."

His wife watched Vickers sympathetically. "Perhaps it will be clear to you if I explain our history in more detail. I am a geneticist and Walter is a microbiologist. When we put aside our work with desert plants many years ago, it was to concentrate on plankton. Those are the tiny, ocean-going life forms which support much of the life in the sea. We thought of releasing plankton in shallow salt ponds throughout the world's desert regions and raising it like soup.

"While working with this idea we happened across an interesting and rather common little freshwater coelenterate named *Hydra viridis*. This particular hydra, unlike its relatives, exists in a symbiotic relationship with a wonderful alga called chlorella. Chlorella is photosynthetic, Mr. Vickers, but it is more than that. In addition to producing its own food, it will also produce enough to keep its host alive.

"When chlorella is not present, the hydra is forced to eat solid food just like its white relatives." Her husband rose and exited through a back door again.

"We became very excited, Mr. Vickers," she continued. "We thought how wonderful it would be if we could genetically engineer a strain of chlorella to be a symbiont with man. We succeeded. The production of food per acre of arable land is no longer a valid problem, Mr. Vickers. Countries like India and China can have as many people as they wish. With our friendly alga as a partner, everyone on Earth can produce enough food for his or her own body.

"Think of the peripheral problems our discovery will solve! Everyone will be a pleasant shade of green. No more raising and slaughtering of animals for food. We're extremely proud of what we've accomplished, Mr. Vickers. Can you blame us?"

"If you're so proud of what you've done, why haven't you and your husband taken advantage of it?" Vickers asked. "Or is it suitable only for ignorant refugees? Mind you, I don't buy a word of it."

"Oh, we wouldn't expect a reporter of your experience and stature to believe anything so fantastic without incontrovertible proof, Mr. Vickers. Rest assured you'll have that proof.

"As regards your first question," Coban continued. "I am sorry to have to say that once a person has reached the age of fifty or fifty-five—we're still not positive where the line falls—the alga does not adapt to its human host. We believe it may have something to do with the decreasing production of fibroblasts as the body ages. With anyone younger than fifty, there's no difficulty in inducing the alga to take up residence in the dermal layers. Furthermore, the alga is transferred via embryonic fluids to the newborn. Chlorella even responds to artificial light, which enables one to produce food at night, if so desired."

Vickers leaned back against the couch, hardly able to keep his eyes open.

"More lemonade, Mr. Vickers?"

Lemonade. Cool, icy lemonade. Tired, so tired.

Shouldn't be this tired, drive notwithstanding. Made up the lemonade in the other room . . .

"Why?" he said thickly as he slid rapidly toward darkness. "I thought . . . you said . . . you wanted your story told?"

"Oh, you misunderstand, Mr. Vickers," she said solicitously, bending over him and inspecting his face with a clinical eye. "We haven't done anything harmful to you. Just put you to sleep. You need a good night's sleep, don't you? In the morning you'll have the proof you require for your story. Think of the headlines you're going to have, Mr. Vickers! HUNGER ELIMINATED! . . . FOOD SHORTAGES HISTORY! . . . MANKIND SAVED! . . . Think of it, Mr. Vickers. You're going to be the most famous reporter in history. You won't be able to help it . . ."

The sun woke him, shooting through the window shades. He was in bed, a real bed with a mattress and clean sheets.

Last night came back in a rush. Lemonade, chanting, ice, smiling old folks a little more than what they seemed, drugged, unconsciousness.

He sat up fast, relieved that he could do so. Everything seemed to work. Experimentally he flexed his arms, then his legs. Everything was in place. The only thing out of the ordinary was a tingling in his right forearm, near the elbow.

He looked at his right arm—and screamed.

Walter Coban appeared at the door, looking concerned. "You startled us, Mr. Vickers. Are you all right?"

"All right? All right! Look at me!"

Coban did so, professionally. "A very nice shade, Mr. Vickers, if I may say so."

Vickers was holding his head in his hands, rocking back and forth, moaning. "Why? Why me? Why did you have to do this to me?"

"Take it easy, Mr. Vickers. You're a strong man. You'd have to be a strong man to have survived all these years in Africa. You can handle a little sea change like this. Besides, the effect needn't be permanent. Were you to spend a few weeks in darkness, your old, useless color would return.

"Don't you recall our conversation last night? You said, despite what you'd seen, that you didn't believe anything we told you. We promised to supply you with unarguable proof of our discovery. You're going to need it in order to convince your editors back in London. This way, they'll believe you, Mr. Vickers. Even those skeptics in the scientific community who ridiculed us will have to believe you, after you've done nothing but sit in the sun and starve yourself for weeks on end without getting hungry or losing any weight. They'll believe you because you'll be your own proof, Mr. Vickers."

"Side effects," Vickers groaned. "What about side effects?"

"We've studied the symbiotic relationship for many years now. There are *no* harmful side effects. Without the change in skin color, you'd never know the chlorella was present in your body. Oh, there is one thing...

"You remarked on our assistant Rala's apparent distaste for the proposed lobster supper? Her disgust? You'll discover before long that the thought of ingesting solid food will make you nauseous, except for the tasteless vitimin and mineral supplements you have to take. Photosynthesis doesn't supply quite everything the human body needs."

Vickers licked his lips and said morosely, "But I *like* eating. I like lobster, and steak, and fried chicken."

"Superficial pleasures at best. You'll see. No worrying about what to eat anymore, Mr. Vickers. Think of the money you'll save. Think of the extra time you'll gain each day in return for spending a little time in the sun. Photosynthesis may not be an exhilarating way of obtaining nourishment, but it's a highly efficient one."

Heedless of his nakedness, Vickers slid out of bed. There was a half-length mirror fastened to the far wall. He gazed in amazement at his lime-green self. Now that the initial shock had faded, he found the soft, pastel coloring almost relaxing to look upon. They might not believe right away when he strolled casually into the London office, but they would certainly sit up and take notice.

He found himself wondering if Rala would find it attractive.

"Try not to take it so hard, Mr. Vickers," said Coban soothingly. "I envy you, you know. Mary and I are the discoverers—the ones who did the dirty, rewardless legwork. You are to be the herald of a new age. You should be proud. Before you die, everyone will look like you. Everyone will be a member of the Chosen."

Coban was right, Vickers knew. The system was too efficient, too benign, to be denied. The only problems in gaining widespread acceptance would be psychological, and he was as sure now as Coban that these could be overcome. After all, the human body was already a reservoir of living things, from bacteria to more complex organisms. Why should anyone object to a few more visitors, especially visitors as beneficial as chlorella?

It really was a most handsome color, he decided.

Coban saw the change come over his guest and relaxed. "There, it's not so bad, is it? We're simply becoming one of our many fantasies, Mr. Vickers, and what a promising fantasy it has turned out to be. We have met the little green men from outer space, and they are us."

About the Author

Born in New York City in 1946, Alan Dean Foster was raised in Los Angeles, California. After receiving a bachelor's degree in political science and a Master of Fine Arts in motion pictures from UCLA in 1968–69, he worked for two years as a public relations copywriter in a small Studio City, California, firm.

His writing career began in 1968 when August Derleth bought a long letter of Foster's and published it as a short story in his biannual *Arkham Collector Magazine*. Sales of short fiction to other magazines followed. His first try at a novel, *The Tar-Aiym Krang*, was published by Ballantine Books in 1972.

Foster has toured extensively through Asia and the isles of the Pacific. Besides traveling, he enjoys classical and rock music, old films, basketball, body surfing, and karate. He has taught screenwriting, literature, and film history at UCLA and Los Angeles City College.

Currently, he resides in Arizona with his wife JoAnn (who is reputed to have the only extant recipe for Barbarian Cream Pie).

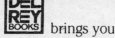 **brings you**
Exciting and Hair-Raising SF Adventure from

ALAN DEAN
FOSTER

Available at your bookstore or use this coupon.

____**FOR LOVE OF MOTHER-NOT**   30511 2.95
Finally, the novel Foster fans have been waiting for. the meeting of Flinx and Pip! Flinx.
a child, recalls little of his past and nothing of his family. Kidnappers capture first.
Mother Mastiff and then. Pip, the only family Flinx has ever known. and somehow he
must save them. A paperback original.

____**BLOODHYPE**   30578 2.50
It was a killer! Bloodhype was the most dangerous drug in the galaxy with instant ad-
diction and no antidote. Thought to be totally eradicated. someone. somewhere was
secretly manufacturing it.

____**NOR CRYSTAL TEARS**   29141 2.75
Ryo. a dreamer in a world of sensible and stable beings. buried himself in his
work—until he came across a letter describing a relative's encounter with a horrid.
two-legged. soft skinned space-going beast.

____**WITH FRIENDS LIKE THESE...**   28242 1.95
A dozen delightful stories from those fabulous adventures of Flinx and his minidrag
Pip.

____**CACHALOT**   28066 2.25
Cachalot. the planet whose surface is one great ocean. where humans were strictly
confined to a few islands and floating towns. But something was destroying the towns.
leaving no clues...and no survivors.

 BALLANTINE MAIL SALES
Dept. TA, 201 E. 50th St., New York, N.Y. 10022

Please send me the BALLANTINE or DEL REY BOOKS I have
checked above. I am enclosing $_____ (add 50¢ per copy to
cover postage and handling). Send check or money order — no
cash or C.O.D.'s please. Prices and numbers are subject to change
without notice.

Name_____

Address_____

City_____State_____Zip Code_____

08   **Allow at least 4 weeks for delivery.**   TA-59